SONGS OF ENCHANTMENT

SONGS OF
ENCHANTMENT

———

BEN OKRI

NAN A. TALESE
DOUBLEDAY
NEW YORK   LONDON   TORONTO   SYDNEY   AUCKLAND

PUBLISHED BY NAN A. TALESE
an imprint of Doubleday
a division of
Bantam Doubleday Dell Publishing Group, Inc.
1540 Broadway, New York, New York 10036

DOUBLEDAY is a trademark of Doubleday,
a division of Bantam Doubleday Dell Publishing Group, Inc.

First Published in the United Kingdom in 1993
by Jonathan Cape Limited.

Library of Congress Cataloging-in-Publication Data

Okri, Ben.
    Songs of enchantment / Ben Okri. — 1st ed. in the U.S.A.
        p.   cm.
    Sequel to : The famished road.
    I. Title.
PR9387.9.O394S6   1993
823—dc20   93-17198
                                                       CIP

ISBN 0-385-47154-8

1   3   5   7   9   10   8   6   4   2

To Silver Okri

'felix, qui potuit rerum cognoscere causas'

Virgil, *Georgics*, Book II, 490

Book One

———

CHAPTER ONE

What We Didn't See

WE DIDN'T SEE the seven mountains ahead of us. We didn't see how they are always ahead, always calling us, always reminding us that there are more things to be done, dreams to be realised, joys to be re-discovered, promises made before birth to be fulfilled, beauty to be incarnated, and love embodied.

We didn't notice how they hinted that nothing is ever finished, that struggles are never truly concluded, that sometimes we have to re-dream our lives, and that life can always be used to create more light.

We didn't see the mountains ahead and so we didn't sense the upheavals to come, upheavals that were in fact already in our midst, waiting to burst into flames. We didn't see the chaos growing; and when its advancing waves found us we were unprepared for its feverish narratives and wild manifestations. We were unprepared for an era twisted out of natural proportions, unprepared when our road began to speak in the bizarre languages of violence and transformations. The world broke up into unimaginable forms, and only the circling spirits of the age saw what was happening with any clarity.

This is the song of a circling spirit. This is a story for all of us who never see the seven mountains of our secret destiny, who never see that beyond the chaos there can always be a new sunlight.

CHAPTER TWO

———

An Unwilling Adventurer

YES, THE SPIRIT-CHILD is an unwilling adventurer into chaos and sunlight, into the dreams of the living and the
dead. But after dad's last fight, after his magnificent dream,
my adventures got deeper and stranger. My spirit-companions
were the invisible causes of this deepening. They persisted in
trying to lure me back to their realm, but now they chose
another method, a method more terrifying than any they had
employed before. They chose to draw me deeper into the horrors of existence as a way of forcing me to recoil from life. But
they didn't count on the love that made me want to stay on this
earth. They didn't count on my curiosity either.

It took dad a long time to recover from his mythic battle
with the man from the Land of Fighting Ghosts. He became
withdrawn, and something about him changed irrevocably.
After dad's fight, and after the good wind stopped blowing,
a new cycle launched itself into our universe.

In those days it didn't rain, but I didn't go to school any
more. I stopped because even at school my spirit-companions
tormented me. Their songs distracted and confused me, and
when I copied down the wrong things I got into trouble.
There was a history class, for example, in which the teacher
was horrified to find my exercise book covered in complex
mathematical equations. I didn't know where they had come
from. When we were being taught mathematics under a dying
silk-cotton tree the face of a penitent oppressor of our people
stared at me from the trunk. On one day I saw the radiant
face of Pharaoh Akhnaton, on another the faces of the unborn. When I stared at them, mesmerised, the teacher

4

flogged me for not paying attention. In the English class my spirit-companions sang polyphonic chorales at me in a blending of seven traditional languages. It became impossible to concentrate. There were even times when the spirits whispered things in my ears and I blurted out what the teacher was going to say moments before he did. The worst thing was that I seemed to know our examination questions before they were set, and I knew the answers as well. The teachers found this very peculiar. Suspicious of the accuracy of my answers, they often failed me because they thought I had been cheating.

In short, my spirit-companions played havoc with my education. They made me seem strange to the other children, and so I didn't have many friends. There was only Ade, but he was succumbing to the world of spirits. His epileptic spells were luring him away from life. I was often lonely. And my spirit-companions used my loneliness to invade my life in new ways. They expanded my being and filled me with mysterious spaces. They insinuated themselves into my vision. In the midst of my new solitude, and particularly at night when I was asleep, they frequently read to me from invisible books of history, science, philosophy, musicology and geography. They poured all manner of arcane knowledge into my head. They filled me to bursting with spirit books of literature, archaeology, quantum physics and advanced lessons in counterpoint and chiaroscuro long before I could even read. They filled me with images of Zimbabwean rock paintings and Nordic gods, with Luo proverbs, Ashante songs, and Byzantine melodies, with Zulu epics and stories of ancient, forgotten heroes. All this made me babble out the strangest things and made my teachers hate me. Tired of being singled out for merciless whipping, I took to sneaking from class and wandering through the ghetto.

Yes, those relentless spirit-companions of mine poured into me the prophecies of Nostradamus and the wild visions of African mystics and the theories of Pythagoras and hundreds of useless facts. Meanwhile I walked barefoot in a world breaking down under the force of hunger. Meanwhile I staggered beneath the demonic smile of the yellow sun which sets bushes and newspapers alight.

CHAPTER THREE

————

Dad and the Luminous Demon

THEN ONE MORNING, more golden than yellow, my wandering found a focus. I went outside to our housefront and saw that the beggars had gone. They had come uninvited to the party dad threw to celebrate his great victory, and he absorbed them into his mythology and set himself up as their champion. He promised to build them a school. But we had been so concerned with dad's recovery that we stopped noticing the beggars, and forgot their special place in dad's political vision. And because we forgot them, they turned against us. Dad had great plans for them. Now they had disappeared. It was with some anxiety that I looked for them everywhere.

I scoured the street and asked everyone I met. I went to Madame Koto's barfront. I searched for them along the edges of the forest, where they scavenged for food and slept in unfinished houses, but I simply couldn't find them.

Late in the afternoon when dad returned from work, reeking of the bags of fish he had been carrying on his head all day, I told him that the beggars had gone.

'Gone?' he asked incredulously. 'How can they go? I'm going to build them a school. I've even started asking about the cost of a plot of land. They haven't really gone, have they?'

'They have,' I said.

Stinking of fish, his forehead glistening with iridescent scales, his boots thick with mud, he bustled out into the street and went looking for the beggars. He didn't even stop to change from his work clothes. I hurried out with him. Great energies swirled around dad. His spirit was fiery. He walked with enormous strides and I tried to keep up with him

7

as he erupted into a torrent of fantastical ideas and schemes. He was going to build a unique school for beggars. He was going to supervise the education of all poor and illiterate people. He said they needed education the most.

'That is how the powerful people keep us down,' he maintained. 'They keep us illiterate and then they deceive us and treat us like children.'

He swore that he was going to teach the beggars mathematics, accountancy, law and history. He said I would teach them how to read. He talked of turning all the ghettoes into special secret universities where the most effective knowledge in the world would be made available.

We went up the street and got to the main road. Crowds of people all over the place were talking about politics. They talked about the forthcoming rally and the famous musicians who would be performing. And they also talked about those who had died in the political violence. We happened to notice a few beggars up the road and dad went and spoke to them as if they were old friends. I heard him asking one of them about Helen, the beautiful beggar girl with a bad eye. I heard him pleading with them to come back to our street and help with the building of the school. He was so fervent and earnest that he must have struck everyone as being quite mad. The beggars were frightened by him, and they fled. Dad went after them, pleading, and they kept running: they must have thought that he was trying to steal what little money they had. Exasperated, dad turned to me and said:

'What's wrong with them? Why are they afraid of me, eh?'

'They are not the same beggars.'

'Not the same beggars?'

'These are different beggars. They are not the ones from our street.'

Dad glared at them. Then he said:

'Let's go back.'

We pushed through the crowds, past bicyclists ringing their bells, cart-pullers groaning with their loads of garri and cement, past the tight throng of traders and marketwomen. At the arena where the great rally was going to be staged carpenters were constructing a mighty dais with a zinc roof. Hundreds of artisans were working at the site, hammering away, sawing up wood, climbing up ladders, carrying thick planks, singing, shouting and arguing. Petty traders sat around selling soft drinks and ready-made food. Dad met some of his fellow load-carriers and engaged them in lengthy political disputations. And when we got back to our street we were astonished to find our beggars sitting round the broken vehicle, as if they had been there all along, and as if we had just re-entered their alien reality. Helen wasn't with them.

The beggars looked at us with dull eyes. They didn't move from their positions and their faces didn't light up at the sight of dad. It was clear that they had reached a decision. Dad felt excluded from the closed circle of their resolution, and he tried to regain their trust, and inspire them with his lofty schemes. But they had heard his promises a thousand times and their faces registered no response. He joked, and laughed at his own jokes, but they remained sullen. He asked about Helen, but they made no reply. He became unaccountably desperate.

'Where has she gone? Has someone touched her? Did she run away? Has she deserted our cause?'

The beggars were silent. Dad stared at them for a long time, apparently confused. Then, muttering something, he hurried back to the house. I went after him. When I got to the room, he was taking off his boots. He told me to polish them till they shone. He went and had a bath and washed the fish smells off him.

While he bathed, mum returned from her day-long hawking of cheap wares. She seemed leaner, her eyes dulled by the yellow dust, her face darkened by the fiery marigold sunlight. After dropping her basin of provisions on the cupboard, she sat on the bed. She did not move. She did not speak. She stank of profound exhaustion.

9

When dad came in from the bathroom he did not seem particularly pleased to see mum. In fact, he ignored her altogether. He sat on his chair and proceeded to anoint himself with coconut oil. He combed and parted his hair. Then he put on his safari suit which used to be white, but which had turned brownish with age. He applied cheap perfume to his face. Something odd had happened to dad after his great dream. He had become more susceptible to invisible presences in the air. It was as if holes had opened up in his spirit through which wisps of malevolence could enter.

When he saw that his boots had not been cleaned or polished, he exploded into a short burst of rage. He chased me twice round the room with a thick belt in his hand. He caught me at the door, dragged me in, and was about to lash me when mum – in a deadly voice – said:

'If you touch my son, you will have to kill me.'

Dad lowered his belt and sat in his chair. He retreated into the barely contained whirlwind of his fury. He poured himself a generous quantity of ogogoro, lit a cigarette and, in between smoking, proceeded to decrust his boots. While he cleaned his boots his spirit boiled and I watched as a strange demon entered him in the form of a beautiful girl with green eyes. The demon-girl moved into dad's spirit and sat comfortably, and then I couldn't see it any more. As he cleaned his boots with fiery vigour, smoking his cigarette with a grim intensity, his spirit rising and swirling, dad lashed us with accusations. Sweating through his suit, his temper seemed to burn around him. His forehead became an agitation of wrinkles. Mum sat very still, listening. While dad was shouting at us an evil spirit went right through our room, on its way to the preparations for the great political rally. The evil spirit, passing through our spaces, made all of us edgy. It awakened deep irrational passions in dad's brain. Fuming, he scraped the dried mud off his boots angrily. His face swelling, his chest heaving, his big muscles bristling, he accused us of betraying him, of not caring enough for his ideals. Mum, he said, only cared for herself. He complained that we had no respect for him, that we didn't even see the importance of carrying on his schemes while he recovered from his fight.

He harangued us as if we were failed members of a government cabinet. He was angry about the fact that we had not supervised the beggars, had not encouraged them, had not fed them, and had not looked after Helen, the beggar girl, whom he said was a princess from a distant and devastated kingdom. He rounded on me because I had stopped spying at Madame Koto's bar. He rounded on mum because she had not been keeping in touch with political developments, and had done nothing to recruit women to his political party. And he turned on both of us for failing to keep alive his dream of a university for beggars and the poor.

Mum said:

'You spend all your time talking about this university for beggars, but what about us, eh? Are we not beggars? Don't you hear how cracked my voice is? From morning till night I walked this ungodly city, hawking my provisions, crying out, while you slept like a goat for seven days.'

Leaping to his feet, dad vented his full fury at mum. Blindly, he hurled his boots at the cupboard. The cupboard door flew open, revealing the pots empty of food. Cockroaches were sent scampering everywhere. Stamping his feet, lashing the air with his big fists, he went quite berserk with shouting. He said mum was entirely devoid of vision and spent all her energy counting her wretched profits, while he tried to improve the condition of the people.

'Improve our condition first,' mum replied.

Dad was momentarily stunned at the boldness of mum's interruption. She continued.

'Where will you get the money to build a school for mosquitoes, talk less of beggars, eh? Will you steal, eh? Do you think money falls out of dreams, eh?'

11

Dad stopped in the beginnings of an antagonistic gesture.

'But what about all the money I won?' he asked, staring at us in utter disbelief, his bewilderment tinged with rage.

We were silent. We had completely forgotten the huge amount of money due to dad for winning the battle with the warrior from the Land of Fighting Ghosts. Worried about his injuries, awestruck by his fabulous sleep, and distracted by his recuperation we had not remembered that Sami, the betting shop man, owed us what amounted to a sizeable fortune.

'WHAT ABOUT MY MONEY?' dad cried again.

'We forgot,' I said.

Mum shot me a furious glance. Dad sat on his chair and kept staring at us alternately, as if we had committed acts of unbelievable criminality.

'Do you mean to tell me,' he said, pressing such menace into every word, 'that you people haven't YET collected my money, eh?'

We dug deeper into our silence. Mum started to fidget. Then dad, jumping up, sending the three-legged chair flying from underneath him, truly unleashed his mistral rage.

'You are not on my side,' he bellowed at mum. 'You are clearly my enemy! You want me to fail! You want me to be destroyed by the world! You go around in dirty clothes, and ugly shoes, and a disgusting wig of a he-goat, when I have hundreds of pounds sitting just across the street! You starve me, you starve my son, you obviously feed yourself in secret, and meanwhile you don't even bother to secure my investments! I carry loads that would break the neck of Hercules. I fight with giants and monsters and thugs. Yes, I fight and get beaten and manage to win – and I win only because of you two – and yet, through all this agony, you don't even bother to look after the fruits of my victory?'

Dad paused. Then he drew a deep breath and, thrusting his raw face at mum, he shouted:

'GET OUT OF MY HOUSE, YOU USELESS WOMAN WITH YOUR STUPID WIG! GET OUT! Go and sell your

stupid provisions from morning till night! YOU ENJOY SUF-
FERING – YOU ENJOY POVERTY! Fine! GO and enjoy
your poverty somewhere else and DON'T COME BACK! I
will not kill myself for an UNGRATEFUL WIFE!'

Mum bore his tirade in a dangerous and stiff-necked
silence. When dad had exhausted himself, mum stood up.
With the movements of one who was enacting a decision
she had reached long ago, she began to bundle her possessions. She gathered her faded wrappers, her moth-eaten
wig, her undergarments, her old blouses, her slippers, her
cheap jewelry, her tin-can of money, and dumped them all
into an ancient box. Having almost reached the end of her
forbearance, she took dad's words extremely seriously.

'Where are you going?' I asked.

She screamed at me, deafening me with the full volume of
her life-long frustration. Dad stamped on the ground with his
boots, downed a shot of ogogoro, and stormed out of the
room. I followed him, but I kept a careful distance between
us. The demon-girl was growing in him, becoming more
luminous and ecstatic.

CHAPTER FOUR

————

A Bizarre Courtship

O UTSIDE, GREEN MOTHS were thickening in the air. No one
seemed to notice. Dad was striding furiously to Sami's
betting shop when he saw Helen. Her beauty was more hyp-
notic than ever. Her blind eye was darker, her good one more
jewelled, and she was sitting on the bonnet of the burnt political vehicle, surrounded by the moths.

As if magnetised by the force of her astonishing serenity,
dad changed direction and ran over to her. He was about to
speak when she turned her strange eyes to him and said:

'It's time for us to go.'

'Why?' dad asked.

'When the time is right we will be back,' she replied,
turning away from him.

Dad pleaded with her to stay. The more he pleaded, the
less interested she seemed. After a while she jumped down
from the bonnet. The other beggars appeared mysteriously
with rotting corn-cobs and mouldy bread in their hands.
They gathered round Helen, awaiting her command. The
moths had concentrated about them as if their poverty and
their wretchedness were a unique kind of light. Without
uttering another word Helen led the beggars up the road.
The moths went with them, their clattering wings sounded
oddly metallic.

Dad stood still for a long moment, watching the beggars
leave. His face was disconsolate and it seemed his dreams
were deserting him. The beggars had gone a short distance
when dad broke the trance of his abandonment and ran after
them. The street watched us. The moths clicked in our faces.

14

Thickly gathered around the beggars, they seemed a kind of shield. Was I the only one who saw the moths? Dad didn't seem to, for he had launched into an impassioned plea directed at the beggar girl. Staring deep into her gem-like eye, he begged her to give him one last chance to fulfil his promise. He blamed his neglect on his recuperation, on me and mum; and swore that he was going to build a school for them as soon as he had collected his money from the betting shop man.

'I will prove it to you,' he kept saying.

But the beggar girl, deaf to his entreaties, carried on walking. Glowing in a new delirium, dad began to praise her beauty and her elegance, her face of a yellow moon, her limbs of a blue gazelle, her eyes of a sad and sacred antelope. He completely amazed me with his declaration of fearless love. In a burning voice, robust and insane, he said:

'I dream of you every day, my princess from a strange kingdom. Everyone else sees you as a beggar, but I know you belong to a golden throne. You are so beautiful that even these butterflies . . .'

'Moths,' I corrected.

Dad glared at me, tapped me on the head, and proceeded with his bizarre, passionate courtship.

'. . . that even these butterflies cling to you as if you are honey. You have the head of a spaceship, your eyes are like those of the wonderful maidens of Atlantis, you belong to the angelic kingdoms beneath the sea. You are a moon-woman come to brighten the earth. Your skin looks like flowers from another planet. You are the mistress of beauty, princess of grace, Queen of the road. Let the flowers of the earth see you and weep . . .'

Dad went on and on, pouring out a stream of contradictory praises. The beggars ate their mould-encrusted bread and laughed at dad's ridiculous words. Helen remained indifferent. Unable to bear her indifference, his face twitching under the assault of the moths, dad finally blocked her path, just before we got to Madame Koto's barfront. He astounded me by saying:

'I want you to be my second wife. Stay and marry me. I will take care of your people.'

The beggar girl went on as if she hadn't heard anything. Then dad – his spirit swirling in the new yellow delirium – boldly declared his intention to honour his promises. He said Helen should come with him to Sami's betting shop, and if all he was saying wasn't true, if he didn't have the money to build them a school, to feed and cater for them, then she was free to go. He made a solemn oath, loudly and with dramatic gestures.

For the first time Helen acknowledged his persistence. She stopped. Dad's face broke into a triumphant smile. Turning to the rest of the beggars, he told them to wait for him. Then he seized Helen's hand and set off with her towards Sami's shop. Pestered by the moths, he strode defiantly through the rumour-making stares of the street.

Just as we were going past our house, mum emerged with her tattered wig on and her ancient box under her arm. Dad didn't notice her. She looked so unlike herself, so wretched and haggard, as if she were a tramp, or as if she were fleeing the compound in shame, that even I nearly didn't recognise her. She followed us a short way and then, loud enough for the whole street to hear, she shouted:

'So you want me to go, eh? So you are throwing me out because of that stinking beggar girl with a goat's eye, eh?'

Dad looked back, saw her through the eyes of the demon sitting comfortably inside him, made a dismissive irritated movement of his hand, and carried on, dragging the unwilling but mesmerised beggar girl with him. The demon that had entered my father had moved in for good. The occupation was complete. I could see his spirit whirling with grand dreams of love. For, as he went, oblivious to the terrible changes he was bringing into our lives, I realised how much

16

dad was brimming over with love, possessed by its secret madness, bursting with love for everything, a wild unholy indiscriminate love, a love so powerful that it made him feel like a god, so vast that he didn't know how to contain it or express it. The love in him had become a double demon and it propelled him towards chaos.

Mum began weeping bitterly, cursing all the years of her privation and suffering, cursing the day she set eyes on dad in the village, during the most beautiful years of her life, swearing at dad for having drained the life out of her in so profitless a marriage. And between them both I didn't know who to choose. Mum went off, wailing, in the direction of Madame Koto's fabulous bar. Dad marched on to Sami's place, unmindful of the destruction he was sowing behind him. I started after mum, but she screamed at me, as if she perceived that I was in alliance with dad. And it may have been because of the moths (which I alone saw as moths), because of Helen and her tattered yellow dress, her emerald eye, or because of dad's polished boots and his bristling demonic love, or because I didn't really believe mum would disappear from our lives, that I chose to go after dad – for with his mad passion lay the greater magnetic adventure, the curiosity and the rage.

And so, watching mum grow smaller in the distance, a slouching figure, wailing and renting her wig, I reluctantly stuck with dad's story, and suffered the choice I made for many nights to come.

CHAPTER FIVE

———

The Demon's Gift

WHEN WE GOT to Sami's betting shop we were alarmed to find that his signboard was no longer posted outside. The main door was padlocked and two planks had been nailed across it. Dad knocked and got no answers. The beggar girl watched from a short distance away, the moths swirling round her head in perpetual motion. Dad banged on the door. Then he kicked it and ran against it with his shoulder. The wood splintered. He raised such a racket with his banging and shouting that the compound people came rushing out with sticks and machetes, fearing that they were being robbed, or that the political thugs had returned to wreak greater oppression on their lives. When dad saw them he asked in an angry voice where Sami had gone.

'He has left, packed away,' one of the neighbours said.

'Packed away? To where?'

'Black Tyger, why are you asking us? He's gone, that's all we know.'

'Gone? Gone? What about my money?'

'Do I owe you money? Why are you asking me about your money, eh?'

'My fight money, my money, where's my money?' dad kept screaming, kicking the door, ripping off the planks, lashing out, foaming at the lips, his rage conquering him.

Such energy and fury swirled round him that he staggered, quivering, under the blind intensity of the demon's gift.

'You are all hiding him! This is a plot! You are all trying to keep the money I nearly died winning,' he yelled, rushing at the compound people.

The men fell on him and hammered him with their clubs and sticks. I screamed. Dad threw punches in every direction, flooring two of the men. The women, howling, pounced on him with brooms and firewood. The other men went to get reinforcements. Soon the landlord came rushing out, clad only in his wrapper, holding a cocked dane gun in his hands, demanding to know the cause of the commotion. But the reinforcements jumped on dad. There was much hollering. A crowd gathered. Dad disappeared under the tumble of bodies. The men hit out indiscriminately, lashing their own. Children cried around their mothers. A little girl was accidentally clubbed on the head by an over-enthusiastic neighbour. The girl's mother clubbed the neighbour back, and the fight widened.

From beneath the crush of bodies I heard a mighty cry, and when the cry reached its frightening pitch the wind cracked a tree branch near us. Helen started to retreat. The crowd swelled, and somehow became included in the scuffle. The rest of the beggars arrived. Seeing that dad was being beaten, they fell in and clawed away at every moving body. They kicked and bit and punched whatever was in their way, till the mountainous tumble became a frenzied hybridous animal of many limbs tortured by its own insanity. The moths flew everywhere, circling the fighting men. And then suddenly dad emerged, his head crowned with mutinous lights, his suit in complete tatters. The beggars were sprawled around him like gigantic insects in mid-transformation. The women groaned about their broken limbs and the men about their battered heads. The landlord stood in the midst of all this, his wrapper torn from round his waist. He was completely naked. His eyes surveyed the chaotic events with controlled disdain. His dane gun was pointed at the writhing centre of bodies. One of the beggars saw his imperious and terrifying stance, and released a strange cry. The landlord, without changing his expression, trained his gun on the beggar; dad jumped in front of him; a child began yelling; and when the moths rushed upwards, surrounding the landlord, when the landlord directed the muzzle of the gun at dad's chest, the lights changed, everyone screamed, the air darkened, a sulphurous tiger of light leapt out into the new darkness, transfiguring the beggars, and a dreadful noise exploded in our ears. Everyone dived for cover and when the noise cleared there was a curious silence punctuated by the clicking sounds of the multitudinous moths. We looked up and saw only the landlord standing, his eyes crossed in dementia, his gun smoking. Totally naked, and hirsute, his head was framed by the distant stars in the dark blue sky, and by the nimbus of angry moths. It was only when a beggar broke the silence with his wailing that we realised what had happened.

I got up and frantically began looking for dad. I could not find him amongst all the bodies. Meanwhile the compound men jumped on the stupefied landlord, disarmed him, tied his wrapper round his waist, and led him back into the house. The women were yelling everywhere. Children were crying. The rest of the crowd rose slowly from their cowering prostrate positions. I turned and noticed Helen a long way up the street. Behind her the beggars were carrying the body of their companion. I watched their departure while still searching for dad. They were almost out of sight when I stumbled over a man lying on the ground. He raised his head, and then stood up, snorting like a wild bull. With bewildered eyes he looked one way and another, muttering something about being in the land of the dead. His clothes were all muddy, sand and leaves were in his hair, his eyes were bulbous, there was an ugly cut on his face, and it was only when I smelt his body-breath of a maddened frustrated man that I realised he was my father.

'Dad!' I cried.

'Where am I?' he asked in a subdued voice.

'The beggars are going. The landlord shot you,' I said.

Then he remembered. With a new agitation he inspected himself. He checked every bone in his body. He felt his neck, his chest, his stomach, frantically searching for a hole the size of a cow's foot. He asked me to look all over him. He suddenly imagined a hot wind blowing through his lower back, and blood pouring from his neck. He howled at the thought of a pain that had opened up at the base of his skull. I looked, and found nothing. And when it became clear that he was all right he promptly forgot about the hot wind and the pain and his money, and ran after the beggars. His arms were jittery at his side.

He caught up with them just as they entered the mysterious darkness of the forest. Helen was weeping. The beggars bravely bore the body of their wounded companion. Shuffling along on the rough earth, with their missing limbs, their soft-wax legs, their bulbous goitres, their monstrous faces of diseased vegetables, they were all of them wailing in a funereal monotone. Dad was distraught at the trouble he had brought them. He kept apologising to Helen, clinging to her hands, trying to hold her back, begging for a chance to make up to them in some way, but she refused to listen, and she did not stop. She led her companions into the deep mysteries of the forest.

The wounded beggar kept twitching. The moths were thick around his wound. Dad tried to help bear his weight, but the others wouldn't allow it. So dad, crouching and walking alongside them, poured consolations into the ear of the beggar. It was a relief to dad that the poor man had only been shot in his bad arm. The arm dangled, and thick blood flowed steadily along the forest path. Dad tried to get the beggars to stop so he could staunch the bleeding. He went on pestering them with his unwanted solicitations till they could bear it no longer. Suddenly they stopped. With her eerie grace, Helen went on steadily into the forest, where the moths were more populous, covering her, propelling her deeper into a haze of green self-illuminating wings.

Having stopped, the other beggars stared at dad ominously. He was confused by the emerald fire in their eyes.

As dad reached out to touch the wounded beggar's arm, a guttural noise rose from the group. And then the wounded beggar turned his twisted head, and spat into dad's face. As if it were a cue, the others joined in. We were stunned. They carried on into the deep forest, shuffling along on the dark earth, singing a nasal lamentation.

For a long moment dad didn't seem to know what to do. Then, wiping their anger off his face, galvanised by the desire to redeem the suffering he had caused, dad went after Helen. She led us deeper and deeper into the darkness. There were whispers and murmurs everywhere. The trees resounded with the chorus of the beggars' lamentation. I saw butterflies with red wings appear from the thick bushes. Long-legged insects leapt across my face. An owl flew over dad's head. Cobwebs became wrinkles on my forehead. The forest was changing. The air turned black. A formation of white bats descended on us and we ducked in terror. By the time we had recovered, the beggars were nowhere in sight. We couldn't even hear their song. The world turned on an inscrutable axis and plunged us into an alien terrain. We heard a tree groaning deep in the forest. Then a fantastic noise shook the earth. Dad rushed on ahead and the next thing I knew I was alone. The darkness bristled. I felt disembodied forms jostling me, whispering numinous words into the pores of my body, as if all my pores were undiscovered ears. I went forward cautiously, feeling the air like a blind man, when a white wind swooped up into my face. And when I looked down I found myself staring into an abyss, a pit of darkness.

Dad was clinging on to the roots of a tree. I could hear his feet kicking the earth and the empty spaces.

'Help me,' he said.

I did my best and after a while dad managed to climb out from the hole. When he regained firm ground he held on to me. We were still. Much more cautiously now, we felt our way through the darkness. I climbed a tree. Dad walked round in circles. I couldn't see anything, and climbed back down. To our terrified astonishment, much as we tramped through the bushes looking for Helen and the beggars, much as we tried, we could not find them. It seemed another realm had swallowed them up. It seemed as if they had stepped out of this reality, and into another. Maybe we need to keep looking at the world with new eyes.

CHAPTER SIX

The Dreaming Forest

'THEY'VE VANISHED,' dad said.

'The world has changed,' I said.

Dad was in a frenzy. My head kept spinning. We sat on the forest floor. All around us in the dark everything was still, and yet everything was moving. I listened to the night, and heard the whispering wind. The leaves rustled and insects were in secret conversation everywhere. I listened to the silence of the moon as it cut a shimmering path through the branches. A rubber tree dripped sap not far from us. The air was sweet-smelling.

'The forest is dreaming,' dad said, lighting a cigarette.

Then he was silent. I couldn't see his face. After he had finished the cigarette, he said:

'Let's go home.'

'There is a river coming,' I said.

The mighty sound of flowing waters, each wave murmuring with human laughter, gathered behind us, deep in the forest. The insect noises became more tumultuous. Birds flew wildly from the invisible trees and shot past us. Dad jumped up.

'Let's run,' he said.

Seizing my hand, he broke into a canter. We ran for a long time. The air turned green. A hyena laughed in the dark. An owl called. Ritual noises surfaced among the bushes. Suddenly, everything was alive. The air crackled with resinous electricity.

'I can't breathe,' I said. 'The air is turning to fire.'

'Just keeping on running,' dad said, 'and don't close

your eyes.'

We ran into a quivering universe, into resplendent and secret worlds. We ran through an abode of spirits, through the disconsolate forms of homeless ghosts. We hurried through the mesmeric dreams of hidden gods, through a sepia fog thick with hybrid beings, through the yellow village of invisible crows, past susurrant marketplaces of the unborn, and into the sprawling ghommid-infested alabaster landscapes of the recently dead. We kept pushing on through the inscrutable resistance of the moon-scented air, trying to find the road back into our familiar reality. But the road eluded us and we troubled the invisible forms of great trees with our breathing, and the spirits of extinct animals with our fear. Our heads pulsated with an infernal violet heat.

We broke into another level of time. I could hear the moon-voices of my spirit-companions calling out to me from the nocturnal choir of insects, the rococo piping of night-birds, and the penumbral cries of agonised trees. Haunting flute-songs followed us. I saw solitary fauns dancing in the dark. Hidden monsters that bred all year round watched us as we stumbled through their living spaces. I looked back and noticed green lights, isolated in the air, following us steadily.

'Ghosts are spying on us,' I said.

Dad lifted me on his back and bounded on through the pullulating darkness of the shadow worlds. We passed a vermilion toadstool, spectral and sentient. I heard the awesome roar of a big jungle cat. Dad ripped through the bushes like a madman, chanting curious incantations. The world went on changing and all kinds of lights kept appearing above the undergrowths. It was impossible to determine how long we had been running, or how far we had travelled. But after a while, it seemed as if dad had been running in a straight line which paradoxically curved into an enchanted circle. We couldn't break out of the forest. It had become a labyrinth of secrets and dreams.

'My head is burning,' dad said.

Suddenly, my forehead caught fire and I screamed; and when I looked up I saw that there were gigantic spirits everywhere. Their thoughts pervaded the forest like scented woodsmoke. I knew instantly that they belonged to the slow migration of the great spirits of Africa. Where were they going? I had no idea. Their dreams were impenetrable, locked and coded in gnomic riddles. In the time we had been running civilisations had risen, had fallen, had disappeared. Transformations are faster at night. In that same time great leaders had been assassinated. I heard their astonished cries. New worlds were bursting out of the egg-shells of a million mutinous dreams. The labyrinth contained them all.

'If only I can find my secret training ground, I will get us out of here in no time,' dad said, his chest heaving, his back rippling.

The wind sighed over us, cooling the fire in our heads. Dad started to slow down. His breathing had become laboured. Then he stopped, and I got off his back.

Standing there in tenanted spaces, looking around, I could only make out the forms of trees moving in the waves of darkness. For a moment the air was still, and the moon had gone. We were silent for a long time. We couldn't even see the sky. There were green thoughts around us everywhere. I heard the river rushing towards us from behind. I said nothing. The wind heaved. A mighty thought shook the earth. I heard padded footfalls. Something cracked above us, and a silver wing cleaved the air. Something brushed against my foot, but I couldn't see what it was.

'What are we going to do?' asked dad.

He was invisible.

'Something has just touched my leg,' he said.

I looked down again and saw the two golden discs of a cat's eyes. Then I couldn't see them any more. Then after a while I saw them in the distance.

'Let's follow those eyes,' I said.

'What eyes?'

I pointed, but dad couldn't see my finger. So I took his hand and led him on. Then he said, his spirit rising:

'I can see them!'

He lifted me on to his back and we followed the golden eyes that kept appearing and vanishing.

'They remind me of Green Leopard,' he said, referring to his defeat of the famous boxer from the land of the dead.

'It's a cat,' I said. 'It's my friend.'

'Don't talk nonsense,' he replied.

'It's not nonsense.'

He didn't say anything. He went on running, pacing his breath, and after some time he cried out and said:

'My stomach is on fire!'

'The river is coming,' I said.

The cat's eyes disappeared and we didn't see them any more.

'Where has that cat gone?' dad asked in exasperation.

'I don't know.'

He stopped. We stayed like that for a moment. Dad looked around, trying to find the cat's eyes. Then something cracked again in the sky and before we knew it the silver wings sliced open the heavens and a flood of water crashed down on us. The water was warm and the wind buffeted us, smashing us against trees, hurling us into undergrowths. We fell and struggled back up and tramped through the loamy water that kept shifting the earth from beneath our feet. The rain thrashed us, blinded and deafened us, flogged us till we were livid all over. As we trudged on, directionless, the darkness kept opening and shutting. When it opened, in a swift deluge of light, I saw a bright city full of sunflower houses and blue streets. And when it shut, the darkness flashed with water. When it opened again I saw, in a crack of incandescence, the faces of three white women with dishevelled blonde hair and dolphin eyes and bleeding lips. And when it shut, dad said:

'Something is biting me all over.'

27

And my body too began to itch furiously. My eyes itched. My brain itched and I couldn't scratch it. The irritation grew more inflamed. I started screaming and dad said:

'I can see!'

The itching ceased. We were still. We found ourselves staring at a fabulous house encircled with red and yellow lights. It had a fluorescent signboard, whose legend I couldn't read from that distance. In front of the house many women, crowned with flowers, their eyes brilliant with antimony, silver bells in their hands, were dancing to effervescent music. A blind old man, with red bracelets and a white hat, played on an accordion and strutted around them. Then we heard flaming laughter and the strangled cry of a moon-slaughtered goat and dad said:

'We are in another world.'

'That is Madame Koto's place,' I said.

'It is! It is!' dad yelled, breaking into a joyful dance.

He made me slide off his back and he lifted me up and put me down; he threw me up into the air three times in jubilation and it was only when he was out of breath that he stopped to rest from the exhaustion of his own happiness. For a moment he too knew the spirit-child's exultation at homecoming.

But his momentary celebration was cut short by the realisation that the wind was cold. The rain had ceased. The silence over the forest was total, as if the land had stopped breathing. It didn't breathe in and didn't breathe out and we waited for the silence to end; and when it didn't end dad carried me on his back again, thinking about all the confusion he was going home to face. We had broken out of the dreaming forest, but the new realities of our lives were before us. We went past Madame Koto's place without stopping. We went up the dry street to our room without speaking. We found our door wide open.

CHAPTER SEVEN

If You Look Too Deeply
Everything Breaks Your Heart

T HERE WERE TWO lighted candles on the table. A mosquito coil burned steadily. Mum was asleep on the floor, under the shadow of the centre table. She had a thin cloth over her. The flickering candle light, making the shadows dance on the bare walls, illuminating the rafters and the cobwebs, revealed to us more forcefully the poverty in our lives. As soon as we stepped into the room, breathing in the stale libations, mum woke up. Dad took a few steps towards her. I saw the plea for reconciliation on his face. He went towards her tentatively, with anxiety on his brow, and when he thought he had her in his arms, when his face relaxed into profound gratitude at being so soon forgiven, mum ducked under his empty embrace. With her eyes wet and shining, she put on her slippers, and hurried out of the room. She didn't come back the whole night.

Dad sat in his chair and for hours he stared at the cupboard with a confused expression. He had the tormented look of a spurned lover. He sat very still, as if his brain had turned to wood, and didn't speak. The itching on my body came and went. Occasionally, my eyes twitched. We sat up all night, with the gloom and the midges thickening in the air, the door wide open, and the mosquito coil dropping its perfect spiral of ash on the centre table.

I went and had a bath. When I came back the room was dark, dad didn't light another candle, and all I heard was his breathing of a great animal in the disconsolate silence. I shut the door a little and brought out my mat.

I lay down, listening to the language of mosquitoes, the complaints of the insistent midges, when I noticed that the spirit of the luminous demon-girl had left dad. There were empty spaces where she had been sitting. The labyrinth and the rain had washed away his insane passions.

All night I watched the spaces in dad fill with a great sorrow, the colour of anguished blue. Dad's colours were of an immense sadness, almost a serenity, and I watched them deepen. I was determined to stay awake with him, but my eyes became heavy. I shut them for a while, and when I opened them again it was morning.

Dad was still sitting on his three-legged chair. His eyes were raw. He hadn't slept all night. I could tell he'd had a bath. He looked a little fresher and had changed his clothes. When he saw that I was awake he said:

'Go and buy yourself some food.'

He gave me some money. After I had washed my face I went and bought cooked beans, fried plantain and meat from the woman across the road. Dad didn't eat with me. I was hungry and ate everything and when I had finished and drunk some water, dad said:

'I'm not going to work, I'm not eating, and I'm not sleeping till your mother forgives me.'

Then he said:

'Read to me from one of those books.'

I selected one at random. It was a book of love poetry. The words were strange to me but when I stopped concentrating too much they made sense. I read as if I were repeating words spoken in my head by one of the several lives resident in me. I read five poems out to dad. After a while he was trembling on the chair, his head shaking, his face contorted.

'Are you crying, dad?' I asked.

He turned his face away and wiped his eyes and then said:

'How come you can read these books at your age?'

That was probably the first time that I felt the doors to my other lives – my past lives, my future lives – opening on me with frightening clarity. Sometimes my other lives would open and then shut, and what I glimpsed didn't make sense. Other times I could see far into an aquamarine past; I saw places I had never been to, saw faces that were both entirely alien and familiar; and my mind would be invaded with the black winds of enigmatic comprehension. The lives in me increased their spaces, languages of distant lands bore my thoughts, and I found I knew things I had never learnt. I knew the charts and tides of the Atlantic, I understood complex principles of higher mathematics, the sign-interpretations of the forgotten magis, the sculptural traditions of the ancient Benin guild, the lost philosophies of Pythagoras and the griots of Mali. Powerful symphonies resonated in me and sometimes I found that I could compose passages of silent spirit-music while I played in the street. The presences in me had been growing vaster, swelling out to include intuitions of other spheres and planets, and the invasions of knowledge had become frightening – and it had all been happening so quietly, so inexorably, that I became sure I was soon going to die. And when dad asked me the question I got up from the mat and put the book on the table and went to him and held his comforting arm, and said:

'My head grows bigger in the night.'

He stared at me for a while. Then he said:

'Don't read any more.'

He lifted me up and held me tightly. He pressed me into the sweet sad colours of his spirit. Deep inside I could hear him weeping. We stayed like that for a long time and then he put me down.

'We have to go and find your mother,' he said.

Leaving the door wide open, we went out into the street.

We searched for mum everywhere. We went up and down all the streets in our area. We asked all the women we encountered if they had seen mum. We asked men lounging outside their rooms, under the thatch eaves of makeshift kiosks; we asked children; we asked old men and young girls. No one had seen her and no one knew who we were talking about. We went to the marketplace where she used to have a stall before the thugs of politics drove her away because she hadn't joined their parties. We asked the market women. They remembered her, but hadn't seen her for a long time, they said. We tramped up up and down the wondrous chaotic marketplace, from the ironmongers to the money lenders, from the fish-sellers to the cloth-traders, from the hair-weavers to the corn-roasters, from the makers of rope to the makers of magic. No one could help us. Dad grew frenzied. He asked beggars and blindmen, little girls on errands and the great matriarchs of the marketplace. We left the market and started wandering without any sense of direction. Dad would suddenly sprint across the road and accost a woman with a basin on her head. He stopped all the women he saw, asking them irrelevant questions, on the off-chance that they might be one of her companions in hawking. Many of them were offended at dad's seemingly impertinent questions and they abused him, suspecting him of trying to rob them in some insidious way. Then he began wandering the confusing streets, the dirt tracks, the rough pitted roads, turning down blind alleys, backstreets, rutted pathways, roads that curved on themselves, following what he imagined to be the secret trail that mum took when she went hawking her meagre wares. How we wandered that day! The world seemed to be a nightmare of streets, a fiendish labyrinth of paths and cross-roads devised to drive human beings mad, calculated to get us lost. The world seemed to be composed of recently invented byways and tracks and dirt-roads created by the endless desire of human beings for shortcuts that elongate journeys, roads that start to induce their own peculiar form of dreaming on the exhausted soles of the feet. There are demons lurking underfoot in all the streets of the world that love to take men on terrifying unintended journeys. We walked that day into places that could only have been created by our own intense desire to exhaust all the routes of mum's daily journey out of the ghetto. We suffered her secret agonies that day, staggering under the blinding glare, stepping on sharp objects, kicking stones, seeing mirages, but never seeing mum.

'Didn't your mother ever take you with her, eh?' dad asked.

'No,' I replied.

We searched further. We wandered into the dreams lurking in all the sand-whorls, our faces dehydrated, our throats dry like leather, our eyes clogged with dust. After a long time, his voice humbler, deep with shame, dad said:

'I didn't know that your mother walked so much every day. Why didn't she ever tell me that she suffered so much to sell so little, eh?'

I didn't say anything. I don't think he really expected an answer. After we had been conquered by fatigue, and had worn out our soles searching, we went to a kiosk and dad bought some beans and soft drinks. He had finished eating when he remembered his promise not to eat or sleep till mum forgave him, and he tried to spit out the food but it had gone inside and I was a little ashamed of him, but I ate and drank because I had made no such promises and because my eyes were throbbing and red with hunger.

We went on searching for mum through the vengeful burnished fury of the ghetto sun. By the late afternoon dad's face was somewhat bony and darkened. Green veins were visible on his neck and forehead. His eyes were delirious. I had begun to sleepwalk in exhaustion. Dad carried me and went from house to house, describing mum to complete strangers, asking carpenters and brick-layers if they had seen a hawker like mum, and some said they had and pointed us in directions that led to creeks and clay villages; and we spent the worst part of the afternoon, when the sun most tormented the earth, wandering in dad's frantic and heroic sadness. And when evening came, when dad began to hallucinate that he was seeing mum everywhere, I said:

33

'Let's go home.'

Dad took us back, staggering, tripping, his head bowed, as if the sadness in his mind weighed more than the monstrous loads he carried at work. When we got near our place dad put me down, saying that he could no longer bear my weight. The dust of the world rushed into my eyes. The bad smells of the street, more intense at my height, crowded my nostrils. Everything I saw drew my spirit away from the world: the poverty and the cracked huts, the naked children with sores and the young women who had accelerated in ageing, the men with raw faces and angry eyes. Dad, with his head bowed, like a giant destroyed by the sun, released a profound sigh.

We had started shuffling towards home when we heard a mocking cackle of laughter behind us. I turned and saw the old man who had been blinded by a passing angel. He had two helpers with him. He wore an ill-fitting green suit, a red cravat and a black hat. He tapped dad on the head with his walking stick. In his cracked funereal voice, he said:

'It is terrible to care too much.'

Dad stared at him in bewilderment. The blind old man, releasing another cackle of laughter that made my eyes twitch, went on to say:

'If you look too deeply everything breaks your heart.'

Then he was silent. Dad grabbed the old man's cane.

'What do you mean by that remark?' dad wanted to know.

'Your wife is working for Madame Koto,' he said, and laughed again.

Dad let go of the cane. The old man brusquely signalled his helpers, and they led him up the street, towards the main road.

'He's talking rubbish,' dad said.

We went home silently. And when we got to our room, with the door still open, we beheld a miraculous sight. The whole place shimmered with cleanliness. The floor had been swept, the walls scrubbed, the bed made with new sheets, the cupboard crammed with food. There was a whole bottle

34

of ogogoro on the table. Fresh stew, excellent pounded yam and choice pieces of fried meat had been prepared. There were new cooking utensils next to the cupboard. There were new curtains over our window. The air, laced with the aroma of incense, smelt wonderfully ventilated and cool. At first we thought we had walked into someone else's room. Then we thought we had wandered into a dream. And then we saw dad's three-legged chair. Dad sat, and looked around in astonishment.

'Maybe a good spirit is helping us,' I said.

CHAPTER EIGHT

Parable of the Peacock

LATE IN THE evening, after we had rested, we went to
Madame Koto's bar to see if mum was there. The bar
had undergone another of its fabulous mutations. The walls
outside had been freshly re-painted in the colours of blue
and yellow. An extension was being constructed at the side
nearest the bushes. The bar was encircled with multicoloured
bulbs. There was a bigger signboard, and it was brilliantly lit.
Madame Koto had transformed her bar into an almost magical
enclave.

Inside, it was crowded with women. They bustled everywhere with large cooking utensils. They were dressed as if
for a feast or a celebration. Madame Koto, who was no
longer seen by the inhabitants of the area, who had now
become so powerful that all we knew about her were the
legends we invented, had completely entered the realm of
myths. She was a colossus in our dreams; her power over
us became demonic. Every day was a celebration in her bar
– a celebration of power, an affirmation of her legend.

The women, wearing identical wrappers and blouses,
were resplendent in their jewels and bangles and amulets.
They were mostly mighty women with enormous breasts
and eyes that were frightening in their invulnerable stare.
They were busy around the barfront, milling about with
tables and folding chairs. Their perfume was delicious to
the nostrils and they bore themselves proudly, like a select
people, or like members of a royal household.

When dad tried to go into the bar, they wouldn't let him.

'I have come to look for my wife!' he said.

36

'Go and find a wife somewhere else,' one of the women replied, stirring laughter amongst the others.

Music started up inside and when we looked through the new curtains of gold and green strips we saw men and women dancing. We saw tables with shining red tops. We saw cages with long-beaked birds pecking away at the wooden frames. Dad kept trying to get in, and the women kept pushing him away. Dad pleaded with them, he said his wife had disappeared. The women replied that it was men like him who made such things happen to their wives.

I went to the backyard. Women swarmed everywhere, busy with what I gathered were the preparations for the great rally. Madame Koto had built a proper kitchen and the rich aroma of stews and roasted chicken hung densely in the night air. I passed the back door and saw a woman who looked just like mum wearing a gold-tricked wrapper and a green blouse. She was dancing with a man who had a bullet-shaped head, a thick neck and a lion-capped walking stick.

'Mum!' I cried.

But the music was too loud for her to hear me. She flashed smiles in all directions, red lipstick burning her face, her arms loaded with bangles. I tried to get in, but the solid wall of women's bodies prevented me. I hurried to the front of the compound and saw dad sitting on the steps.

'There is someone like mum in there,' I told him.

He stared at me with dull eyes. He didn't move. I sat beside him and listened to the parrots squawking above the music. Three peacocks, their tails dazzling like rainbows, sauntered past and stared at us. Dad looked at the peacocks. One of them took a sinister interest in me. I threw a little stone at it, and missed.

'Leave it alone,' dad said.

The peacock scurried away and came back, leading the rest. It had silver-tinted eyes whose colours kept changing.

Looking at me curiously, it came over and pecked at my foot, drawing blood.

'That peacock is a witch,' I cried, knocking it away.

The peacock spread its wings and released a startling, almost human cry. The women in the bar came running out. Some of them went after the peacock, caught it, and began to say soothing words to the bird as if it were a special being. The other women towered over me and asked what I had been doing to the peacock. I showed them what it had done to me. One of the women knocked me on the head and dad regarded her with dull, menacing eyes. The woman tried to hit me again, but I clung to her leg and bit her and she fell over. The others came after me and I gave them the slip. Having no choice, I ran into the bar, into the smells of sacrificial blood and ritual herbs, the juices and rich potencies of bark and earth. At first I was entirely confused by the parrots noisy in their cages, the chained monkey jabbering away, and the demotic music. Wherever I turned a peacock spread its shimmering wings in my face. Wherever I looked women were passing away into empty spaces. I nearly ran into a blue mirror at the back of the bar. On the ledge, over the mirror, I noticed the shell of a tortoise. The constant movement of women pressed me against the wall. Something slid down my face. I yelled. I turned and saw snails on the wall. One of them dropped on my foot, and broke its shell on the floor. Blue water flowed out of its fragmentation.

Looking for the face of my mother, I struggled through the bodies. Women danced as if in a heated trance. Women sang quivering political songs that spoke of the new era of money and power. I couldn't get very far, so I retreated behind the counter. I climbed on a chair and surveyed the revelling. Suddenly, the music stopped. The parrots began squawking again. The tortoise on the ledge moved. The chief peacock strode into the bar and everyone made way for it. The peacock strutted all around the bar and came over to where I stood and stared up at me. Then a loud voice said:

'What is that boy doing here? Grab him!'

The women moved towards me. I got down from the chair and the peacock pecked me again on the thigh, drawing blood a second time. I lashed at the peacock and it fell against the mirror and all the voices cried out in horror as if I had committed a monstrous crime in broad daylight. Faced with the angry wave of bodies rushing towards me, I fled into the darkest corner of the room, behind the counter. A white cloth hung over a newly constructed alcove. I ran behind the cloth and something knocked the lights out of my head. When I came to a moment later I found myself in the presence of an enormous woman seated on a black chair. She had red sunglasses on her alabaster face, a yellow cape on her shoulders, a large fan of eagle feathers in one hand, a flywhisk in the other. The voices had stopped behind me.

The woman was perfectly still and exuded a presence both menacing and ancient. For a moment I was transfixed by the snails crawling up her face. Then the monkey broke into its erratic jabbering. The peacock came flapping into the corner and the red sunglasses fell off the woman's face. Instead of eyes I saw two red stones in her sockets. When the women outside the niche raised their voices at the violation of a sacred corner, when the wind lifted and turned green in my head, raising images of deep forests and places where the dead ride elephants – something exploded at my feet. I drew back. One of the woman's eyes had fallen from its socket. The red eyestone palpitated on the ground in front of me. With an intent that only animals have, the peacock lashed the air with its wings, quietened, stepped forward daintily, pecked at the eyestone, swallowed it, and fell, choking and kicking. Then it was still.

A darkness bluer than the depths of godless rivers closed over me before I could utter a sound.

CHAPTER NINE

———

The Conquest of Death

WHEN I OPENED my eyes the bar was empty. Flies sizzled in the hot air. Mum kept appearing and disappearing from me in the darkness of old rivers. Moths flying past my face opened lighted terrains where, as an unwilling adventurer, I saw Madame Koto growing bigger and vaster than the night. She was bloating, her face was mask-like, and her skin, peeling away, revealed a yellowness underneath. As the lights went on and off, she kept summoning me. I noticed the eunuchs around her, washing her skin in the milk of young girls, bathing her swollen body in the oil of alligators, washing her feet with rosewater. They dressed her in a velvet robe and when she stood up the men fell to their knees in prostration. Women appeared out of nowhere and decked her in cowries and golden necklaces. At the door to the outer chamber, kneeling down, waiting to be summoned, to be accepted into the secret circle of power in our new age, was my mother. She looked very small in that great space.

Madame Koto was encircled with this yellow power. Her radiance set the night on fire. Mum sweated all over, as if she were being fried in dread mysteries.

Startled by deep coughing outside, I waded through the darkness. I seemed to be making good progress when, looking up, my eyes burst into another realm of adventures, and I beheld the awesome sight of the converging spirits of the continent. I saw them in their transfigured procession. I saw the great spirits of all the ages, from all over the world, from all realms, saw them pressing closer, approaching with deep sounds in the air, coming together for their

40

mighty convocation, bringing their spirit-mysteries, their oceanic wisdom, their gnomic lore distilled from countless incarnations, bringing the jewelled terror of their immanent foresight, and their understanding of the secret forces and balances in the universe. I saw the spectral forms of these master spirits as I went slowly out of the bar, with the mosquitoes whining in the heat. I walked into a wall. The lights came on in my eyes and in another realm I saw my mother with medallions in her hair, a garland of coins and cowries round her neck, pound notes stuck to her body, as she advanced deeper into the long room, crossing the inviolable threshold, moving towards Madame Koto, whose face quivered in a weird ecstasy. I turned and went back into the bar, not knowing why. I walked into benches in the dark. My thigh hurt where the peacock had pecked me. And when I heard the forest sighing I felt freer and moved towards its breathing, and heard the night birds singing and the wings of the flying insects, and smelt the peculiar harshness of dad's cigarette.

He was sitting on the steps, his face weighed down by the night. It seemed he hadn't moved since I last saw him. When I touched him, he laughed.

'I have been sitting her for three nights and they still won't let me see your mother,' he said, dragging on his cigarette.

I didn't understand. Had I been dreaming? Had I somehow woven in and out of three separate nights compressed into a single memory? Had time been so different for us? Or was he exaggerating?

I sat beside him and he put his heavy arm round me. His sweat-smells made me more awake. I said:

'The blind old man was right. Mum is working for Madame Koto.'

Dad put out his cigarette.

'Then we have to save her,' he said, rising.

We went home without saying a word. The night followed

41

us and deepened as we entered the room. Dad tried to light a match three times, and failed. The night seemed to be conquering our attempts at creating illumination. All around in the darkness Madame Koto was growing. She was growing in our room. Her great invisible form surrounded us in the dark, filling out the spaces, deepening in the corners, breathing in the air of our spirit. Her body encompassed us and wherever we tried to go her shadow was there, listening to us, watching us from the heart and eyes of mum's love, following the motions of our spirit. My heart suddenly began to beat faster. Dad said:

'I can't light the match.'

'It's the night,' I said, in an old voice which startled me. 'She's everywhere.'

'Who?'

'Madame Koto.'

'Nonsense.'

'Her body is eating up the night,' I said.

'Come and light this candle,' dad said.

I tried to move forward but Madame Koto's shadow was everywhere. I stretched out my hand and all around me the darkness was a solid space.

'I can't move,' I said.

'Move!' dad commanded. 'Move like a soldier!'

'I can't. And we're losing mum,' I said.

'Come and light this candle then I will do something about your mother.'

Madame Koto's form flowed around me. I could hear her heart beating. It pounded in the air like the heart of an elephant or the great bull of night. Her heartbeat of forest drums made my ears ache. The pain pierced my head and when I recovered I momentarily found myself deep in the nation of her body. I saw great waves of people in the darkness, their heads disembodied and faintly lit up by the dull flames in the air. They poured in one direction. They moved in ritual organisation, as if sleepwalking.

They walked backwards, and a robed political leader commanded them. They turned into soldiers. The Head of State, a General, barked out orders and they lifted their guns and shot down all the living dreams of the nation. The darkness flowed around them and around me, and I understood the secret of living within the body of the leviathan-spirit of our age. With no choice, resorting to the freedom of the world of spirits, I began to mutate. I turned into a fish: I swam upwards. My scales were of gold. I turned into a butterfly: the air helped me on. I turned into a lizard, and scampered up the body of the night. I fell from the ceiling, hurting my back, and landed at dad's feet. For an instant I had rediscovered the powers of transformation locked in my spirit and in my will, powers that only came awake because mum was moving deeper into the long room, through the ritual thresholds, changing from a woman full of love and suffering into a half-woman half-antelope, her milk turning sour, her body wrinkling under the force of the night.

When I landed at dad's feet he kicked me gently and I rolled over and he said:

'What's wrong with you?'

'Mum is changing,' I said.

'Light this candle,' he said.

As I searched for his hands in the dark, Madame Koto offered me cowries. I took them. They burned my palms.

The mosquitoes whined.

'Shut the door, dad,' I said.

'Leave the door alone,' he growled.

Madame Koto offered me money – it turned to liquid in my hands. She offered me gold, which turned black, and thickened into wax, and flowed down my arms. Dad was crying. I didn't understand. Eventually I found his hands and took the box of matches. The wind sighed in the room. Dad stopped crying. I lit a match twice and the night ate up the brief illumination. The third time I succeeded in lighting the candle. At the door, sitting on its tail, was the shadow of a

43

cat. Then the apparition vanished. The candle light fought the darkness, fought the wind, and managed to stay aflame while new forebodings breathed into our lives. Dad looked at the candle with wonder in his shining eyes. He was still standing. Even with the light in the room, light enough for me to see dad's half-darkened face, and the cobwebs thickening in corners of the ceiling, the room was still occupied by Madame Koto's presence.

I drew near to the light. So did dad. We were silent. After a while, dad said:

'The air has changed in our room.'

'What are we going to do about mum,'

'I will do something,' he said.

He looked tortured. His face was shrunken.

'Get some sleep. I'll be watching over you. Our spirit is strong, you must fear nothing, you hear?'

I nodded. Fear nothing? I knew he was afraid, but he didn't know what he was afraid of, so I said:

'Something is happening.'

'Something wonderful,' he replied.

His voice had no conviction. The fact is that a weird anti-magnetism was operating on our lives, pulling everything apart. Dad got up and began pacing the room, stirring his spirit, uttering incantations, filling the place with his energies.

'The secret of strength is in the spirit,' he said. 'Life is often like fighting, and sometimes you have to draw power from your eyes or your toes or from your heart.'

He sat in his chair. I got out my mat and spread it on the floor.

'Tell me a story,' I said.

He smiled, stayed silent for a while, and then began speaking in the voice of a story-teller who can spread power with words.

'There was once a man who suffered all the bad things that can happen to a human being. He was a good man in a world full of wickedness. When a new bad thing happened

44

to him he refused to lose heart and he tried harder to live the good life. Then his only son died. His house burned down. His wife left him. He was sacked from his job because he refused to be corrupt. He was crossing the road one day when a cow kicked him and broke his face. He lived in the streets and bore his suffering with a smile in his spirit. Then he fell ill and began to die. While he was dying a mosquito landed on his ear and said, "If you stop being a good man wonderful things will happen to you." "Like what?" he asked. The mosquito replied, "You will be rich and famous. You will have many beautiful wives and lovely children. You will have power. Everybody will love you. And you will live a long and fruitful life."'

'So what did the man say?'

'He said, "And if I don't stop trying to be good?" The mosquito replied, "You will die when the sun comes out."'

'Then what did he do?'

'He knocked the mosquito away, got up from his bed in the street, and he went from house to house asking people if he could help them in any way because he was going to die that night. He helped the weak to fetch firewood. He carried loads at the night-market and gave the money away to beggars. He went to hospitals and spoke kind words to people who were also waiting to die. He settled quarrels between husbands and wives, between friends and enemies. And he preached everywhere he went, saying that people must learn to love one another because death was coming. He did a lot of things in that night, more in one night than in his whole life.'

'Then what happened?'

'Morning drew nearer. When he saw dawn in the sky he went and lay down on his bed in the street. His heart was full of peace. His face suddenly looked younger. His body was surrounded with a powerful and gentle light. Then a dog came to him and licked his feet. Then a goat came and licked his hands. Birds settled round him and began

45

to sing. People whom he had helped saw him and drew a crowd round him. Then the mosquito came and landed on his ear and said, "Your time is up." "Good," the man said. "I am not afraid." "Why not?" asked the mosquito. "Because", he said, "love is the real power. And where there is love there is no fear." The mosquito became very unhappy. It started to cry. The man said, "Why are you crying?" The mosquito answered, "It's because you are not afraid. I have brought death to thousands of people, but you are the first person I have met who is not afraid of dying." "But I am not going to die," said the man. "Why not?" asked the mosquito. The man then pointed to the birds and the animals and the human beings gathered round him. "Because", he said, "I have given them my life. I used to be one. Now, I am many. They will become more. How many of us can you kill? The more you kill, the more we will become. So you have done me a great favour and I thank you." Then the man drew his last breath and shut his eyes and the sun came out. All the people buried his body in a special place and his spirit became the guide of all those whose hearts are pure.'

When dad finished there was a silvery silence. Then, in a different voice, he said:

'Stories can conquer fear, you know. They can make the heart bigger.'

In the new silence I noticed that Madame Koto's presence had receded from around us. Dad's story had driven her away. His story made the candle burn brighter and seemed to have increased the serenity of his own spirit. He no longer looked tortured. His eyes shone and sweat glistened on his forehead. When I looked up I noticed a sentient silence among the cobwebs. The spiders had also been listening to dad's story.

'So get some sleep, leave the door open, and when you need me I will be here.'

He blew out the candle. I didn't hear him leave the room. He went out, but a form the exact shape of his body – only larger – remained sitting in his chair. Through the night the form grew even larger, filling out the room. It became lighter and cooler, a gentle shade of gold.

When I woke up in the morning the room had again been cleaned. There was food on the table. A pleasant aroma lingered in the air. I knew that dad hadn't returned, but I wasn't afraid. And I wasn't afraid because the good spirit had been visiting and keeping our lives company while dad did his penance and I stayed alone.

CHAPTER TEN

You Must Also Learn How to Fail

F OR THREE DAYS I followed dad in spirit. I followed his penance and I circled him in his journeys. In the daytime he went away. At night he would tell me a story. When he left, his other form in the chair grew more powerful and it protected me. The good spirit would tiptoe into the room while I was asleep and clean the place and prepare the most savoury dishes. Dad didn't sleep for seven days. I didn't see him eat. I ate, and grew leaner. The fleas harassed me. The mosquitoes fattened themselves on my blood and died from over-nourishment.

The wind kept trying to blow away dad's other form. The harder it tried, the lighter dad's other form became. It seemed like water. The intentional wind blew it one way, and it flowed, and re-formed in another space. The war between the nightwind and dad's secret form went on during the periods when dad left the house and carried mountainous loads at the docks, or mighty bales of cloth or bulging bags of garri at the markets, or broke rocks for the construction of roads.

The harder the wind blew, the harder dad worked. He seemed to be punishing himself, filling with suffering the empty spaces where the demon-girl once resided. He starved. He didn't drink any alcohol and didn't smoke any cigarettes. He didn't get into any fights and when provoked he allowed himself to be beaten. He came back a strange man every evening. He would rest a bit, pace the room, and tell stories about people who were dying and who went around helping others who were also dying and the mosquito said different things to the hero on the dawn of his transformation. Sometimes it was a lion that licked the good man's feet. Sometimes it was a tiger. Sometimes an elephant bore his body deep into the forest and to the land of spirits. Other times it was a giraffe that bore him on its cushioned hump into the kingdom of pure spirits on the great dawn of his coronation.

For three days I followed my father in spirit as he worked to earn mum's forgiveness. I never knew that dad also had many people inside him. He grew taller. His eyes became sunken, but they shone brighter. His unshaven look and the broken expression on his face kept making me want to cry. But a moment before I might have started to weep, he would begin a story. And when he left the house, staggering from his loss of weight, I realised that as he grew thinner his other form in the chair became so vast and powerful that it was soon bigger than the whole compound. It was a mystery. The other tenants, for no apparent reason, became kinder to me. They brought me food and kept touching my head fondly. Then one day a most curious thing happened. I was alone, playing in the street, when an old man with reddish teeth came to me. He stared into my eyes, smiled, and made a prayer over me, and went away.

My father carried loads with a vengeful determination. His neck shrank. His boots looked sad. He took to clearing the accumulations of rubbish in our street. He gave the money he had suffered so much to earn to families and total strangers who were poorer than we were. His penance became a new kind of demon. He offered to wash clothes for over-burdened women. He fetched water from our well for everyone. He dug gutters, he helped to build wooden bridges over marshlands near us, he worked on building sites, he visited our poor relations and took them medicines and fruits during their illnesses, and he came back every night with his head bowed, his eyes raw, unable to forgive himself.

On the third night he came home sadder than usual. He said:

'My son, I have been unable to gatecrash your mother's forgiveness.'

I stayed silent. Dad was disappearing. He hadn't eaten and his body was growing hollow.

'There is a red wind in my head,' he continued. 'When I was carrying loads today a fly sat on top of the load and I fell down and couldn't get up. No one in the wide world came to help me. I stayed on the ground the whole afternoon. The owners of the load came and kicked me and called me a dog. I didn't retaliate. Then an old woman came to me and said, "You can't hide your head from life. If you succeed you will lose your head. You must also learn how to fail." Then she left. She was a messenger from my father, the priest of Roads. But, Azaro, my son, I don't understand the message.'

He stared right through me. The door creaked open gently, as if the wind wanted to come in and listen to a story. I didn't like the wind any more. It had chilled me, and it had not stopped waging war on my father's secret form. But something made me want to turn round.

'Don't speak,' dad said in a low voice that made me think he was dying.

His face hung down, his jaws were slack, but he stared at something behind me with a glittering intensity in his eyes. When I turned right round the sight of the black cat sitting on its tail, its eyes alight, frightened me. When I screamed, the cat disappeared.

'You have driven our visitor away,' dad said sadly.

'It was another messenger,' I said.

'What was the message?'

'Go and beg mum,' I replied.

Dad was silent. He shut his eyes. He didn't move for a long time. I blew out the candle. For the first time in seven days, dad slept. He slept in his chair. That night, as dad slept precariously in his three-legged chair, I saw his other form gradually grow smaller. The gentle haze of gold diminished and settled in him and I never saw it again. I knew then that dad had found a secret way back into the immeasurable invisible happiness that is mixed like air into the long days of suffering, into the nights of agonised sleep. I knew then that he had somehow re-discovered the magic substance which the great God sprinkled in us and which sings with the flow of blood through all the journeys of our lives. And I dreamt that a large handful of that wonderful substance was sprinkled on us as we slept in the truce of the nightwind.

I woke to find that dad had bathed, shaved, combed his hair and put on his French suit. He was also singing. When I sat up the first thing he said was:

'My son, today is Madame Koto's day. Get ready. We are going on an interesting journey.'

CHAPTER ELEVEN

The Quest for Madame Koto

No ONE HAD SEEN Madame Koto for a long time. She existed only in rumours and in our dreams. Her absence had increased the force of her legend. The road was asleep when we set out to find her.

We made enquiries at the bar and the women gave us directions to one of her great stalls in the marketplace. When we got there her shed was shut. A woman directed us to another market. The same thing happened. Dad was not discouraged. We received many directions which sent us up and down the city. At one of her shops, where jewelry and lace materials were sold, a little girl told us she had just left. It was late in the afternoon before we arrived at a shop which Madame Koto rarely visited. It was a small shop, with a few tables of trinkets outside. We went into the shop and met a lean woman with a bandage over one eye.

'We have come to see Madame Koto,' dad said.

'Which Madame Koto?' the woman asked.

Dad was confused.

'How many Madame Kotos are there?'

'It depends,' the woman said.

We looked around the shop. It was bare except for a few chairs. The place stank of sweat and urine and human misery. The woman stared at me with her one eye. She seemed rather intent on me. It made me uncomfortable. Dad said:

'Maybe we have come to the wrong place.'

The woman didn't say anything. A child began crying in a room at the back of the shop. The woman went out and my eyes cleared a little and I suddenly noticed the political posters in the deep shadows of the walls.

'Let's go,' dad said. 'This is the wrong shop.'

He started to leave when I heard other voices at the back, the voices of women whispering in a corridor. While I was straining to hear what they were saying, a goat wandered into the empty shop from the front door. It stared at us. Then the goat moved towards me, and edged me to the wall. It had big eyes, unfathomable and curiously human. I pushed the goat away, but it came back at me, its head lowered, its green eyes glittering.

'Leave that goat alone,' dad said.

The goat turned to dad and subjected him to a long intense scrutiny. Then it went out through the front door and soon afterwards the woman with the bandaged eye came in and said:

'Wait.'

Then she was gone. I listened to the bustle of the main road outside the shop, the voices calling, the hawkers drawing attention to their goods, car horns blasting, news vendors rattling out the sensational headlines of the day, music playing all over the distances. While I listened dad touched me on the head and I suddenly had the distinct impression that Madame Koto was in the shop. I could feel the awesomeness of her body. She was breathing in the air. Her legend surrounded us, watching our every movement.

Dad sat on a bench. I stood beside him, conscious of the disquieting notion that Madame Koto had somehow multiplied in the spaces where we waited. Then the wind shifted in the shop and a big man, draped in a cheap agdada, strode in. He eyed us and went through the back door, leaving behind flashes and hints of indecipherable possibilities. These were intensified a moment later when the woman brought in a tray of food – pounded yam and spinach stew, rich with dried fish, fried chicken and goat meat. She put the tray down on a low table which she dragged out of the shadows. She brought water for us to wash our hands. We didn't touch the food. The woman watched us. Dad's face was stony; he registered no bewilderment. After a few moments of silence the woman said:

'Follow me.'

We rose.

'The boy first,' she said.

We followed her through the back door, along a corridor, into another house, up a winding set of stairs, across a landing to the top floor of a two-storeyed building, down another set of winding stairs, and back into the same shop we had originally set out from.

'What's wrong with you, eh?' dad growled. 'Are you playing games with us?'

The woman smiled. She indicated the bench. Dad sat down. The food was gone. The room was somehow different. The woman left and soon came back with a crying baby. She left the baby on a chair and went out again. The baby shrieked and made us feel quite scared. I went over to the baby and played with it, trying to get it to stop crying. I touched the baby's face and it stared at me with deep fearful eyes. I realised in an instant that it was not an ordinary baby. I was playing with its tiny hands when, with a sound in my head like the roaring of an enraged lion, it suddenly scratched me, drawing blood. Then it flashed me a radiant toothless grin. I showed dad the scratches.

'Let's go and get you a plaster,' he said.

'That baby isn't human,' I said.

'All babies are strange,' dad replied.

We went out and bought a plaster and when we got back the shop was full. Chairs and benches were packed tight with visitors, traders, hawkers and children. Loud voices made the crowded spaces quiver. There was a perpetual din of heated arguments. The spaces were jammed with all kinds of human beings and the intra-spaces were packed with all kinds of shadows. The goat wandered amongst the strange crowd

54

and no one seemed to notice. The evening drifted into the shop and everything slowly darkened. The walls yielded up their secret colour of green; the political posters were gone; the screaming baby was no longer there. The people went on arguing, gesticulating, and I couldn't understand what anyone was saying or what their gestures meant. My head fairly whirled in the changed atmosphere of the airless shop. The goat rubbed its head against the legs of the men. Dad leant against a wall and lit a cigarette. The darkness pressed down on us.

'We are under the sea,' I said.

Dad was silent. The goat attempted to walk between dad's legs, and I drove it away. Standing a short distance from us, the goat suddenly reared on its hind legs and gave vent to a chilling cry, like a woman in agony. The voices stopped. The woman with the bandage over her eye pushed her way over to us and said:

'Follow me. Madame Koto will see you now.'

Dad crushed out his cigarette. We followed the woman down three long corridors. Animal skin lined the walls. In the third corridor there were drums at intervals next to the closed doors. Mirrors vibrated over the lintels. The corridor seemed endless. We went deeper and deeper, as if into another reality. The air smelt of cloves and river banks. In one room there were many goats. In another room there was a white horse with the heavy-lidded eyes of certain politicians. At the end of the corridor there was a sign which told us to take off our shoes. Dad took his off. I remained barefoot. There was pepper in the air. My eyes watered; I sneezed. We entered a big room. The walls were completely white. The ceiling was low. Dad had to stoop. On the walls there were preternatural feathers and flywhisks, empty bird cages and spears, animal hides and the head of an antelope. Beyond that room was another one in which a tumultuous gathering of women was holding a meeting. They fell silent when we came in. They had suffering faces, scoured with the religion

55

of misery. They were petty traders, women without children, women with ailing children, women with angled faces and hollow cheeks and sober eyes, faces that never smiled. They were waiting to be called in to see Madame Koto and they had been arguing about who was next, whose case was more urgent.

When we passed out through the narrow door the women began arguing again. In the new room we saw an order-ly queue of women, all surrounded with the grave aura of people who had travelled vast distances to have their problems heard, people who had been waiting with great patience all their lives and who were waiting patiently now. They had brought food with them. They eyed us with pro-found indifference. We went past them into a smaller room potent with ritual smells, the smells of power, of the earth liberated by rain, of a mighty woman, of gold and perfume, of childlessness, sweat, eunuchs, virgins and pitchers. A great white veil divided the room. Beyond the veil seven candles were aflame. Two men were fanning a leviathan figure on a regal chair. Young girls were combing and plaiting the hair of this figure. We heard water being poured. Ritual chants reigned in rooms behind rooms. Somewhere a sheep was being slaughtered, a man screamed as if branded, a child wailed, women laughed. Everywhere I looked shadows were changing places.

The bandaged woman retreated without a word. The darkness in the outer room where we stood became thicker. I noticed the stained-glass windows and the kaoline-painted floor. When dad coughed the leviathan figure made a sign. The white veil was drawn aside. One of the men motioned us to approach. We waded through the dense air of legends.

Madame Koto, like an ageless matriarch, was sitting on an ornate chair, with the seven red candles surrounding her. She had a yellow mantilla on her shoulders. She had grown so enormous that the large chair barely contained her bulk. She wore a deep blue lace blouse and volumes

56

of lace wrappers. She had acquired gargantuan space. As the evening darkened, her presence increased. Power stank from her liquid and almost regal movements. Behind her, in a large golden cage, was a shimmering peacock.

The men went on fanning her in slow motion, as if the fan of giant eagle feathers were very heavy, as if they were working monstrous bellows. She studied us in silence and then, with a light gesture of her fat arms, dismissed the men. Drawing up the sleeves of her blouse, she revealed the beauty of her skin, which was the mahogany blue of the forest at night. Her face was large, her eyes big with deep secrets, and her features – serene like the bronze sculptings of ancient queens – defied memory. She neither registered nor betrayed any conceivable expression – as if nothing in the world could stir the great mass of her spirit. I had not seen her in a long time and she looked abnormally resplendent. Her face burned with health. The jewels round her neck bathed her in ghostly lights.

'I know why you have come to see me,' she said to dad, while looking at me.

Her voice was unrecognisable, deep with the tones of a bull. She cleared her throat.

'You have stopped coming to my bar,' she now said, addressing me directly.

'You have been growing in our room,' I replied.

'What?'

'Are you the nightwind?' I asked.

'Shut up,' said dad, pinching me.

I fell silent. Madame Koto stared at us.

'Both of you have caused me a lot of trouble in the past.'

Dad began to fidget. Madame Koto didn't say anything for a while. Her silence made me sweat. Then she motioned for me to approach her. I did. She held my hand. Her palms were hot. I started to shiver.

'I am dying,' she said eventually.

I was astonished.

57

'What is killing you?' I asked.

Several thoughts, like dark winds, blew across her face.

'The children in my womb,' she said. Then after a moment, she added: 'And high living. Money. Power. Responsibility. My own success is pressing me down.'

'What about my mother?'

She smiled and let go of my hand. I went back to dad. He put a protective arm on my shoulder, tilting me in the direction of his peculiar madness. Madame Koto made her reply to dad.

'I will let your wife go on one condition.'

'What?'

'I want your son to come and sit in my bar again till I give birth.'

'Why?'

'Same reason as before. He is a strange child and has good luck.'

Dad shook his head vigorously.

'But you are not a good person,' he said.

Before he could unburden himself of a torrent of recriminations, Madame Koto interrupted him with an imperceptible movement of her arm.

'You don't have to agree with my politics,' she said. 'I just want your son to come to my bar as he used to. If you don't make trouble for me, I won't make trouble for you. I am not well. I am dying and maybe your son is the only person who can help me.'

Dad was confused.

'Go home and you will find your wife waiting for you. Don't say anything about your quarrel. She is working with me for as long as she likes. But from now on I want your son to come and sit in my bar any time he wants.'

Dad thought about her proposal. I followed the confusion in his spirit. I pulled his hand and he leant over to me and I whispered mum's words into his ear.

'All things are linked,' I said.

Dad remained like that for a moment, leaning over, thinking about what I had said. Then, slowly, he straightened. He nodded his agreement to Madame Koto's condition. When she made another cryptic movement of her arm, the men fanning her returned. The bandaged woman came and led us through the maze of corridors and rooms. I saw mum fleetingly in one of the mirrors above a door. She was decked in gold-braided clothes. I turned round swiftly, and saw only darkness behind me.

———

CHAPTER TWELVE

The Fore-runner

As WE NEARED home we saw a woman sitting on our doorstep. I thought it was mum, and I ran over, and discovered it was only a beggar. She was very old and had a dirty veil covering her crushed and bitter face. As we went past her into the room she lifted up her veil, revealing her poisonous eyes, and held out a green bowl.

'I heard you are a good man,' she said, in a rattling voice.

Dad instructed me to give her some of our food. I dished a modest portion of the food that the good spirit had made for us. The old beggarwoman ate it all quickly and asked for more. Dad nodded. Three times she asked and three times we complied. When she had eaten her fill, and nearly all our food, she stretched out on our doorstep, and fell asleep. Dad told me not to shut the door. The beggarwoman's filthy clothes stank unbearably and she snored like a monster all through the night.

'What if she comes in when we are asleep?' I asked.

'We are protected,' dad said. 'Nothing evil will cross that door.'

He sat up all night waiting for mum to return. He was very anxious and kept pacing. Every sound outside made him jump towards the door. After much fretting and wearing himself out with anxiety he went and had a bath, combed his hair and dressed up in his best clothes in anticipation of mum's return. All through the night the wind whistled above our rooftop. The old beggarwoman at our doorstep kept groaning and twisting. Then deep in the night she started to sing. Dad went out and gave her a covercloth and a pillow. The woman didn't thank him. When dad got back in the woman started grumbling loudly about all those who had beds, who had rooms, and who allowed old people to sleep at their doorsteps. Dad was afraid of some sort of superstitious retribution. He got very worried and asked me if we should invite her in. His eyes were big with fright. He didn't wait for my reply; he brought the woman in, and I noticed how sharp and bitter her eyes were in the candlelight. Her hands were bony and they kept shaking. Dad offered her the bed, but she refused. She said she would sleep on the floor. I brought out my mat. I sat and watched the beggarwoman – old and skinny, her fetid smells overpowering the room – as she slept not far from me. I tried to stay up and keep an eye on her as dad dozed off in his chair. Then I nodded and found myself in a classroom. The other students were cattle-egrets, sunbirds, an elephant, a giraffe and a goat. Our teacher was a tortoise. The class went on for a long time. I got bored with the teacher's drone. We were being taught about the history of the world backwards, from the end of time to the forgotten original dream. I looked up and saw branches with red fruits. The fruits fell, turned into flowers, and wounded me when they landed on my head. I tried to escape from the flowers, but I ran into the arms of the goat. It began to kiss me. I kicked the goat and the beggarwoman cried out. I opened my eyes and found a heavy form over me. I fought to get out from under the form. I couldn't breathe. Then I heard harsh laughter in my ears and smelt rotting teeth and I struggled fiercely and threw the form off.

'You have sweet blood,' the form said in the dark.

I lit a candle. Dad was snoring on his three-legged chair. The beggarwoman had gone. I went and looked outside. The compound was empty. Up in the sky, I saw a star falling. I went back in and woke dad up.

'The woman has gone,' I said.

'What woman?'

'The beggarwoman.'

He turned his head away. Then, craning his neck towards me, he said:

'You mean Helen?'

'No,' I said. 'The old woman.'

'There wasn't an old woman. Go to sleep,' he said in an exasperated voice. I left him alone. I sat on the floor with my back against the wall. I heard the house breathing. Dad lifted his head suddenly and asked:

'Has your mother returned?'

'No.'

He went back to sleep again. I stayed up, watching the room, till dawn broke. All through that time I was struck by how free our air had become. Madame Koto's presence did not enter our nightspace. The strange wind didn't battle with dad's spirit. I heard the birds of sunlight singing when I fell asleep.

CHAPTER THIRTEEN

An Indirect Miracle

PLAYING ALONG OUR street the next day, I saw my friend Ade rolling a bicycle wheel. I started towards him and he turned and ran. I pursued him into the forest and caught him near a well. I held him tight. He was breathing very hard, he was wheezing and gasping. I said:

'Why are you running away from me?'

He was silent. He hung his head low. He looked pale and lean. His eyes were heavy and dull. His face was unanimated and he looked like a child who was being starved. I knew about his illness, his spirit-child epilepsy. I also knew he was implacably willing himself out of life. I had heard about the numerous ritual treatments he had undergone in the hands of herbalists, all of them trying, and failing, to break his resolve to die.

'Where have you been?' I asked.

'They say I am all right now,' he replied.

'So why are you running?'

'Nothing.'

We stood there in the forest, in silence. He didn't move. Nothing in him moved towards me. I watched him for a long time and felt him already entering the world of spirits and I left him standing there in the forest and went back home.

I sat on the platform of our housefront and saw the future invade our street. The invasion took place silently. No one noticed. That day dad returned early from work. He brought with him the odour of raw fish. He had a little bag on his back.

'Has your mother come back?'

'No.'

He looked very sad and I followed him to our room. The door was wide open. The room was different. Someone was asleep on the bed.

'It's that beggarwoman,' I said.

The woman turned over. I sat on the little centre table. Dad faced his chair towards the bed, and sat down. Rocking the chair back and forth, nodding rhythmically, a sublime smile lit up his face. Mum lay asleep on the bed as if she had never left. Her things were all in their normal places. The cupboard groaned with food. There were sacks of garri everywhere. Basins, crammed with stockfish and dried meat and peppers and onions, were stacked up next to the cupboard. We sat and watched mum sleeping, full of wonder at how she had re-entered our lives so silently. We didn't wake her up and we didn't move. We stared at her sleeping form as if she were a miracle. After an hour of silence dad, in a low voice, said:

'I went to work today and carried twenty-seven bags of garri, twenty bags of fish, and ten bags of cement. Then I went to the river with a friend. I threw his net into the water and caught twelve fishes. Our life is changing for the better.'

Mum slept easily, breathing gently, her face serene, her skin lovely. Dad couldn't take his eyes off her. He sent me to buy some ogogoro and he made libations, in a whisper, to our ancestors. He prayed for another hour. When he finished, he said:

'Your mother needs rest. We have been bad to her. Look at how lean you are and she has been gone only seven days. From now on we will be good to your mother, you hear?'

I nodded. Dad slept on his chair again, with a beautiful smile on his face. The room felt new that night.

Book Two

———

CHAPTER ONE

The Invasion by the Future

T HEY SAY THAT when strange times are coming the world
takes on the aspects of a dream. They always say this with
hindsight.

Mum slept for two days. While she had been away,
while she slept, the future had been pressing down on us.
Without knowing it our lives had slipped into a new dark
stream of terrible ancient legends. Dad seemed unaware of
it all. Under the enchantment of mum's mysterious return he
made attempts at living an exemplary life. He went to work
early, came back early, fetched water for everyone, washed
all our clothes and cleaned the house. He even prepared our
food. He was a dreadful cook. He would sit in the kitchen,
surrounded by the bemused women of the compound, and
try to light a fire. Instead he almost set the whole place alight.
Using firewood which was still damp, pouring kerosine on
the wood when a little strip of rolled paper would do, he
plunged the entire compound into the pungent smoke of his
ineptitude. The women, delighted at the novelty of dad in the
kitchen, gathered and watched him from a distance, passing
hilarious running commentaries on his disastrous attempts at
cooking. But dad persisted, and managed to burn everything
he prepared, and succeeded in over-salting the stew, the yam
and the beans. He ate in excellent spirits. I hardly ate at all.
He didn't notice. He didn't notice anything except mum's
presence on the bed.

The day after mum returned we heard that thugs of
the Party of the Rich had killed a man at the other end
of our street. There were retaliations that afternoon. The

street boiled with an old rage. My head swelled with visions. The sun seemed to burn the earth with an inexplicable fury. Everywhere I looked I saw unoccupied spaces filling out with new beings. The street had been invaded by alien presences. Everywhere seemed crowded in a way I couldn't fathom. Strange people had been moving into our area without our knowledge. Houses suddenly appeared in previously empty spaces. New tenants rented the rooms. We didn't know who the new people were.

While all this was happening the trees were being felled every day in the forest. We heard the stumps screaming in the evenings. The word went round that the spirits of the forest had turned vengeful. No one was supposed to go there at night. A curfew reigned over its dwindling terrain. Sometimes we heard wild irregular drumming and banshee wailing and the animistic clashing of machetes among the trees. And sometimes we heard female voices singing sweetly in its darkness. There were stories that a beautiful maiden of the trees had been luring people into her indigo abyss. The people were never seen again. The forest became dangerous. It became another country, a place of spectral heavings, sighs, susurrant arguments as of a council of spirit elders, a place with fleeting visions of silver elephants and white antelopes, a place where elusive lions coughed – a bazaar of the dead. And because the forest gradually became alien to us, because we feared the bristling potency of its new empty spaces, we all became a little twisted.

We grew more suspicious of one another. Everyone began to suspect their neighbours of being witches and wizards. People no longer shared their food, no longer left their doors open, no longer had parties, no longer smiled at one another. Things we couldn't explain turned swiftly into superstition. Children died mysteriously. The rain brought typhoid, and malaria snatched off many people. Nebulous imputations abounded.

Our minds turned strange. A woman in our street went

to the market in the morning and returned in the evening wailing that spirits were taking over the place. She claimed that mighty spirits were occupying the area from the garage to the market, from the spot where the rally was to be held right up to the beginning of our street. She said that some of the spirits had diamond spears, some held aloft books that quivered with emerald lights, and one of them, a child, bore a golden tablet of rock on which had been inscribed certain forgotten laws of life. She couldn't remember what the laws were. She said many of the spirits were great kings and seers and healers and leaders. None of them seemed happy. No one believed her.

For a whole day the woman tramped the streets telling of what she had witnessed. She said the spirits had white cars and lived in flaming yellow houses and that they were converging in the air, watching us. She said that when one of the spirits noticed that she could see them it blew a white wind at her that knocked away her hawker's basin. The woman went everywhere, telling her tale, warning us that something terrible was going to happen. She talked of floods, of fire, of hot winds, dying children, people going blind, the blind recovering their sight, lame people flying around on machines, women levitating and men dancing on the moon. The inhabitants of our area came to the conclusion that the woman had wandered off into the country of madness. That evening her voice ceased altogether. People said that she had joined the maiden of the trees. That night we heard two female voices singing in the forest. They wounded us with the beauty of their song.

CHAPTER TWO

Of Signs and White Antelopes

SIGNS MULTIPLIED ALL over our area. Ade had another epileptic fit in front of our compound, and when he was calmer he complained that spirits were marching through him. Later he saw yellow birds flying in diamond formation over the forest. He said the birds were on fire. Afterwards children began to have strange fits along our street. Women talked about the yellow birds they had seen rising from the earth in the morning. The dreams of the road became frightening. In the afternoons, when everything was somnolent, the bushes caught fire. Even patches of the road burst into flames. The fire didn't burn for long. Later we heard that chickens and goats had mysteriously combusted. That night it rained and in the morning our street was shivering with frogs. Then the oddest thing started to happen. Women began to disappear from their husband's houses. Young girls vanished. At night we heard the haunting threnody of multiplied female voices from the impenetrable screen of trees.

While all this took place, mum slept, and woke, and didn't speak. She went about as if she were in two places at the same time, her body here, her spirit somewhere else. And during the last day of her sleep and the first day of her silence – politics returned to our area with its loudest voice yet. The vans of the political parties were bigger than before. The noise they made was worse. They brought great truck-loads of supporters. And they now resorted to using a perversion of traditional masquerades to scare us into voting for them.

At night the masquerades of both parties bounded up and

down the streets with whips and sticks, pikes and machetes. Terrorising us, banging on our doors, they shouted our names in guttural voices: they warned that they had people watching us in the polling booths to report on who we had voted for in secret. The political masquerades, the thugs and the supporters invaded our lives and changed the air of the street. Soon no one was sure who was really the enemy. People died from inexplicable poisonings. Meetings were held by elders of the street to discuss the new terror, but the political masquerades disrupted one meeting and set the house on fire. We became afraid. Every day we listened to endless rumours to find out which side had become stronger overnight.

During all this Madame Koto had become more remote. People began to say they couldn't even remember what she looked like. Then we heard that her fabulous bar was now the ghetto headquarters of the Party of the Rich. When the dreaded masquerades chanted at night, with thugs clanging their machetes on our doors, we thought of Madame Koto with mounting bitterness. The people of the area avoided her bar, but she grew more prosperous anyway. She sent the children of five poor families to school. She gave a scholarship to a blind girl. She had long queues of people at her bar who had travelled vast distances to bring their impossible problems for her to solve. Women who wanted her protection came with gifts and paid homage. Her fame had travelled a hundred secret routes and had spread all over the country. Her legend had become so pervasive that we could no longer give her a human face.

The women who disappeared into the forest, whose poignant songs set fire to our dreams every night, grew greater in number. In fact we could no longer distinguish their different voices, and so we had no idea how many they had become. Those who were out late at night, who suffered the agony of the women's piercing melodies, said that sometimes they had caught fleeting glimpses of white antelopes with glittering eyes in the forest. The antelopes were ghostly and splendid and when they saw human beings they vanished into the trees. No one had caught any of the antelopes. The trees went on being felled and the women's voices became more painful in their beauty. And on the day mum woke from her sleep we heard it said that a hunter had succeeded in killing one of the white antelopes. The next day it was rumoured that he had been sacrificed to the road, run over by one of the trucks of politics.

CHAPTER THREE

The Invention of Death

MUM ROSE FROM her sleep as if she were emerging from a mythic river. Her hair flowed brightly round her face. Her skin had been washed a marvellous roseate colour by her dreams. Enchanted, dad kept staring at her as if she had once again become the very image of his first love. Mum rose from her long sleep and bore herself with the serenity of a princess. She was beautiful and silent, as if her sleep had given her strange powers. Her eyes were gentle and her poor clothes shone on her. Dad wasn't sure how to treat the new apparition that was mum. He bathed at dawn, combed his hair, polished his boots, and made me read to him from volumes of love poetry while he stared at mum with wondering eyes, nodding his head in silent astonishment at her enigmatic transformation.

Dad changed. He woke early, went off to work reluctantly, and rushed back earlier than normal. He stopped drinking and alarmed me by cleaning his teeth with chewing sticks almost every hour. He started using perfumes with odd smells, he bathed far too often, washed his clothes too frequently, and began to doubt his appearance. He kept asking me if I thought he was handsome. For many days he did not know how to behave towards mum. He didn't know whether he had been forgiven. Something new had entered mum's spirit and because we couldn't comprehend it we were a little afraid of her. For days dad spoke to her tenderly, self-abasingly even, but she remained within the nimbus of her silence. There was always an enigmatic smile on her face. A glimmering light danced in her eyes.

In silence she cleaned the place, scrubbed the floor, washed our clothes and aired the room. She brought flowers from the edge of the forest and arranged them in bottles. She lit sticks of incense and watched the smoke-spirals occupy the air. Everything she touched shone.

Our lives brightened. Good air and wonderful lights flowed through our room. We moved about in the limpid atmosphere of mum's bliss. In the mornings her singing woke us up. She sang us to sleep at night. Her spirit soared around us. She developed a curious magnetism. One morning a white bird flew into our room and landed on her shoulder. With a smile on her face she took it in her hands and the bird stayed with us for three days. Afterwards she took to wearing white dresses and white slippers. Her hair dazzled with health. She even moved soundlessly. When she went to the market she brought back the most amazing fishes, lovely vegetables, and bread which had in it the perpetual essence of childhood. Her cooking tasted sublime. When she fetched water from the well the water seemed luminous as if it contained an invisible star, or as if it had come from a heavenly fountain. Candles she lit burned blue. Her spirit superceded dad's, and her radiance drove all the darkness away. Her silence healed our unrest, dissolved our fears. We were never ill, and we slept beautifully. We were so happy in our silence and with our poverty that one day I said to mum:

'Death is coming.'

She touched me on the head, and said nothing. But that night, while dad was polishing his boots and staring at her as if at a special being who had come to bless our lives, she took me in her lap, fondled my hair, and told me this story.

'Once upon a time,' she said, in a voice that was also a mood, 'human beings were happy and they lived for ever. They did not know death. When it was time for them to change, a light would surround them, and a bird would fly out from the centre of the light. At that moment the person was being re-born – sometimes in the same place, sometimes in another. Human beings understood everything. They had no language as such. With their thoughts they could talk to trees and animals and to one another. There were no wars. People didn't travel far. And they understood the language of angels. They could actually see angels.'

Mum paused and looked at me with twinkling eyes. She smiled again, and continued.

'Then one day a rainbow appeared on the earth. It was very beautiful. Where it touched, the earth turned into gold. Then a young man said: 'I saw that rainbow first. It is mine.' The men began to argue. They fought. The young man killed his best friend in the fight, and claimed the rainbow. When he claimed it, he became different. He knew hunger. Darkness entered him. He wanted new things, new places, new experiences. He saw the women differently, and he wanted them. There was one in particular whom he wanted more than all the others, so he didn't even bother to go to the chief, her father. He went straight to the girl and said: 'If I can have you, I will give you half of my rainbow.' It came to pass. The girl became different. She too wanted new things, new experiences. She hungered for dark unknown places. The young man and the girl caused trouble everywhere with their new desires and their ambitions. And because of them fighting broke out and blood was spilled. There were retaliations. And people's time came up when it wasn't supposed to and they were re-born too quickly and so they didn't live long. Corruption came upon the people and grew fat. Diseases dwelled in them and Misery had many children amongst them. The world turned upside down. Creation became confusion.'

Mum paused again. Dad had stopped polishing his boots to listen to her story. He stared at her with eyes wide open, his gestures frozen, every part of him alert and listening, caught in mum's spell. Touching me again on the head, the smile still playing on her lips, she carried on with the story.

'God saw all this misery and darkness, and was not

happy. So he sent Death down amongst human beings to remind them of the miraculous life they had before. Death lived amongst them. Everyone was miserable, but Death was happy. In fact he was very happy. The people did not recognise him and did not listen to his message. They went on as before, increasing their misfortune, making things worse. Soon things got so bad that the people no longer understood the language of trees and animals. They no longer saw angels and came to believe that such beings had never existed. They no longer understood one another. They became greedy. They broke into tribes. They had wars all the time. And they moved away from the great garden that was their home and travelled far out into unknown darknesses. Death became so angry because human beings did not respect him and did not heed his message that he decided to take the law into his own hands. He drove them deeper into the darkness. He laid waste their habitations, destroyed their means of living, and scattered them all over the earth. Some went to places where ice fell from the sky, and some went to where the sun blazed from the heavens. But Death became the king of the world. He was a very wicked king. He punished human beings and trees and animals for every conceivable reason. His punishment was final. There was no appeal. And then he sent out his children to be the kings of all the scattered tribes of humankind.

'God, seeing that Death had not only disobeyed him but also tried to rule the world, was not happy at all. So he sent a little blue bird down to earth. When the bird arrived, it turned into a child.'

There was another pause.

'Then what did the child do?' I asked.

'The child travelled to the kingdom where Death was King. He found the King and said: "I have come to kill you." The King in fact nearly died from laughing: "How can you kill Death?" he asked. The child smiled and said: "With love." Then the child left. Afterwards Death became angry at the threat and rode through the world killing off people. He poisoned people's hearts. He destroyed everything that was visible till there were only skeletons everywhere. He did this out of arrogance; he thought that because he could kill therefore he was God. And when he had completed his destruction of everything the child came to him and said: "You did what I expected you to do. Your work is finished. New human beings are being created from the old. From now on you will be king only over those who believe in you. God has put one new thing into people and that is love. If people find it in themselves and keep it, they cannot die. If they lose it, they are yours." Then the child became a bird again and flew back up to heaven. And that is how Death was killed by a small bird,' mum said, ending her story.

'So is Death dead?' I asked.

'Death is everywhere, listening, waiting to jump on those who believe in his religion.'

When mum finished her story dad was smiling. We were all silent for a long time. Then dad got up and laid out our food. Mum didn't eat. She watched us with shining eyes as we ate. When the plates had been cleared, and when we were sitting again in a semi-circle of silence, I told mum about the good spirit who helped us while she was away. Mum didn't say anything. Dad said:

'Good spirits are always on our side, my son.'

Mum got up and prepared the bed. Dad lit a stick of incense. I fetched my mat. Soon mum was asleep. We watched over her as she slept. Dad didn't dare get in the bed with her. It had been like that for a while now. Dad slept with me on the floor instead. Throughout that night, unable to contain his new awe of mum, he kept saying, in the mischievous voice of a child:

'My wife has changed! God has given me a new wife! She has been touched by angels!'

* * *

That same night, as dad lay asleep beside me on the floor, mum came and woke me up. She looked very intense, as if her illumination, her serenity, were a higher kind of flame that was burning up her aura. She took me to the far side of the room and, in a low voice, said:

'I know what is going to happen. I have been shown it all. Don't be afraid.'

She sat on the bed and didn't say anything for a long while. Her eyes were brilliant in the dark.

___

CHAPTER FOUR

The Precious Stones of Sleep

DEATH AND IRREGULAR miracles found our street. In the forest the singing of the women grew more elysian. Lightning struck one night. The sky split open. I saw fishes swimming in the cracks.

People in our area claimed that the women of the forest were seers, that they had powers of transformation, and that they turned into white antelopes. It was also claimed that the women had discovered the secrets of herbs and bark, of the earth and the night. They understood the language of trees and butterflies. It was said that an old woman was their leader. No one knew who she was or where she came from. The men of our area began to suspect their wives of belonging to a new, secret sect. More women disappeared from their homes. It was whispered that the women of the forest could see into the future. Some said that the old woman, their leader, was blind. Some said she was an owl. Others maintained that the women, seduced by the spirit of the forest, were against Madame Koto and her ascendant cult. And mum surprised me one night by telling me that the women were singing of the forgotten ways of our ancestors. They were warning us not to change too much, not to disregard the earth.

Things got so confused that when we heard that the Party of the Poor forbade anyone killing the white antelopes we didn't know what to believe any more. We didn't even know if it were true that some men, unable to bear the sublime voices of the women, had run off to join them in the forest. Then one night a green leopard with burning copper eyes was seen sitting on a branch. Not long afterwards night-runners with their flaming masks and their silver machetes invaded our area. They pursued children and women, and chanted songs of terror. Some say Death danced with them and took away three of their victims.

With the world changing, my mother silent, my father struck dumb by her transformation, and with bizarre omens populating our lives, I became very lonely. I went to Ade's place and I wasn't allowed to see him because he was being treated by herbalists. I wandered up our street, towards the main road, and got lost. Then I came upon the timber-workers, the carpenters, and part-time road-builders who were engaged in the construction of the magnificent dais for the great political rally. I watched them for a while, not noticing anything unusual in the air. And then I found my way back home, troubled by a feeling that the world was be-coming overcrowded in ways I couldn't perceive.

For many nights dad couldn't pluck up the courage to sleep with mum on the bed. Dad looked sadder as mum became more beautiful, more aloof, like a seraphic priestess. Every night dad dreamt up a new strategy for finding a way into the bed, and every night he failed. He told us endless stories. Many of them were about marriage and love and were so convoluted and full of impenetrable hints that they lost me altogether. Mum didn't seem affected by them either because when dad finished his stories she got up, lit a stick of incense, went to bed, and slept instantly. Dad took his failure badly. He vented his foul temper on me. When mum had gone to sleep, dad would twist and turn, curse and writhe, on the hard floor. One night, he suddenly hit me on the head.

'What's wrong with your mother, eh?' he asked gruffly.
'I don't know.'
'Hasn't she told you anything?'
'No.'
'Azaro, tell me the truth.'
'She said she knows what is going to happen.'
'To who?'

'I don't know.'

'What about me? Did she say anything about me?'

'No,' I said.

He hit me again.

'Find out about me, you hear? Ask her about me.'

'I will try.'

Dad turned and creaked his bones all night in his misery. When he began snoring mum came and shook me again. We went to the far corner. She seemed feverish in her strange happiness.

'Look!' she said, directing my attention with her voice.

I beheld a kaleidoscope of white and rainbow lights in her hands. She said she had brought these jewels and precious stones and luminous cowries from her dreams. Her cupped hands glittered with wondrous colours, iridescent stones, pearls whose brilliance opened up lightning flashes of joy in the eyes. The lights from the stones illuminated her face. Drops of sweat glistened on her forehead. Turning the lustrous stones over in her hands, she said:

'They are gifts from my best friend who lives at the other side of the world. The people there are white.'

'How did she give them to you?'

'In my sleep. I was dreaming and then the next thing I knew we were standing on the top of a mountain that shone like a star. She broke off some of the mountain and gave these to me. We talked for many hours. She said I should bury them in the forest.'

I marvelled at the stones.

'Don't tell your father,' she said.

'I won't,' I said, remembering how he kept hitting me.

'I also saw my grandmother. She is forty-one years old and she lives near the sea in another country. She is well. All of our ancestors are well. But they are worried for us.'

'Why?'

'Trouble is coming. My grandmother told me to beware of the seven-headed spirit.'

81

I was silent.

'Don't be afraid,' she added. 'In the end we will all be happy.'

It was her turn to be silent for a while. Dad twisted and turned on the mat, and mum covered the stones and the room went dark again. When dad resumed snoring in a higher register, mum said she was going to plant the precious stones of her dreams.

'Where?' I asked.

'In the forest.'

'What about the women singing there?'

'These are special stones. They protect me.'

Then a cool mysterious breeze blew across my face. I felt around in the darkness. Mum was no longer there.

I waited for her a long time. Dad stopped snoring. I lay down and listened to the silence, and breathed in the air of incense and precious stones. Then, after a long while, I felt an intense mood in the room. I smelt trees and herbs and moonlight on a wind that came in through the door. I got up and found, to my amazement, that mum was asleep on the bed.

CHAPTER FIVE

———

Riddle of the White Antelopes

AFTER SHE HAD planted the precious stones in the forest, mum became different. In the mornings she went to work and helped with the general preparations for the forthcoming political rally. She was listless and sluggish in the daytime; her eyelids drooped as if she never slept at night. We began to worry about her. Her wonderful serenity waned. Her skin turned pale, her face grew bonier, and her clothes hung on her, making her look miserable. She became a sad mystery. At night, however, after she had slept a little in the evening, her spirit irradiated like a star. Her buoyancy returned. Her mystery deepened.

We did not know what to do with her, or how to reach her. She spoke little, and worked hard. She did not complain about anything. One day dad couldn't bear her silences any longer.

'How is Madame Koto's bar?' he asked.

'Fine,' mum replied.

'How are the preparations for the rally?'

'Fine.'

Dad looked at me. I looked away. On another evening, when dad was out, mum said:

'My son, I have forgotten why I am living.'

The remark made me very unhappy. I refused to eat that evening. When dad returned he was in a good mood and he told long stories which drove me to get out my mat, and which did not help him get into bed with mum.

'What's going on in my house?' he grumbled.

No one said anything.

'Are you two conspiring against me, eh?'

We remained silent. He paced the room, stamping, and eventually calmed down. We went to bed early. That was the night I became certain mum kept disappearing. It had been going on for some time, but at first I wasn't sure. So I took to pretending I was asleep and would watch the bed in the dark. For three nights she tiptoed out of the room. She didn't stay out too long, but it was long enough to make me suspicious. On the night that dad had accused us of conspiring against him, I sneaked after mum on her secret journey into the new enigma of the forest.

I followed her up our street, towards Madame Koto's bar. I hung in the shadows, and the shadows whispered at me. I hid behind clumps of bushes, and I heard the leaves talking. Mum hurried past Madame Koto's bar as if afraid of being seen, and paused near an ensemble of wild flowers at the threshold of the forest. Then she moved on, slowly, looking backwards all the time. The elysian women broke suddenly into song. Their celestial voices made me notice that there was a full moon in the sky. There were no stars out and the sky itself was oceanic, serene in its immanence, and of the deepest blue. I came to the harmonic cluster of wild flowers. They seemed to contain their own light; and their colours – red and blue and white – had the soaring patterned illumination of medieval paintings. I was gazing into their mysterious beauty when a voice in my head said:

'Pluck the flowers.'

I plucked some of the flowers and put them in my pocket. As I did so I was struck by the absurd notion that the wild flowers were somehow connected to the blood of the wounded beggar. They had grown all along the path. The deeper into the forest I went in search of mum, the more beautiful the flowers were, the brighter their centres. The darkness of the forest seemed to bring out light in things which concealed their light. A special corona, almost silvery, shone around mum. I saw spiders asleep on their cobwebs. A curious imperceptible radiance kept spreading and diminishing about me as if it were a coded message for the initiated. From all around, from the trees, the earth, and the sky hidden by branches, the voices of the women poured forth like a divine choir. Their songs were an irresistible perfume on the wind. Everywhere I looked white flashes kept disappearing from view. When I stopped trying to look, I saw white antelopes out of the corners of my eyes. They were like beings that existed only in glimpses, creatures that were real only in the margins and tangents of vision.

Mum skirted the pit into which the beggars seemed to have vanished. Beyond the pit was a boulder. The moon, shining on its massive form, made it resemble the head of a forest god carved by unknown masters, guardian of ancient mysteries. It was a mighty head, with wise and indifferent eyes where the moon chipped the great rock. I hid behind the boulder, soothed by its timeless shadow. Then a voice from inside the stone said:

'The less you look, the more you see.'

I fled from the rock. Mum had disappeared. I made a careful detour round the great stone and came upon a white pot with three eggs and two pieces of kaoline inside it. Another voice said:

'Rub the chalk on your face.'

I rubbed the kaoline on my face and everything went dark all around me. The sky seemed everywhere. The moon had gone. I pushed on till I heard a rattling sound, and saw a snake coiled round a tree. I wasn't afraid. Further ahead I tripped on a stone and felt my big toe bleeding. When I got up the light tinkling of bells on the wind was all around me. I heard the dense beating of wings. A bird flew past my face. Holding my breath, I stared deeply into the darkness. Only the wind spoke. I walked into its polyphonic whispers, and soon found myself at a clearing. Then everything went silent. And in the silence I beheld a gathering of white antelopes with jewels around their necks. They were in a white circle.

In the centre of the circle was a tree that resembled a rhinoceros. The antelopes didn't move. Their stillness was uncanny. Their heads were craned forward as if they were listening to an oral rendering of wise old legends. The jewels and precious stones glittered round their slender necks with many beauteous colours which the wind kept changing. The moon re-appeared and the sky withdrew from over my head. The antelopes stood white and wondrous in the clearing, with the rhinoceros tree in their middle, and with the bells gently tinkling in the wind. The voices had stopped singing. Incense wafted from the open spaces. Something felt hot on the nape of my neck. I turned, and saw the glassy green eyes of an owl. I drew a breath. The wind circled my head. The owl gave a piercing hoot and then flew up into the sky with a flurry of beating wings. The antelopes all looked up, and froze. The owl circled the air above me, hooting its alarmed cry. Suddenly, there were many eyes on me in the forest. It seemed that the trees and leaves had eyes, that insects were watching me, that the darkness was intensely populated with eyes, all concentrated on me. I couldn't hide. Crouching on the earth, I felt water flowing beneath my feet. I looked down, and saw nothing. I could have been standing over an abyss. The wind rose and I looked up and saw a blue mist obscuring the antelopes. And then I saw women in the mist, with jewels and precious stones twinkling round their necks. The women wore white. They moved towards me.

Then I heard a growling from a frightening animal with fire in its throat, and I began running. I ran and tripped and got up and went on running. Footsteps multiplied around me. When I got to the boulder, the white pot had gone. Lost among the trees, I heard the beating of wings and the whisperings of the wind and hooves and footsteps everywhere. In the margins of my vision I saw open doorways with lighted interiors. I saw children playing joyfully round fountains of golden water. I saw naked men and women, entwined, flying through the air, flying out of visibility. Dreams swirled around me. I stopped. The hooves and footfalls also stopped. I moved gently and all the noises moved gently. The tender bells started up again. The owl flew past, its eyes glittering with alarm, the eyes of a watchful old woman.

I ran in a straight line and after a while I saw the lights of Madame Koto's bar through the trees. The feeling that I was almost safe brought a rush of blood to my head, and I fell. As I got up the growling was so hot on my back that I cried out and ran with such desperate fury that it was with a shock I collided into a solid figure carved out of a mass of darkness. I was sent sailing through the air, my head swirling. And when I recovered – astonished to find myself swaying in a world of muggy lights, where worms had wings, where skulls had painted faces like old women at a fair, where jackals were dancing to the antiphonal music of a warped harmonica – it came as a surprise to see that I had knocked over the blind old man. My heart wildly drumming, I rushed and tried to help him. He cursed, and stood up and dusted himself. When he lifted his face at me, I nearly fainted at the yellow lights that glowed in his eyes. With frightening speed he grabbed me and shouted, in the voice of an exhausted bull:

'What on earth are you doing in my dream?'

CHAPTER SIX

The Blind Old Man's Dream:
a Prophecy

I OPENED MY mouth, and the hot wind blew in. No sound came out. My insides burned. I screamed, and the blind old man hit me on the head. I was about to hit him back when I saw that he had feathers about his neck, and quills and glow-worms on his face. His arms had bony wings, as if he had been trapped midway in transformation from a skeleton into a bird.

'Answer me,' he shouted. 'What are you doing in my dreams?'

He had the eyes of a bull and the feet of a dog. He kept beating his bony wings, with an expression of tormented ecstasy on his bristling face. I was trying to wrench myself from his calcified grip, when something unpleasant happened to my eyes. I found I was no longer in the forest. I started to scream again, but I heard my own sound somewhere else. The old man laughed. He had the tongue of a cat. He waved his wings over my face and an excruciating pain shot through the back of my eyes and when I looked I saw fierce soldiers behind him. Everything had changed. It was a burning day, and the soldiers were clubbing men and women in a crowd. They hit the women till they became a mass of writhing worms. The pain went through me again and the scene transformed and I saw men bound to stakes, the great ocean behind them, soldiers with guns in front of them.

'Fire!' the blind old man commanded.

And the soldiers shot the men for what seemed like

three generations. Then things began to change horribly. I felt myself flying at terrific speed, the wind almost snapping my neck. The blind old man flapped his monstrous wings in the heated air. And I became absolutely terrified because I realised for the first time that I had accidentally hurled myself into the blind old man's dreams.

I flew into a world of violence, of famine, of pullulating hunger, with beggars swarming the city centre, with maggots devouring the inhabitants, with flies eating the eyeballs of the children who were half-dead with starvation, with traffic jams everywhere, and people dying of hypertension at their steering wheels; with gases burning in the air, multiplying the ferocious heat of the sun; with housing projects built by corrupt businessmen collapsing and crushing to death their inhabitants all over the country; with soldiers going mad and shooting at people, emptying their guns at students, butchering their mothers, while riots quivered all over the landscapes; with the prisons overcrowded and exuding an unbearable stench of excrement and blood; with children poisoned by their mother's milk, the mothers having been poisoned by just about everything; with the rich and powerful gorging themselves at their bacchanalias, their feasts of twenty-one slaughtered cows, their sweat reeking of vintage champagne, seven bands playing for their perfumed guests and weaving their patron's names in fulsome songs, while the food spilled on the polished floors and the guests trod on them, while the choice delicacies changed into the writhing savoury intestines of the dying children and women, which were gobbled up in celebrations without end.

I saw soldiers in armoured trucks rolling into the city, I saw coup after coup, till our history became an endless rosary necklace of them, each new bead an assassinated head of state, or the secret numbers of failed coup-plotters, executed at dawn.

I saw history as a madman with a machine gun, a madman eating up the twisting flesh of the innocent and the silent.

I saw the blind old man administering potions for warding off evil projections directed at the master politicians.

I saw the blind old man changing, and I knew his secret identity to be that of a master transformer, who could turn into a bat and spy on his enemies.

The old man took me through the insurrectional afternoons, the boiling nights, through days and years merged together, with great events and ordinary happenings taking place simultaneously, and with his robotic grip fixed on my wrist.

My eyes were burning now with so much forbidden sight that I couldn't see myself. Through the fire of such sight I suddenly found myself on a battleground deep in the country, deep in the dream of the unborn nation, and I saw a bloody war raging, a war without beginning and without end, whose origins formed a self-feeding circle like the oroboros. I saw soldiers stick their bayonets into the eyes of their countrymen. I saw bombs explode, laughing, while limbs scattered about the place in unholy jubilation. Blood spurted from the trunks of palm trees. Limbs, intestines, eyeballs and pulped torsos grew from the earth and writhed and crawled amongst the rain-washed undergrowth. Flowers sprouted out of slit and rotting throats. Mushrooms bristled out of the suppurating anuses of the dead. The battleground became a liverish carpet of sliced tongues and slug-infested hearts. The blind old man turned into a skull, the skull exploded, and blood washed down on the earth. Detonations growled, and trees – dancing – were splintered. I saw a young man with his face melted by grenade heat. He ran howling through the cinderous village and women fled from him. The war raged and the blind old man turned into a mosquito, spied on the rebel troops, and reported back to the army chief who had hired him, whose emblem was a white lion. I was on fire all over with the horror, and the more violently I tried to get away, the greater was the metallic grip on my wrist.

Then an incandescent flash lit up everywhere and I saw

a glowing yellow carpet on a beach, with the green ocean swelling and dreaming all around. And on the yellow carpet I was surprised to see a fervent mass of men and women tearing the blind old man's body apart, eating his entrails, gorging themselves on his divinatory head. And when they had finished devouring him, his sorcerer's blood drove them mad and they jumped into the ocean and drowned in a choir of ecstatic voices. The maddened waves washed the carpet away and deposited on the beach a new thing, a new image, a being, wriggling like a great horrid worm – the blind old man, reborn as a baby, regurgitated from the sea. His muscles were bunched-up, his head was mighty like a Nimba sculpting, his eyes were raw and intelligent. He had two sexual organs, his prick was monstrous and erect, his vagina was tiny, like a comma.

The ocean became calm. I saw the baby growing, and it saw me, and stared at me. I was knocked about in the old man's dream of a dying country that had not yet been born, a nation born and dying from a lack of vision, too much greed and corruption, not enough love, too many divisions.

And when I looked I saw the baby impregnate itself: it grew into a man-woman, and struggled for many generations trying to give birth to itself, to its own destiny. The sky changed, and the earth heaved, and when the period of parturition was over, I noticed at the feet of the man-woman a bizarre birth, a birth within a birth. Everything was still. The man-woman had delivered several babies who were joined at the hips. They were all different, they had few resemblances, their hues were dissimilar, and they were secretly antagonistic to one another. It was truly frightening, this pullulation of babies with different voices, different eyes, different cries, different dreams, similar ancestry, all jostling, all trapped within the same flesh, pulling in conflicting directions. Unable to escape one another, growing at incompatible rates, some dying as others grew fatter, some dragging the corpses of their siblings through the days and nights, feeding off the dead amongst them – this horrible sight made my head swell in the infernal labyrinths of the blind old man's dreams.

Time accelerated. The original man-woman had disappeared into its hybridous offspring. And I saw them, with their unnumbered legs, their multiple arms and heads, seldom thinking together, suspicious of one another, condemned to wander as one, to build as one, to destroy as one, yet always trying to be separate from one another, always failing, for they were all of one body, one ancient and forgotten ancestry, their destinies linked – in union or division – for ever.

My soul was so wounded with the agony of witnessing such strangeness that I turned to the blind old man, all feathered and half-transformed, his phallus erect, and I said:

'I want to go home.'

He laughed, but no sound issued from him. Then I realised that in his dream he could see but paid the price by being deaf and intermittently dumb. There were glowing pinpoints all over him. And when the lights became lurid in his dreams I noticed that he had eyes all over his body: he had eyes in his feathers like a peacock, he had an eye in the middle of his forehead, and he had a necklace of them round his neck. My fear had become intolerable, and I panicked. Then a voice said to me:

'Be still.'

I was still. The voice said again:

'Eat the wild flowers.'

I ate the wild flowers. Nothing happened. The blind old man tried to seize them from me, but he couldn't. He hit me on the head, and I grew strong. He hit me again, and I grew stronger. I held him by the throat and throttled him with all the herculean might the flowers gave me. And when he eventually let me go everything first went white and then black, and I felt myself falling. I fell for a long time through many undiscovered universes. I fell, but I did not land, I did not hit the earth. Instead I found myself leaning against a tree. My body blazed all over with livid agony. It seemed as if I were entirely covered with bruises and welts, as if I had been flayed. My head throbbed as if I had been hammered with a mighty stick, my eyes were full of fire, and my wrist seemed raw with exposed nerves. All this was the price I paid for sensing and suffering the future on my living flesh.

The lights were still on in Madame Koto's bar when I hurried past. I heard the strains of the blind old man's accordion as I fled across his darkened domain. An owl flew overhead, watching me. When I got to our room the door was open, the air was suffused with mosquito coil smoke, and dad was asleep on the mat, his legs spread wide apart. Mum was on the bed, asleep, as if nothing had happened. Lit up with pain, I lay on the mat beside dad. After a while of breathing in the familiar smells it seemed as if time had not moved at all. But I also felt that the world had turned. The new angle of things was strange to me.

CHAPTER SEVEN

The Serenity of the Foreseen

MY BRUISES BECAME visible. Dad enquired about them and I told him that I had hurt myself playing in the forest. Mum pressed the stinging juices of poisonous herbs on my welts and lacerations. Poison fought poison and two days later the bruises lessened noticeably. I marvelled at mum's herbal lore.

That evening a message came from Madame Koto. She asked why I hadn't been visiting her bar as we had promised, and demanded that I begin the next day. Dad was worried. Fighting had broken out everywhere, and it had become dangerous to wander the streets. Party thugs continued to terrorise people. The world was at a new angle to the sky, but the old violence had returned. People were beaten at street corners for giving the wrong political passwords. The nights became populated by strange men with hard faces and bad smells. Madame Koto's bar was now the acknowledged centre of mobilising our area for the elections. Her new driver had been fitted out with a superb uniform. As Madame Koto's personal driver he was a powerful figure in his own right and, like his ill-fated predecessor, had taken to speeding up and down the road, blasting his horn, frightening old women and babies learning to walk.

Dad was worried, but mum said nothing. It was as if she accepted that what would happen had already been foretold. Her serenity in the face of the new violence infuriated dad. There was nothing he could do: mum had entered a new domain of her spirit and dad was scared of her. And so he took out his annoyance on me. He made me wash his

94

clothes. He made me polish his boots twenty times in one day. He made me split firewood with an unwieldy axe and he towered over me, breathing heavily in his comic rage. Then later, in the evening, he relented. He carried me around on his shoulders and told me stories about the village which I entirely forgot because I was still angry with him.

CHAPTER EIGHT

New Angles of the World (1)

O N THE DAY I went back to Madame Koto's bar a rainbow appeared over the forest. It had rained that morning. All through the day the sun shone and the rain poured down steadily. People said that somewhere an elephant was giving birth. The rainbow was very clear and distinct. It made me think there was a great big jewel in the sky that light poured through. The people of our area stared at the rainbow in wonder. They spoke of signs. The rainbow of the forest was solid, but it had a twin. The second rainbow, which seemed to originate from Madame Koto's backyard, was not distinct, nor clear. It was a half-rainbow, and its colours were all a little vague and washed together like an incomplete manifestation.

From a distance it seemed as if Madame Koto had now entered the god-like business of creating rainbows. Our respect for her grew. But when I drew nearer to her bar the rainbow, like a spirit seen by those who are not part-spirits, seemed to vanish altogether. I heard people whispering that her power now depended on space, on distance, on silence, which was why no one saw her any more.

The way people talked about her made me scared of going to her bar alone. It was as if she had multiplied in some way, as if she had conquered our dreams. I kept delaying having to go there. I wandered around a bit, approaching her forecourt and retreating. Then I decided to go and see my friend Ade. The herbalists had apparently finished the first course of his treatment. What did they know of his condition? My friend was lean and pale, his lips quivered, and he broke into subterranean voices when I wasn't looking. He had been told not to wander far from their house. Boredom was de-hydrating his spirit. An intense light had entered his eyes. He was like a child who knew something very evil, but in his case it was as if he knew that something hot and beautiful was approaching his soul. I knew that every day he was willing himself to die. He had that look in his eyes. The world had no power over him. His sense of freedom was awesome and terrifying. And when he broke into the hoarse cavernous voices of his spirit-companions a black wind blew through my mind.

'Let's go to Madame Koto's place,' I said.

'I am not afraid,' he replied, irrelevantly.

'Of what?'

'Of rainbows.'

'Why should you be afraid of rainbows?'

'When there are four rainbows in the sky, the flood will come.'

'What flood?'

'I won't be here then.'

'You're talking nonsense again,' I said.

He gave me a strange smile. The smile grew bigger and a happy expression filled his face. Then he began to tremble. His limbs shook and he was bathed in radiance, as if his fit were a sweet juice that he was drinking, or as if it were sunlight to the feverish. I became scared. He burst into laughter, the jubilant laughter of death. I slapped him. He stopped for a moment. Then I grabbed him by the collar and dragged him to his father's workshop and left him there, afraid that he might do something dreadful to himself in his unearthly ecstasy. I called his parents and when they came out and saw their son, I fled home.

In the evening the drizzle ceased. The half-rainbow dis-appeared from Madame Koto's backyard. I set out for her establishment. As I drew closer I was surprised to see a weird towering structure in front of her bar. At first I thought that this structure was responsible for the half-rainbow. People had gathered and they kept pointing at the new phenomenon. It was a gigantic red Masquerade, bristling with raffia and rags and nails. It had long stilts for legs and two twisted horns at the sides of a wild jackal's head. The red Masquerade held aloft a shining machete in one hand and a white flag, emblem of their party, in the other.

This terrifying colossus was so tall that even adults strained their necks looking up at it. No one knew who had built it, who had brought it there, or when. No one could explain the dark enigma of how the Masquerade stood upright on its long wooden legs without being blown away by the wind. And as if all these things weren't astonishing enough, no one amongst the gathered people could explain the most puzzling fact of all. The Masquerade had the head of a jackal, with fiercely protruding jaws, and it had the twisted horns of a ram – but it had human eyes. The eyes kept looking at us, turning in their sockets, regarding us with intense hostility. It was when people noticed the eyes that they began to be really mesmerised with horror. A man suggested, in a whisper, that there was a human being high up in the Masquerade. But another man said it was impossible and wondered how someone could be up there so still, in a space as small as the head, trapped in raffia and nails. It occurred to me that the eyes were familiar. At first I thought they belonged to the blind old man. Then I thought they were Madame Koto's. But none of these seemed likely. And as our speculation increased so did the palpable malice in the eyes of the red colossus.

We were so fascinated by the gigantic apparition that we didn't notice another enigma that stood right in front of us. The enigma was a white horse standing near the door of the bar. It looked docile, its head bent low. It was a big handsome horse, with a wonderful mane, and it shone in the evening light. We stared at the white horse and the red Masquerade for a long time, speechless, overcome with an indefinable sense of dread.

The evening darkened. The wind made frightful noises as it blew over the head of the Masquerade. People hurried to their homes and heard the first mutterings of an exodus. I went towards Madame Koto's bar.

When I passed the white horse it lifted up its head and gazed at me with green eyes. Then, unaccountably, it started kicking the air with one of its front feet. Convinced that it was threatening me in some way, I fled into the bar and into a completely new reality. The place had undergone another of its cyclical transformations. There were no long benches and tables. The counter had gone. The bird cages, the chained monkey, the mysterious peacock and the screened corner of the glass-eyed image had all vanished. The spaces inside were more expansive. The place had acquired a weird sort of domestic elegance. Red cushioned chairs had footstools beside them. Little tables had replaced the long ones. Spears and daggers decorated the walls. There were almanacs everywhere. Tinsel trailed down from the ceiling. Batik materials served as curtains. And, as always, the place was crowded. Women with almond eyes, long fingernails and lace dresses floated past holding cigarettes in their hands. There were short men with powerful heads and small eyes, tall men with servants who fanned them, stocky men with bleary eyes. The red lights made everything seem unreal and I kept going up to people and touching their stomachs till one of the women caught my hand and said:
'Sit down and don't move!'
I didn't see mum in all the commotion of lights and loud music. There seemed to be more voices than there were people. Some of the voices were very guttural. I couldn't understand anything that was being said. The longer I sat in the bar, the weirder I felt. It was as if I were asleep and awake at the same time, as if my body were at home and my spirit were under a red sea. Strange violent energies wandered around in my head. My eyes began to pulse. My

99

throat tightened. I suddenly realised that I couldn't breathe. I screamed, and heard the sound at the other end of the room.

While I was trying to rally myself, a stocky man with big eyes and an elastic grin came over. He gave me a piece of fried chicken and tapped me on the head. I was about to eat the chicken when I heard mum's voice saying:

'Throw it away.'

I threw the chicken on the floor and the man came back and knocked me on the shoulder. I felt better. I got up from the bench, pushed past the crowd and went to the backyard for some air. The man came after me. There was a full moon over the forest. The man pointed to the moon, and when I looked at it, he laughed. I turned to him and became aware that he had holes in his eyes. He pointed to the moon again. I looked. The wind blew his voluminous garment. I smelt rotting flesh. When I turned to him again, his eyes were normal. His grin was still elastic. There was something distinctly odd about him and I didn't know what it was.

'Give me back my chicken,' he said.

'It's inside,' I told him.

'Go and get it.'

I went in and picked up the chicken from the floor and when I went back outside he was gone. I looked for him and couldn't find him. I threw the piece of chicken into the bushes and heard a subdued growl from the darkness. I went back into the bar and searched for mum. She wasn't there. Neither was Madame Koto. The wind blew decomposition into the bar and when I sought the refuge of the backyard the man emerged from the bushes, with holes in his eyes, holes all over his face, and holes in his neck. He smiled at me. Then he laughed. And through his mouth, right through the back of it, I could see the moon. Then it dawned on me that the man had died a long time ago. Before I could do anything he went into the bar and I did not see him again. I asked one of the women about him. She looked at me as if I were mad, and said:

'I told you to sit down and be quiet.'

I couldn't. The voices, all alien, and the lights, all garish, made me feel ill. I crept out to the backyard again. The moon was riding a white horse of a cloud. I was standing there, listening to the flourishes of drumming and tinkling bells approaching, when for the first time I became aware that a red haze of light surrounded me. I moved, and it followed me. I couldn't step out of it and couldn't shake it off. The red haze sent fiery visions through my head. Heat swept up my spine in vicious waves, filling my brain with the fury of hot nails. I tried to escape from the red haze framing me, but it stayed. It began to obsess me. I felt trapped in its violent peppery heat. But when I slipped back into the bar the heat ceased and the red haze vanished.

But I couldn't stand it inside. The smells grew worse. The men smiled knowingly at me. The women's hands were cold. And an agonised cry started from the barfront. Dogs began barking. When I went to the barfront everything was silent except for the dogs. Then I realised that the elysian voices were not singing in the forest.

I was about to return to the bar when I saw red spirits clambering up the fretful white horse. The wind made the Masquerade's jackal head cry out. People rushed from the bar to see what was happening. The shining machete reflected moonlight on us and the horse neighed, rearing. Tossing its head, the white horse kicked out and raged in an inexplicable access of terror. The red spirits clambered on it and the horse galloped insanely round the Masquerade and one of the women shouted:

'Someone control that horse!'

Then one of the men – tall, impressive, with a bullet-shaped head and elongated eyes – stepped out towards the horse, his hands outstretched. The red spirits jumped off the horse and on to the man and they vanished in him, as if his body had absorbed them. And then the horse trotted over to the man, its head lowered, as if ashamed. The people clapped, and the dogs stopped barking.

When everyone had gone back in I noticed white spirits clambering all over the red Masquerade. The moon burned in its enraged eyes. I had retreated to the backyard when the wind, blowing hard, caused a weird jackal cry to issue from the Masquerade. The cry was so powerful and strange that for a long time afterwards all the nocturnal animals, the dogs, the cats, the weeping children, were utterly silent till the wind had passed and the coded cry had been carried away to the distant regions of the forest.

CHAPTER NINE

New Angles of the World(2)

A T THE BACKYARD, bathed in the sheen of moonlight, the red haze appeared round me again. But before I had time to be scared, the flourish of drums, the tinkling bells and the rhythmic feet materialised. I saw many women, dressed in black, with white kerchiefs, dancing in a circle in the backyard. The blind old man was in the centre of the circle, orchestrating their movements. In his hand was a fan of the brightest eagle feathers I have ever seen. He had his harmonica, he was barefoot, and he danced with the fury and vigour of a wild young man. He whipped the air with his fan. He sprang one way, bounded in another, spun in the air, stamped irregularly on the earth, and lashed their spirits with ageless ritual passion, as he guided them through the cultic dances of the new season.

He led them through the Peacock dance, the dance of the Jackal, the movements of the Bull, and the cornucopia dances they must perform so flawlessly behind their leader on the night of the great political rally. With the exemplary vigour of a bull-leaper, he displayed the requisite motions, foaming at the mouth, yellow liquids gathering at the corners of his eyes. His chest was bare and covered with hieroglyphic markings, his neck was stringy, his stomach twinkled with antimony. He had kaoline on one side of his face and a red cloth with three cowries tied to his upper arm. He made the women stamp to the war songs and the party chants with mad and unbounded energy. He was a mystery of signs, riddles, power and time.

Mum stood apart from the circle of women, the veins bulging on her forehead. She didn't seem to notice my presence, and I couldn't get to her because she was on the other side of the circle. The blind old man went on leaping and capering with the energy of a young lustful bull, his voice thick and harsh. And after he had exhausted the women, he sent for some palm-wine. The women dispersed, holding their hips, hobbling. With a severe expression on his face, he came and sat on a stool near me. Kneeling down, a woman handed him a half-calabash of palm-wine. He took it, and dismissed her. Before he drank he turned his old yellow-watering eyes to me, and said:

'You ugly spirit-child! The next time I catch you in my dreams, I will eat you.'

Then he gulped down the half-calabash of palm-wine, and burped. The dogs started barking. I tried to move as far away from him as possible. I moved surreptitiously, hoping he wouldn't notice. But after a while he turned to me again and, in his harsh voice of a half-transformed bull, said:

'Come here, and let me see with your eyes!'

I fled to the barfront and sat near the door. The white horse breathed over me. The moon burned the eyes of the Jackal-headed Masquerade. The red haze round me began to grow hot again; soon I felt my flesh on fire. I couldn't move. I heard the blind old man laughing in my head. Then I became aware of him staring at me maliciously through the eyes of the Jackal-headed Masquerade. A curious sand-hot wind blasted my mind. A cat ran out of the bushes and leapt across my face. The white horse uttered a piercing scream. The wind became still. Several voices began speaking in my head at once, whispers of hoarse women, the growls of old animals, the screeching of children. I smelt the old man's presence all around. Then I felt eyes on me in the dark, rooting me to the floor. The angry waves of an invisible river roared behind me. My brain began to itch with insurgent passions. The red haze around me grew more intense. Then I had a distinct sensation that the Masquerade was moving. Its raffia trailing rustled in the alien wind. And then, all over the area, I saw them – the great spirits, in blazing lineaments, pouring in one direction, with the golden spirits of butterflies vibrating in orioles round their heads, their drums thundering on the silent air.

The insurgent voices in me grew worse. I wrenched myself up and the moon became obscured and I heard the mighty hoofs of the Masquerade stalking me. I ran and fetched some stones and threw them at the Masquerade and I hit its eyes three times, and three times I heard the blind old man cry out in the backyard.

The red haze tightened round me, scorching my flesh with itches. Unable to bear it any longer I cried out for mum. After a while the moon was clear again in the deep sky, and I heard footsteps approach, and I saw mum surrounded by a blinding glow. Her eyes were serene as if she were conscious of her own sleep-walking. She stretched out a bony hand towards my head, and for a moment I was afraid. She did it with a bizarre stillness, as if she were possessed by a secret powerful goddess. Fortified by light and wind, she said in the voice of one returning from a distant dream:

'No one will hurt my only son!'

And with a new cry mum seized the red haze around me. With a quick movement of her wrists she gathered it together and held it like a hoop, and dispatched it into the air. I watched the red hoop spinning like a strange disc: red into blue, it vanished slowly into the dark sky. And then I felt the cooling clarity of the moon and wind. When I looked around, mum was gone. I saw nothing except the white horse, its head held up, regarding me with surprised intelligent eyes; and the Jackal-headed Masquerade, its two ram horns askew, its eyes of the blind old man glaring at me in puzzlement and fury.

I was standing there in the calm field of moonlight, confused about where I was and what had happened, when I felt a concussive light in my head, a white searing agony, brief and strangely beautiful. In the horrible brilliance of that moment it seemed I crossed a threshold, a time boundary, adventuring into chaos and sunlight. Still spinning, I was startled by voices behind me. And when I turned round it was suddenly broad daylight. The afternoon sun was burning on the surviving bushes. The streets were populated with people I had never seen. Cars went up and down the perplexing criss-cross of roads, blasting their horns. Bicyclists jingled their bells. Hawkers went past me, smiling, singing out the items of their trade. A lorry shot past, raising dust from the untarred street. Children were playing games in raised voices. A water-tanker drove into the yard of the house next door and sold water to the house-owner. I noticed the aluminium tank in front of the house and a signboard which belonged to a tailor. Then Ade came up to me, his face long and lean, his eyes mischievous.

'What has happened?' I asked.

'Look,' he said, pointing at the chaotic grouping of bungalows and zinc abodes.

'Look at what?' I asked.

'The forest has disappeared,' he said, smiling in an irritating, almost patronising manner.

'Where has it gone?'

'You are a fool,' he replied.

'Why?'

'Things have changed.'

I looked around again. There was no white horse, no Masquerade, no Madame Koto's bar, no forest; just a dry dust-saturated ghetto with sand-coloured houses, unfinished buildings, the signboards of a hundred small professionals everywhere, naked children playing, and flat-breasted women wandering the streets. The wind was hot, the sun unbearable, the smells of rotten eggs and open gutters terrible in the nostrils, the sky a burnished expanse of yellow heat. Ade hit me playfully on the head and went down the street, chuckling. Then, suddenly, the growling blast of a car-horn sounded behind me, freezing my heart, darkening my sight. I jumped, landed heavily, and fell. When I got up it was night again, with the red and green bulbs shining in Madame

Koto's bar, and the voices of the women scorching the forest air. Bewildered, I turned and saw the white horse regarding me. It seemed quite pleased with itself, as if it had carried out an insinuated threat. A sharp pain roamed my head, and I realised I had been kicked. Without thinking, I ran into the bar. I screamed, and fought my way through the squat men with toad eyes and women whose perfumes masked their wickedness. I rushed to the backyard, trampling over the blind old man who was smoking a pipe, and jumped into the arms of my mother, into her protective serenity. She stood with magical grace in the moonlight. Her eyes were dazzling. She had the sweet scents of crushed herbs about her. She held me tight and, after a brief silence, said:

'It's time for us to go home. Trouble has become our neighbour.'

She said her goodbyes to the other women, took her basket and white shawl, and carried me safely across the street swarming with the ghosts of golden-eagles, and sunbirds, and one-eyed goats, and chickens without feathers. She bore me safely past the mouth of the forest, where the women were singing again in angelic waves, lulling me towards sleep.

But as we neared home I saw over mum's shoulder the sight which was to bring terror into our lives. The Masquerade was stirring, its jackal head tossing, as if animated by a vengeful demon. I heard the anguished howls raised from its elongated mouth by the wind which was blowing new horrors into our living spaces and dividing time for us, for ever.

CHAPTER TEN

Dark New Age of Enchantments

T HAT NIGHT WE heard the stampeding hooves of an old
bull. We heard the jackal howls and the wild neighing
of horses.

Dad sat up most of the night staring at us, not
speaking, studying me and mum as if we were conspirators who were going to kill him as soon as he fell
asleep. His demented concentration unnerved me. Mum
remained serene. She laid out our food. Dad struggled
with his frustration. He refused to eat. I ate all his share
of the food and he sat hunched in his chair, snarling at
me. Mum cleared the table with the ghost of a smile on her
face.

Dad didn't sleep that night. Mum lay on the bed and I
stayed on the mat, and I heard dad grumbling obsessively,
twisting his great body, creaking his neck, freeing trapped
energies along his spine. That was when we first heard
the bull bellowing, the horse neighing, the jackal howling, the
night-runners pounding the earth, the drums thundering,
the machetes clashing, the dogs barking, and a woman
wailing three houses away from us. The wail was sliced in
half at the same time that all the dogs stopped barking. I
heard dad stamping towards the door. Mum said:

'Be careful. They are very powerful, you know.'

'They don't call me Black Tyger for nothing,' dad boasted,
and swept out of the room.

He came running back in a moment later, panting heavily.
I lit a candle. Dad looked perplexed. Standing at the doorway,
he had a terrified expression in his eyes.

'Put out the light, or they will come here next,' mum said, calmly.

I blew out the candle and found myself circling in a moonlit space and I saw the Jackal-headed Masquerade riding the white horse, swiping the air with its silver machete, the white flag fluttering in its grasp, its jackal mouth slavering, its eyes red. The white horse galloped furiously in the night-spaces, through the forest. The Masquerade slaughtered the trees, felling them, cutting down invisible enemies that cried out and were silent. And when the jackal eyes saw me and the horse turned and rode towards me, shaking its great head, I screamed – and mum lifted me from the mat and made me lie down with her. Dad sat still, dazed, more afraid than I had ever seen him, his eyes wide open, his neck stiff. The air in the room was heavy, as if there were no longer any boundaries between the world outside and our private lives.

The next day we heard that seven dogs were found beheaded in our area. Five people had been killed. We saw the corpses of three women in white robes with jewels round their necks. Their rigid bodies were borne by some of the men of the street, borne into the forest. The men never returned.

Mum's spirit became darker. Dad grew more fearless as the day wore on. It rained all afternoon. The people of the area were too scared to spread rumours, because a new force had seized control of our spaces. For three days during which it rained, and the street flooded, we stayed in, hungry and silent, our spirits raw and beaten. The voices were temporarily silenced in the forest. And there were no heroic acts of resistance to give us the hope of ever sleeping peacefully again at night for as long as we were poor and defenceless.

CHAPTER ELEVEN

The Masquerade's Kingdom

ON THE FOURTH day dad's spirit, daring the dread of the new season, soared in our room, and that night he spoke to us with the voice of a child. We didn't understand him. Mum had become smaller, her powers had curiously diminished. She no longer disappeared at night. It was dad's voice, speaking from his dreams, which gave us hope.

The next day I went to Madame Koto's bar. Apart from us, no one had yet seen her and people had begun to entertain doubts as to whether she had ever really existed. The Masquerade towered at her barfront, its eyes had become more human, more tyrannical, its face more vicious. It had acquired another pair of horns. Its wooden legs had become the feet of an ibex. We noticed with alarm that gore dripped from the machete which it clasped in one hand like a conquering and ruthless god. In the other hand the whiteness of the flag had been stained with red. The white horse was nowhere to be seen.

The celebrations in the bar that afternoon reached dark bacchanalian proportions. When I went in every available space was crowded. There were numerous crates of beer on the floor, kegs of palm-wine on the tables, yellow banners on the ceiling, enlarged photographs of the Party leader on the walls. There were even pictures of Madame Koto everywhere, her eyes piercing, her face big. She held a mighty key in one hand. There were four men in traditional robes fanning her.

Men and women were dancing and talking excitedly about their victory. I didn't understand. The bar filled out to bursting point, people slipped in secretly through the back door, roast meat was passed round on white trays, drinks were opened, and toasts were made to a new era of power. It wasn't until I began to recognise faces from the market, sellers of charms, women who burned their days hawking cheap provisions under the dehydrating sun, carpenters without work, fishermen without nets, tailors without clothes to sew, neighbours along the street, it wasn't until I recognised them that I understood the nature of their victory. The new powers were winning converts. People who had opposed them – those whose lives had been shrivelled by their night fears, women who had borne too many children, men who had no money and no hopes left, whose children had died of under-nourishment – had all joined the Party, had all accepted Madame Koto's invisible patronage.

Their numbers were swelling, and their celebrations drew more people, drew those whose hunger had been defeated by the promise of wealth and instant protection, drew those who didn't want to suffer and wait for justice any more. The new converts celebrated the most vigorously, for it seemed they had been homeless all their lives and had now found a home, had been denied the comfortable life and had now found a utopia, had been alone and were now amongst many.

Their celebrations were louder than the music. The drunken initiates spilled out from the bar into the street, dancing with palm-wine in their glasses. They danced round the Jackal-headed Masquerade as if they had found an acceptable god who understood their hunger.

Wearing shirts and blouses imprinted with the logo of the Party, the new converts chanted the songs of their faith, weaving and staggering, intoxicated with their initiation, possessed by the awesome spirit of the Masquerade. The faces of the converts – our neighbours and fellow sufferers – had changed. Their faces had changed with their initiation, with the acceptance of their new uniforms, with the meat they ate, with the palm-wine they drank. Their faces had become more brutal and more indifferent, it seemed. Their eyes were harder, as if they had seen a new kingdom of reality. Their eyes resembled Madame Koto's in their ferocious, imposing disdain.

They mocked the crowds of street people outside. They laughed at their wretchedness. The gathered inhabitants of the area stood confused by the rowdy celebrations of the converts. The inhabitants looked ragged, powerless, trapped in bitterness. They looked small, doomed, their faces pinched, their hair dust-coloured, their skin pale. Madame Koto's invisible presence had seeped into their lives, sucked away their dreams, sapped their vitality. They stood defenceless against wind and rain, unprotected from hunger, vulnerable to the bulls of the night, the curfew-making of political thugs, the thundering drums, the caterwauling of the totemic political Masquerade.

Mesmerised by the stomping and chanting of the converts, I saw that other celebrations had begun. They had begun all over the city, all over the country, in small villages, in new ghettoes, along the streets and highways. The forthcoming elections had already been forewon. Fear and strange noises had swept the souls of the country, and those who didn't have anywhere to hide were naked.

Standing there, I saw it all in a sudden swooping flash. The flash blew open the spaces in my mind. My spirit rose in height and I found myself in the mind of the Masquerade. I saw the world through its eyes. I surveyed its extensive, universal kingdom of fear. Dread for those who oppose, protection for supporters, nightmares for the silent. I saw far across the lands, into the heart of nations whose heartbeats had accelerated and had been taken over by the powers of fear. All those who didn't support would lose their jobs, be thrown out of their houses for mysterious reasons, would come home to find that their houses had moved, and their wives or husbands deserted to better pastures. I saw through the terrible eyes of the Masquerade and I realised that it was merely one of a thousand universal manifestations: each land has its own kind of Masquerade, some more refined than others, the principle the same. I saw that its kingdom was under the aegis of a banished god, a fallen semi-deity, ageless, raising the pitch of the heartbeat of nations, preventing them from being born, or being regenerated. For in the chaos of nations and historical periods, in their inability to be born, lie power and wealth for the supporters of the Masquerade. And in being born, in becoming what they can become, in their fullness and regeneration, in transforming into great nations, mature entities, creating power for all, in all this, the powerful are deprived of more power. Through the Masquerade's eyes I understood that there is a war always going on in our night-spaces, a battle between those who become more powerful because of the millions who refuse to be born, refuse to be, and those who *are*, who have been born, who carry on becoming, and who bring the dreams of a possible paradise and an incremental light to the earth.

The Masquerade's kingdom is a mighty one, its armies can never wholly be defeated. They are part of the world for ever. They make the other, wiser, forces necessary. They make it more crucial for the great good dreamers and the slow secret realisers of great dreams to be stronger, to hold fast to the difficult light and to transcend themselves and become the legendary hidden heroes who transform the destiny of peoples and nations for the better.

The supporters of the Masquerade's way are themselves unknowing agents of higher gods of light, who understand the pressure and secret constancy and earth-nourishing silence that creates the diamonds of the universe. But I also realised that if the people of the world saw things from the Masquerade's unconquerable eyes they too would be dancing their support, celebrating their initiation, under the noonday sun, their fears banished, their enemies outnumbered.

CHAPTER TWELVE

Laughter in the Kingdom

AND AS I stood there, seeing the world through the Masquerade's eyes, an excruciating horror coursed through me. Revolving in the sky, high up above the people, I found myself looking down on the perforated zinc rooftops. My head was swirling, there was fire in my brain, and acids in my spirit. Evil whisperings flooded my mind. Horrible incantations of ritual power were breathed into the Jackal's head by the blind old man, sorcerer of manifestations. Weighed down with hideous spells, I realised with the greatest terror I have ever known that I had entered the universal mind of evil things, numinous things, the thoroughfares of indescribable forces that were spreading their empires over the air and night-spaces of the world. I had entered the Masquerade's mind, I was trapped, and didn't know how to get out.

The Masquerade's head was a mighty house. It was not one mind, but many; a confluence of minds. I wandered in its consciousness and found a labyrinthine kingdom. I saw its pyramids, its cities, its castles, its great palaces, its seas and rivers. I saw its moats and marshlands, its architectural wonders, its splendid dungeons and torture-chambers, its vast armies and police networks, its slaves, cabals, mind-engineers, spirit-distorters, reality-manufacturers, history-twisters, truth-inventers, soul-transplanters, dream-destroyers, courage-grinders, love-corrupters, hope-crushers, sleep-eaters, hunger-producers, money-farmers. I saw its great universities, its infernal libraries, its arid museums, its numberless colleges of spies, its control centres, its government-creating agencies, its heresiarchs, its unbelievably beautiful gardens and radiant plants, and astonishing canals, its numerous orchestras for the production of poisonous music, its cunningly seductive art, its spirit-mangling paintings, its negation-breeding poetry, and I even read some of its brain-scrambling books, written in the most hypnotising calligraphic hand. What shocked me more than anything else was the uncanny sense of order in the kingdom. There was no chaos, no confusion, no alternatives, no dialectic, no disturbances. It was almost peaceful, almost – paradisial. It was a strange kind of utopia. The wind was serene, the sunlight blessed, the water brilliant, the grass pure, the earth fertile. There were no dreams in the air, there was no tension, no poverty, no yearnings, no hunger. And there was, mostly, silence. Many minds flowed into the kingdom of the Masquerade. They flowed there from all over the world. They also flowed outwards. I could see the waves spreading to all nations. I saw the invisible Masquerades of the western world, saw their worshippers of order, money, desire, power, and world domination. I saw the great white Masquerades of the eastern nights, the goddesses who ate children in desert towns, the gods who ate their offspring in machines and secret wars. I saw the diverse goddesses of fear and nightmares, who were worshipped with the blood of dissenters, worshipped in dreams. I saw the powers of the Kingdom, how it manufactures reality, how it produces events which will become history, how it creates memory, and silence, and forgetfulness, how it keeps its supporters perpetually young and vigorous, how it protects them, seals their lives with legality.

I wandered lost and frightened, my entrails turning into fire, my feet bleeding on the invisible broken glass paths of the kingdom. I wandered the infernal mazes, with pepper bursts in my being, and I saw eyes opening in the air, following me, spying on me. Separated from my body, trapped in the Masquerade's kingdom, I began to weep.

I wept for my terrible fate. I saw at once that if I lived I would have to struggle for ever and without much hope against the insidious permeating extensions of the Masquerade's kingdom. I would have to fight against it, never certain of succeeding, never sure of companionship, possibly always betrayed by love. I would have to fight, to help spread some light which the darkness would devour, and I would run out of candles and lamps and all proverbial forms of illumination, till I found a way to incarnate light, to become a new illumination, shedding light and seeing by it, burning fiercely and gently for all the world that I had come to love, for all that I wanted to see, burning my being away, without rest, and without the certainty of transformation. I saw how my mother and father were doomed in the struggle. And I understood what mum meant when she buried her jewels in the sacred earth of the forest. And my heart grieved for all spirit-children, for all who had once been children, and for those who are children now – for in the Masquerade's kingdom the world seemed so hard, the struggle so unremitting. My being always aches for joy. And it seemed better·to return to the spirit world and play by the fountains with the beautiful fauns than to struggle against the empire of the Masquerade's dominion, and to do this for ever, hoping every day that a miraculous light would emerge to make the world grow more beautiful for all.

As I wandered in the labyrinths I stopped and burst into the most profound weeping, and laughter echoed back at me from the immensity of the kingdom, from its glacial silence. I realised that my weeping was turned into laughter. And the laughter multiplied everywhere, blowing a volcanic wind through the Masquerade's mind, regenerating the immeasurable negative powers all over the earth. And then I stopped weeping: I saw how my wailing was feeding the kingdom.

I was listening to the wind when a gentle voice said:

'Who invited you here?'

I turned, and saw the white horse.

'I got here by accident,' I replied.

Another voice, behind me, said:

'You can't come here by accident. You must know how to enter.'

I turned, and saw Madame Koto. She was enormous and extremely beautiful. She wore a golden robe. Her eyelashes shone with antimony.

'I was in front of your bar and I looked up and then I found myself here.'

'Liar!' a harsh, more ancient voice cried.

It was the blind old man. He looked handsome and healthy, and was covered in silver bracelets. He was carried on a litter by nubile young women. Around him was a retinue of servants, and the resplendent peacock walked in front of him. The blind old man was a great chief in this kingdom.

'I want to go back,' I said.

'Go back to where?'

'I want to get out of this place.'

'Get out then,' the blind old man said, chuckling, as if he were an old antagonist, older than my memory, which on days when my body's light dims goes back a thousand years.

I turned to Madame Koto for help: she had vanished. I turned to the white horse: only its black shadow remained. I turned to the blind old man, and the wind blasted volcanic ash into my eyes. The searing agony, eating deep into my spirit, made me scream. Tossing and shouting, I realised in a flash of intuition that, before it turns into wailing, laughter might release me from the spell of the kingdom. And I kicked about and fought and contorted and laughed on the sand, till someone threw water in my face and a woman's voice said:

'What is wrong with you? Are you mad?'

Someone else whacked me on the head. I opened my eyes and saw a red ghost peering at me and I screamed again and jumped and ran and found myself in the empty bar. There were flies all about. Dad was sitting in the shadow of a far corner. He had a green hat on his head. His face was lowered. He was mulling over a calabash of palm-wine.

CHAPTER THIRTEEN

The Invisible Censorship

'COME AND SIT near me,' dad said, 'and let me tell you how I am going to rule this country.'

Drying my face, I went over. My eyes were sore. He didn't look at me. He stared into his glass. A fly had died in his palm-wine. He didn't seem to mind. He drank the palm-wine and after a while he spat out the fly.

'Bad things can never get to our spirit,' he said, smiling.

Then he was silent. He was silent for a long time. My eyes cooled. The heat and agony in me slowly dissolved. His presence was immensely protective. His blue soothing light, awakened by his new rage, was large in the bar. For a long time no one came in. After a while he said:

'Where is your mother?'

Mum came in through the back door. She had a basin on her head.

'Don't eat the food,' she said. 'Don't touch the meat.'

'Why not?' I asked.

She went out again, without answering my question. Before dad could say anything the bar darkened, and the wind blew in a pregnant goat. The goat wandered over to our table and stared at us and went out through the front door.

'That goat walks just like Madame Koto,' dad remarked, laughing.

The wind blew the goat back in. It regarded us for a long while. Then it sauntered out again.

'Something is going to happen,' I said.

'Something good,' dad said.

I looked up at him. The volcanic wind rose in my mind.

'Your eyes are red. I will treat them later,' he said.

He had barely finished when the curtains were swished aside and customers crowded in: converts in disguise, spies, informers, thugs who were off duty. They called out for service. They eyed us surreptitiously. The lamp in the bar, creating jagged and elongated shadows of their presence, made them look almost ghoulish.

'This is where I will get the most voters for my Party,' dad said.

'Here?'

'Yes, here,' he said. 'Here in the very home of the enemy.'

Then he got up, glass in hand, and went over to the largest group, and launched into a long speech about politics, about his Party, and about his plans to build a university for beggars. He talked for fifteen minutes, denouncing the major political parties, chastising the Party of the Rich for terrorising people, attacking the Party of the Poor for cowardice and vengefulness. While he talked the bar listened to him in total silence. The lizards and wall-geckos froze, astonished at his blasphemies. I felt invisible feathers growing on my neck. My face crawled with bristles and itches. I was afraid. Dad was stirring a new wind.

As he talked, mum came into the bar, momentarily breaking the spell of motionlessness. She heard dad's insurrectional speech and went out, untouched, unafraid, as if she had foreseen it all. I noticed for the first time how sad she had become. Her luminosity had diminished. Only a terrible dignity, an anguished grace, and a curious fearlessness remained.

When she went out dad felt her after-presence, and he stuttered. A wall-gecko fell from the ceiling into his palm-wine glass. It struggled there, and dad didn't notice. He was looking at the backyard door, anguished at mum's absence, and when he re-entered his speech, talking louder, more daringly, making incoherent statements about the need to regulate the childhood of the nation, I understood the reason why dad had come into the bar, why he had decided to dare the powers eating up our dreams and draining our body's will to rebel.

Unable to find a way back into mum's bed by telling stories, he was trying a bolder method to impress her. So he talked himself into the heart of a bizarre mythology. While he talked the bar filled out with menacing presences. There were moments when I didn't hear dad's voice. The people who came in – tall men with rock-like heads and severe eyes – had the curious effect of making me not hear anything at all. The flies thickened round dad's face. The smell of corrupted flesh blew in through the front door. Then, out of the negation, I heard dad speaking.

'Why don't we use our powers wisely?' he asked the room at large.

No one answered him. Some of the people who had materialised in the bar silently gathered round his table. He seemed unafraid, but I could feel his muscles tightening.

'We can use our dark and our magical powers to create good life for our people instead of oppressing them, starving them, or killing them, don't you think?'

There was a deep silence. Dad began to say something new when he cried out suddenly, leaping from the bench and looking all about him. No one had moved. The wall-gecko in his glass of palm-wine went on thrashing and one of the men seized the glass and threw it outside. Dad sat down, glared at everyone suspiciously, and took off his green hat. Making sure that no one was behind him, fixing his gaze on a milky-eyed man in front of him, dad said:

'We must use our deep powers to get rid of poverty, not to create it. Poverty makes people strange, it makes their eyes bitter, it turns good people into witches and wizards.'

He paused. The flies were silent. I heard the women singing outside in the backyard. I heard them moving basins, chopping firewood, pouring water and praising the beauty of the meat they were about to roast. Dad went on with his speech, his voice rising in waves of intensity, as if he were addressing an invisible plenum of adversaries.

'In the country I rule the machetes of the people will be blunt, the guns unloaded.'

Someone laughed at the door. It was Madame Koto's driver. Short and reckless, his skin patchy, his face like a lizard's, he wore his new uniform of power, swaying at the door, disturbing the light, a bottle of beer in his hand. He staggered in and collapsed on the chair in front of me. Then he lifted his reptilian head and glared at me with his big drunken eyes of one who is certain of protection.

'If you cross my path, I will run you over,' he said maliciously.

Then he sank his head into his arms, and fell instantly asleep.

Dad went on, in a rough voice, talking about the laws he would create in his country. He would stop drivers running over dogs as a sacrifice to their hard deity. He would outlaw the killing of antelopes, lions, leopards and elephants. Everybody would be a farmer. Everybody would be a herbalist. Everyone would have free education and would study the numerous philosophies of the land. There would be a special tax on illiterates. We would produce what we eat. We would create things we need from our own natural resources. We would find ways of using mosquitoes, rats, cockroaches and frogs to be of benefit to us. He talked of training mosquitoes as international spies. He talked of using flies as messengers. He spoke of our people as the ones who carried the weight of the world on their heads. He said Africa has so much of everything, gold, diamonds, diseases, hope, hunger, food, cocoa. He maintained that even our diseases can help to transform our destiny. I wanted to ask him how. Dad spoke of making the nation learn the art of concentration. People who would be in his government would regularly have to pass the severest tests of special sorcerers to make sure that they were not corrupt. He said the whole continent should be one great country. He had just completed that statement when the Jackal-headed Masquerade howled, bringing incoherence into the bar. The darkness, conquering the evening, swept inside on the waves of the air. Dad denounced the Masquerade and said power should be about freedom and food, not about frightening people into voting for one side or another.

While dad spoke, his voice rising and receding, as if the darkness were cancelling out his words, I kept seeing long-legged spiders out of the tail of my eyes. When I turned and looked, I saw nothing. But they kept moving closer, like crabs or a phalanx of Roman soldiers, changing positions with the movement of my head. The mosquitoes flitted round me. A lizard scuttled across dad's hat. The mosquitoes flew into my ears and whined in my brain. The driver stopped snoring. The Masquerade's kingdom began to invade my mind. I felt its gigantic presence in me, alien and dark, like the shadow of a compacted mountain in a small room. I felt the spaces in me crowded out, stretched and bursting with this unholy occupation. A grotesque form, composed, it seemed, of pullulating debris, the essence of the Unborn, the lust of the machete, the darkness of eyes that see without limit and without pity, compressed itself into me. And for the first time I became aware that just as I could unintentionally enter the spirit of things, they too could enter into me. And the Masquerade, howling in my mind, watched dad through my eyes.

My thoughts were all shadows. I saw dad as a luminous tiger, small and snarling with light in the frightening expanse of a dark forest. There were faces on the bark of the trees, spears in the branches. An abyss was at his feet in the illusion of shadows, and boulders hung poised in the clouds above him. Dad turned his face to me and I saw his scowl of an enraged tiger, his tongue red, his eyes yellow, his teeth bloodied. And then I saw him as he was,

123

talking incoherently, whipping his hands in the air, his face twitching, tortured by flies. Dad went on so long and so vigorously that the spiders began to climb up my neck. I couldn't get them off. I cried out and fireflies darted into my mouth. Mosquitoes and irascible insects made me come out in bumps. I itched furiously all over. My skin felt furry, as if covered in rashes; but when I inspected myself, I found nothing. Dad continued with his visions of an African utopia, in which we would pool all our secret wisdom, distil our philosophies, conquer our bad history, and make our people glorious in the world of continents. The more the flies tortured him the more intense and visionary dad became. A fierce energy concentrated round his mouth; his head was surrounded by fire. Dad burned and didn't know it. We mistook the smoke for the smell of meat roasting on the spits outside. Dad's hair caught fire and I tried to move, but the mountain of shadow sat solidly in me. When dad stopped speaking to draw in breath, the fire vanished. He put on his hat and called for palm-wine, and a woman came in with his request, along with a plate of roast meat. She came in a fraction of a second before dad had called her and the meat had a delicious aroma and I tried to speak again but a light flashed in my eyes, blinding me for a moment. The spiders had climbed up on my hair and become entangled and I attempted to pull them out but succeeded only in tearing off clumps of my hair. Dad saw me struggling and he came over and said:

'What's wrong with you?'

I couldn't speak. He knocked me on the head and my brain cleared.

'There are spiders in my hair,' I said.

He looked. After a moment's inspection he pushed my head away lightly, saying:

'There's nothing there. Come and have some of this wonderful meat.'

He went back to his bench. The people who had gathered round him in concentrated solemnity went on watching him. Dad was encouraged by their apparent fascination and he began talking again, somewhat vehemently.

He said that as a people we must have more respect for death; that in the country he rules he will make sure people don't take death too lightly. He lashed out at the political party for filling the people's minds with too many ambitions, with greed and selfishness, promising them land and cars and government jobs if they voted for them, instead of filling their minds with self-respect and regard for hard work and service and love, and with thoughts of how to make the people strong, healthy and well-fed. Dad went on and on. The wind howled outside. One of the men pushed the plate of meat and the palm-wine gently towards dad. A strange spirit entered his head and I saw him trying to shake it out and he burst into ranting about how in the country of which he would be the ruler people would take exercises every day. He would discipline the old and the young, girls and women. He would toughen the bones of the citizens and make their bodies supple. And rituals would be used for reasons that make us take life more seriously and more joyfully, instead of being corrupted into instruments of terror.

CHAPTER FOURTEEN

Dialogue with the White Horse

I T WAS AT this point I became aware of the curious invisible censorship that had come to exist in the air and objects of Madame Koto's bar.

'Africa is the home of the world, and look at how we live in this world,' dad said vehemently, knocking over his glass of palm-wine in a sweeping accidental gesture.

The people who had gathered round him stared at dad as if he were both mad and amusing.

'Poverty everywhere, wickedness, greed, injustice all over the place, goats wanting to lead the country, cows running for elections, rats scheming to become governors. This could be the great garden of the earth, but it is now a backyard,' cried dad.

He launched into a torrential philippic on politics, poverty, drought, history – and the flies plagued him, hanging on his every word, buzzing round his ears, mocking his eyelids. The curious censorship of Madame Koto's powers was such that when dad stopped blustering, the flies stopped pestering him, and the spiders stopped digging their way into my brain. But dad didn't stop for very long. When, however, he fell silent for a while, I found I had suffered tremendously for his courage. Mosquitoes, bugs, mean little insects, beetles with thorn-like pincers had all bitten me and made a meal of my flesh. Even the wooden chair managed to lacerate me. The vicious insects that exist only in the crack of vision had punished me mercilessly for the politically blasphemous things dad had been saying.

By now the darkness had gained complete dominion over

126

the bar. I could barely make out dad's head, with the low flame burning around it like a crown of fire. There was a long silence. Dad was waiting for a response from his audience. They said nothing. And so dad resumed his speech, with renewed vigour.

'We are all fighting to be born, fighting to have our souls sit correctly in our bodies. So why don't you sensible people vote for me, eh, instead of wasting your votes on a party that keeps oppressing us. Believe me, to be born, to stay alive, and to turn into a destiny is a long and great struggle.'

And then, with the truly dramatic enthusiasm of a street salesman, he shouted:

'Let us liberate our future, now!'

I heard the women cheering outside. Inside, the darkness dissolved the forms and mixed everything up, scrambling shadow and substance; and the bar – awash with the brackish waves – became a completely different terrain. The tables began moving like animals, the chairs shifted position, the wind re-organised spaces and objects, blowing the silence of the forest into our midst. After a long while of struggling against the current of disorientation, I heard dad speak.

'Someone has been knocking me at the back of my head. My hat has disappeared. The darkness has eaten the meat.'

'There's no one here apart from me and you,' I said.

There was a pause.

'How do you know?'

I wasn't sure. But I felt something stirring at the doorway, an inexplicable transfiguration. Then the wind whipped swirls of leaves past the curtain, and I beheld a towering luminous form.

'How do you know?' dad asked again.

The luminous form dimmed, and became a solid shadow.

'Madame Koto is watching us,' I said.

'Where is she?'

'At the door.'

'That's not Madame Koto,' he said.

'What is it?'

'It's a horse.'

Then suddenly the horse snorted and burst out with a startling sustained whinnying cry. Tossing its great white head, snorting, it trotted into the bar and filled the place with its moonlight and its horror and its quivering flesh. Dad staggered back in the dark and fell over a chair. I didn't move. The horse stood in the middle of the bar, its pungent animal smell making its presence massive. Its eyes shone. It was completely still, an apparition that rooted us with its great size and its horsehair stench.

'Put on the light!' dad bellowed.

I slid from the chair and crawled under the table. I hit my head against something, and dad cried out. I couldn't see. Everywhere I looked there were discs of yellow light. A hand grabbed me in the dark; I kicked upwards, and at a far corner of the bar dad cried out again as if I had struck him. The hand let go and I scrambled over the shadows, through the dense smell of the horse's skin, and managed to make it to the backyard door. Outside, two women with green body paint on their faces sat in front of a fire with the curious serenity of people who are asleep. I touched one of the women and the second one cried out. Butterflies rose from the bushes and grew brighter as they ascended into the sky, as if the darkness increased their illumination. The first woman turned her sleepwalking eyes to me and said:

'What happened to the meat I gave your father?'

'The darkness ate it.'

The second woman laughed without moving her face.

'Do you want some more?'

'No,' I said.

'Have some.'

'No, thank you.'

'You don't like us.'

'I don't know you.'

The second woman laughed again. Dad began calling me from the bar.

'The horse is inside,' I told the women.

'Inside where?'

'The bar.'

'What horse?' the second one asked.

'The white horse.'

'What does it want?'

'I don't know.'

'What do you want?'

'I want light.'

'Light?'

'Yes.'

'What kind of light?'

'Light for the bar. My father is with the horse.'

'Doing what?'

'I don't know.'

The second woman got up and turned the animal roasting on the spit above the fire. When she stood up I saw something her body had been concealing from me. At first I thought it was a sack. Then I saw its lovely legs, its small and delicate head, its open eyes twinkling like jewels in the fire-light, and when I realised that I was looking at the corpse of a white antelope everything changed in my head. Suddenly I noticed that the first woman had one eye in the middle of her forehead. The second woman had the legs of a furry animal. I backed away slowly.

'Have some meat,' she said gently. 'It will make you wise.'

'No, thank you,' I said, backing away and trying not to reveal my panic.

The second woman came over and gave me a black plate loaded with sweet-smelling meat. I took the plate and went into the bar and put the light on, and found dad asleep. The horse had vanished. Not even its wildsmell lingered. But sitting in a chair where the counter used to be, smoking a pipe, with yellow sunglasses on his face, a piece of kolanut clamped between his teeth, was the blind old man. He looked up at me, his eyes changing beneath the glasses.

'Put out the light,' he commanded.

'Why?'

'Your father and I are talking.'

'About what?'

'Politics.'

'Where is the horse?'

'It turned into a dragonfly and disappeared into my mouth.'

'You swallowed the horse?'

'Yes, and I will swallow you too if you don't put out the light.'

I didn't believe him about the horse, so I went to the barfront and looked for myself. The horse wasn't there. All over the place, on poles, on strips of wire, were banners and flags of the Party. The Masquerade seemed to have grown mightier with the darkness. Its head was so high up I couldn't see its jackal eyes. The cleaver in its left hand shone with the silvery rays of moonlight on metal. The big red flag was indistinguishable from the night. The Masquerade now had five feet, all of them belonging to different animals, to bulls, elephants, antelopes, and it had one human foot so monstrous that it could only have come from a cyclops. Hurrying back into the bar, I found dad sitting in the exact position he had been when he was talking to the gathered people. There was a plate of meat on the table in front of him. In his upright glass of palm-wine was a dead wall-gecko. When I recovered from my astonishment, he said:

'I have been dreaming that I was talking rubbish to seven statues who sat around me, drinking palm-wine.'

'What were you talking about?'

'Politics, and philosophy.'

'Then what happened?'

'Then I had a white hat.'

'Are you sure it wasn't green?'

'No, it was white.'

I paused.

'Then what happened?'

'I knocked over my glass. The driver came in and began to snore. Your mother warned me about the meat. I talked till someone started banging on my head as if it were a drum: I turned round and saw no one there. They started playing loud music in my dream and I had to shout to be heard. And then something strange happened.'

'What?'

'You had spiders in your hair. I pulled them out and the statues ate them. Your mother was covered in jewels and she was dancing in the forest with white antelopes surrounding her. I called her, and you answered. The dream changed and a white horse trotted into the bar and started talking to me.'

'What did it say?'

'It talked for a long time.'

'What did it say?'

'You won't understand.'

'Tell me anyway.'

'It said I was talking nonsense about politics. It said people need magic more than they need food. I laughed. The horse said people don't know what they want; and that people must be kept ignorant. Give them food, give them promises. Without promises people go mad and they revolt. The horse said that the only way people listen is if you fill their lives with signs and omens. People only understand fear. Death doesn't frighten them any more. Not many people really want to be born, the horse said. Not many people can handle the fire and ice of being born. The responsibility is too much for most human beings. It turns them to ash. It freezes their blood. It confuses them. They wouldn't know what to do with power. They would use it to burn down the houses of their enemies. Stronger people should use their power for them. But first the people must be afraid.'

Dad was silent. I didn't think I should press him on, so

131

I listened to him thinking. Then he jerked up his head as if he had suddenly remembered the rest of the monologue. He continued.

'The horse said that once the people are afraid you can make them do anything. Fear is at the heart of power. Fear is a black stone in the brain. When the lights come on the black stone turns into a diamond. Keep the lights off. Never allow the lights to come on, the horse said. Never allow the lights to come on in the minds of the people. Or you have chaos. They start to ask too many questions. Then you have confusion. Too many voices. Irresponsibility. Too many theories and ideas. Ignorance. The many diseases of freedom. Greed. Madness. Everything upside down. Customs destroyed. Strange new useless inventions. You mustn't have too many suns on the earth; too much light will burn the trees, destroy the air, kill the night – and the night is the secret mother of power, sister of the earth, one of the gods of the universe. The horse ended by saying: Keep the light off, stop fighting us, and don't come here to talk rubbish.'

Dad was silent again. He stared at me.

'Then what happened?' I asked.

'You came in with meat on a plate and you put the light on. When the light came on, you vanished. Then I saw the blind old man in the chair over there. He was smoking a pipe. Butterflies lifted out of the pipe when he lit the tobacco. Then I realised he was not smoking tobacco but butterflies. And they were alive. I told him to put out the pipe. He did.'

'Then what happened?'

'He got up and left. And then you came in just now.'

Amazed by what he had told me, I didn't know what to do. So I ran into his arms and he caught me and lifted me on to his shoulder. Then he put me down. He got up from the chair, saying:

'I've had a lot of strange palm-wine to drink.'

'Let's go home,' I said.

'What about your mother?'

'She is waiting for us.'

Dad looked round the bar and shook his head, as if to re-align himself with reality. Then he took my hand and led me out. The darkness was solid around the Masquerade. I looked back and saw the two women. They were still in front of the fire. The forest was silent. As we turned into the street, the lights went off in the bar. Dad laughed.

'I've been talking to myself all evening. Rehearsing.'

He laughed again.

'An eloquent spirit entered me today. All the things you've been reading to me from those books kept flashing and changing in my head. One day I will learn to read,' he said.

I listened to the darkness growing. Then dad spoke again:

'The mind of man is bigger than the sky. All of us together somehow invent this world. I don't understand how we can agree about anything. There is a bit of madness in politics.'

He paused, breathed deeply, put his arm round my neck, fondled my hair, lifted his head to the sky, and said, in a voice quivering with mystery:

'But, my son, I think we have the WHOLE UNIVERSE inside us when we are joyful and full of life.'

I felt happy listening to dad talk. His words were bright in the darkness and they helped me see my way over the pits and stones and treacherous things of the road. His words helped me then, especially as my eyes hurt and seemed to burn the colour of a heated yellow from having seen the world for a single moment through the eyes of the Masquerade. I was happy listening to dad because his words cooled my spirit. It was balm over my eyes. And the silence of the forest, with the moon hanging over it, no longer frightened me so much. And for a brief deep moment I was radiant with joy because I had discovered that without trying, and wholly at random, I could also enter my father's most extraordinary dreams.

CHAPTER FIFTEEN

———

The Perfumed Abyss

WHEN WE GOT home there was a hurricane lamp on the table. It gave off a wonderful moon-glow in the room. All our possessions were illuminated and even their poor condition was touched with the benediction of bright light. Mum was sitting on dad's chair, staring straight ahead of her. The light bared her lean neck and made the bones of her face more prominent with shadows. She didn't move when we entered. But she turned her eyes on dad, then on me. Dad said:

'I don't like that light. It spreads ghosts everywhere. I want candles.'

Mum blew out the lamp. Waves of darkness washed me backwards, my head reeling. Dad stumbled, and cursed. Mum lit three candles and passed our food. While we ate, mum watched us. When we finished she cleared the table and went to the backyard. I went with her. There was no one around. Our neighbours had locked their doors early and put out their lights. The moon was strange that night. It was yellowish and had been bitten in a jagged half by another planet. I told mum about it and she looked at the moon and said:

'The sun and the moon are quarrelling. There is going to be trouble.'

When we got back to the room we found dad ensconced on the bed. He had a determined look on his face. Mum didn't acknowledge his determination and I saw a dangerous mood gathering in dad's spirit. The room was fiery with his desire. He was brusque with me, ordering me to lay out my mat and get some sleep immediately. Mum lit a mosquito coil and dad spoke angrily to me about not helping my mother with household chores. In a tone of stern command he wanted me from that day on to wash the plates, cook the food, buy household items from the market, clean the room, wash all the clothes, in short to make sure that mum never had to lift a finger. He worked himself into a displaced rage and pursued me round the room with his boots, threatening to knock my head off, hoping, it seemed to me, that his rage would encourage mum to come between us.

Mum was sitting on the floor, in a corner, with her knees brought up to her breasts, her eyes shut, her face shadowed with an impenetrable sad bloom. Dad caught me, made two feeble attempts at hitting me, gave up, and went back to the bed. I lay on the mat, watching the lighted coil, while dad tossed and grumbled, while mum sat on the floor, her outline like a dwarf's, silent in the dark, spreading her bloom over the air, forcing something new to secure the foundations of our lives. Dad tossed. And kicked. He abused me. He cursed Madame Koto. He muttered something about the obligation between husbands and wives. He grumbled about money and politics. He sucked his teeth in uncontainable frustration, and then he got up and lit a cigarette, his head restless. He inhaled with a lustful noisy violence, and exhaled with the sigh of an angry beast. He got up and paced the room, dispersing the forces mum was concentrating around us.

As I lay on the mat, watching them, there came from the compound front the deranged twang of a shattered musical instrument, a guitar, or an accordion. Dad stopped pacing, his head cocked. There was a long silence. Then he sat in his chair. The mosquito-coil smoke circled his head. I watched the smoke turning blue round his head and then suddenly we heard a long deep cry from the forest. It was a cry so extended that it couldn't have been maintained by a single breath. And then it stopped. And then another wail replaced it, deep, unfathomable, communicating a grief beyond description.

135

It was a wail without anger or rage. The frightful sound seemed to emerge from the earth itself, so profound was its sustained song of inconsolation. The wind carried the lament to all of our hearts and when it stopped mum said:

'Azaro, shut the door!'

'Leave that door open!' dad ordered, in a voice that had forgotten about desire.

And all at once voices spouted from the earth, voices and songs of such sweetness that they could only have emerged from an abyss perfumed with roses. They were the voices of the incandescent women of the forest, whose songs burned brightest with the funereal accents of a dying moon. The songs brought heat-bursts on the air. As we listened it became harder to breath, for the melodies pulled at our insides, scorching the depths of our spirits with the flaming proclamations of the deep. The melodies, in the voices of repentant witches, became so piercing that they began to hurt, they began to grate and tear at our entrails, and everywhere I felt a concentration of restlessness. The air became dense. The songs became so beatific – rising from the earth with the anguish of animals dying, of spirits leaving the earth for ever, of hopes expiring in the birdsongs of the deep forests – that there opened in the room the vision of a field devoured by fire, with the flowers roasting, and people melting in their sleep of fear. The field vanished, but the songs became ugly in their sweetness. They became the opposite of music, with their gnashings and their harsh accents of horror and hell. The room was hot, the mat was damp, smoke blew in and overpowered us with its smell of forbidden things burning. The smoke was red and peppery, chafing the lining of our throats, cutting off our voices as we choked in silence.

And when the voices stopped, leaving a single song sustaining the peal of an old bell (resonant with the warning that every domination is an illusion which we accept) – a thunderous crash, the shrieking of metal on metal, and the silver lash of a whip cracked in the air and cleaved the song in half, one side still resonating in the silence afterwards, the other side entering a void, never to re-emerge. And it was when I heard the neighing of horses, the cantankerous snorting of hallucinated bulls, that I first had the inkling that a vehemence vaster than the fury of torrential rains had been unloosened over our lives.

CHAPTER SIXTEEN

———

Madame Koto's Dream-lust

T HAT NIGHT SAW the great convulsions of incendiary powers. Spirits roasted in the inferno of the air, while the sun
raged its anger on the moon. Our area became a vast beast
in torment; it writhed and twisted. The houses shook with
the vibrations of mortars exploding on our collective flesh.
The roads arched their backs like mighty snakes in their last
agonised heaving for life. Huge drums thundered in the air.
Elephants crashed on trees, trees crashed on houses. Every
noise was a picture, and every picture was mined with dread.
And as I listened, the noises stopped, and a cold wind swept
over the rooftops. And in the glacial silence of the yellowing
moon an iron ritual rode through the air on red horses.

That night the Jackal-headed Masquerade, surrounded
by its multiples and companions of hyenas and panthers,
chanting with the voices of possessed men, wreaked an
incredible violence on the forces of wind and forest, slaughtering the spirits and the insurgent women, murdering the
trees and our silent protectors, the dormant gods sleeping in
our dreams. And while all this happened the future burst on
me and I saw tanks rolling over the wounded roads; I saw
armoured trucks and jeeps and great military lorries, and I
saw swarms of soldiers in dark places of the country, while
the rest of us dreamt of a new domination.

A twisted African way invaded us that night as the Masquerades and the political sorcerers rode all the seasons of
our future in advance, spreading terror and curfew, disease
and the stench of charred earth, destroying the paths, ripping up the roads, lifting rooftops and breathing oil fumes

138

on the sleeping inhabitants, wrenching electric poles from the ground, entangling cables, creating pestilential accidents on highways. The Masquerades woke up the terrible ghosts of our deep past and the air howled with freed deranged spirits of hunger and injustice. The Masquerades rode red horses and bulls, slaughtering the spirits, destroying the potent shrines, killing the guardians of the jewelled forests and their secrets of complete rainbows.

It was the worst night of the political Masquerades, as spirits died in the air with strange moanings, as the clash of machetes sent electric sparks through the darkness, as farmyards and good harvests caught fire, as metal cut through bones, and as angels – scorched by the fury of the new powers – flew away from us, higher into the sky, beyond the burning moon.

I found myself circling the cataclysm and I saw the blind old man turn into a green vulture with blazing eyes. The vast span of his bony wings created mighty gusts of boiling air as he flew over our rooftops, slobbering, reviewing the nakedness of our lives. His laughter was harsh and infectious, for the hyenas and the terrible ghosts of our past laughed as well. And when the Jackal-headed Masquerade laughed three hundred children died in the country in secret ways, and many fathers went berserk, and for the first time in many years some of our women commited suicide. And the oracles and luminous stones of secret shrines burst into twisted laughter, breaking out in livid prophecies of butterflies dying in the air, birds turning into stone in mid-flight, prophecies of monstrous births, of wars that make mothers go insane, catastrophes and freak earthquakes, prophecies of madness-making wealth, of oil bursts alongside famine. The oracles laughed while the winds raged and the glass tombs split open and wooden cages caught fire, roasting their trapped birds, and churches collapsed, and fountains of blood burst out from white concrete floors in empty army barracks, with animals delivering eggs of metal, birds giving birth to snakes, donkeys giving birth to frogs, as if the cycles of life and death had gone mad. And it wasn't till I saw the Jackal-headed Masquerade with an erection of obscene size, riding the red wind, with the moon burning, and with the butterflies that escaped the incandescent air turning into stars which flickered every fifteen seconds, that I began to understand the illusion of the new conquering force.

The wind cooled suddenly. The silence was broken by the cry of the wind on the taut cables. I looked around our room in the darkness and found myself somewhere else, in a long hallway. The rooftop was gone and the sky was empty. A door opened, blowing me through the walls into another room where I saw Madame Koto asleep, completely naked, her mighty breasts heaving like gargantuan bellows, her great legs quivering. A sound cracked my head from behind, spinning me round into a new space where I saw Madame Koto, dressed in a golden nightgown, naked underneath, riding a yellow horse, burning on the saddle, in pursuit of the Masquerades. I followed her heaving form in the air, overwhelmed by her heated lust smells, by the deep essences of her enormous body stewing beneath the constraints of her convulsive flesh. Her craven volcanic desire made the air demonic. Around her lashed the fury of a lust that had been rising all her life, hurtling her deeper into the powers of her spirit, making her flesh blubbery with the over-ripeness of days without lust and release. It made her eyes sharper in their penetrating insight into the weaknesses of men. It made her centre riper, richer, voluptuous and soft. It made her face mask-like in the solidity of self-control and manipulation. It deepened her command of the psychic centres of men and women and invisible forms of power, drawing to her great body the magnetism of the earth's hunger for fertilisation. And it turned her from a woman into a Queen of nights, protector of the strong, creator of new rituals, guardian of women's forces, controller of witches and sorcerers. She became a mediator between the women of secret cabals and the spirits of shrines drenched with potent menstrual blood, an encounter which fertilises stones and gives birth to new monoliths with faces and features of alien beings.

Her awesome desire, which had survived the penetrations of dream-sorcerers who clambered up her spirit-body and got locked inside, and who were released only when they surrendered all their powers; her robust desire of years without rich release drove her on obsessively, drove the yellow horse to distraction, as if it too were in pursuit of the great white mare, maddened by an unearthly lust. I watched her go, her face contorted, her golden nightgown flapping and creating agonised noises in the air. And I had no idea of her destination, or who it was that could so arouse her mountainous desire, or who could satisfy it without getting lost, or drowned, or being swallowed altogether, or being crushed by the weight of her myth, or destroyed, burned to ashes by her volcanic consummation.

On and on through the air of her dream she went, her skin smooth, freshened with milk baths, her hair silken, her body fleshy, rude in health and prosperity. On and on she went, seeking the giant love story hidden in the flesh of all our agonies, the love between her powerful beating heart and a being or a god worthy of impregnating her with offspring that could command and concentrate the minds of men and women and nations, and possess their dreams and affect their realities. Offspring that could be myths and deities who would extend her powers, offspring worthy of her ancient blood, a blood as old as oral history. I saw her wild and raw, saw her massive heaving buttocks above the saddle, her tumescent palpitating breasts, her lust-steamed breath; and then for a while, as she flew, creating mists from desire, she became obscured from me. And I found myself back in our room, with sinister explosions crashing around us.

Dad was silent in his chair. And mum, sitting crouched on

the floor, began to utter gnomic words. Her feverish voice somehow frightened us more than the upheavals all around, the dogs barking, the cats screaming. And all through the chants of the Party's night-runners, mum spoke about hidden ancestors, priestesses of unnamed religions, bearers of eternal signs. Then she spoke about the sons and daughters of howling shrines, whose objects of worship lead to hallucinations, sexual fevers, possessions by demons. The contortions of these sons and daughters, she said, would invade many realms, brightening the dark antipodes with the dual potencies of their inheritance. And then she spoke of the puzzling children of the new-born country, of the new age, of all difficult crossroad ages: children with pale, long faces; victims of the epilepsies of the epoch, vulnerable to possession by spirits and sleep-runners; children of war, with faces dyed the colour of an unmentionable sensibility; children whose early years would be blighted by undernourishment, and who would suffer in their flesh and souls the future burning cross of the squandered nation.

When mum had finished uttering her prophecies, her voice quivering, a dense silence reigned in the room. And the silence closed my eyes and sent me spinning and I saw Madame Koto being fecundated by the Jackal-headed Masquerade, while the blind old man, transformed into a vulture with the feet and feathers of a peacock, played a dreadful harmonic accompaniment from his infernal accordion. And the consummation was effected and apotheosised by new crescendos of violence, of screeching birds, choked cries of sacrificed goats and sheep; and then the colours of Madame Koto's dream became livid, incendiary bright, for she unleashed an ecstatic cry so fearsome that the night was silenced. In the long stillness which followed I saw that she had given birth to three baby Masquerades in her dream, children who spent their lives divided, warring against each other, fighting for their mother's milk, savaging her breasts, and tearing her apart in a bizarre, incestuous and greedy rage – while Madame Koto, the new Mother of Images, heaved gently, asleep, on her mighty bronze bed.

CHAPTER SEVENTEEN

———

Night of the Political Magicians

THE WORLD ABOUT us heaved in dread and death, but
dad completely refused to shut our door. The wind blew
in the smells of blood, the noxious odours of triumphant Masquerades, the bitter scents of wood-sprites dying, the fumes of
our hopes burning in the streets.

Dad sat now on the bed, watching the door, watching
the leaves and dust blow in. And mum, her utterances ended,
sat in a dim silvery glow. Meanwhile the deep chanting
of mask-heads dominated the air, speaking of new armies,
eternal converts, the victory of fear over silence. Every
now and then we heard cats howling, unable to escape
the hooves of the night-runners and the multiple phantom
images unleashed in the dark by the blind old man, master-
sorcerer. He had crowded the air with apparitions of our
fears, materialising our terrors, converting our cowardice
and anxieties into concrete bestial forms that wreaked havoc
without any mercy.

I saw the blind old man that night, in a black suit and black
shoes. His head was shorn, he had a yellow tie round his neck,
a yellow umbrella in his hand. He went round in his new
master guise, supervising the carnage inflicted on our area,
on the torn-up streets, the dead animals, and on the men
caught wandering about lost or drunk or homeless on that
night of the artificial curfew. The blind old man inspected the
evidence of his powers. He strolled up our street, proprietori-
ally looking at the damaged houses, the wrecked huts, and at
the fallen trees that had ended their domino-like catastrophe
on the buildings where the inhabitants sat huddled in corners

144

of their rooms with branches in their living spaces. He inspected the twisted forms of animals, the contorted shapes of women caught in the forest, the quivering maniacal rage of his followers and party supporters in their unholy bacchanalian possession. Their faces were covered with masks from whose tight nostrils they breathed in fumes that fill the brain with rampant visions of power without end. The masks possessed the wearers with the images of menace carved on their dread-manufacturing features. The wearers became their masks, and the masks took on their own true life, enacting the violence of the blind old man's sorcerous dictates.

He wandered the streets, surveying his new domain, with the tentative gait of a perfect gentleman. He looked into our houses, saw us cowering in our rooms, surrendering ourselves to his kingdom. And over the places he passed, great winds howled, multiplying the furies behind him. I followed him as he consecrated the manifestations of his powers. I followed his spirit's delight as he blessed his desecrations, believing them to be for our own good, believing that the superior manifestations are the best ones and therefore always victorious. As he went deeper into the city, passing the new houses and the skyscrapers and the grand highways of Independence, I knew the exhaustion of his spirit. I knew the price he felt of containing and unleashing such powers, saturating the air with such demonic insurgencies. I knew the agony of having so much power in such an old body, unnourished by new blood. I also knew his spirit's despair at not being able to find worthy successors to his secret might, thousands of years old, a lore of might that wrought leadership changes in old empires, a force at the service of dynasties of kings and queens, or against them; a force that brought rain or withheld it, that dimmed the moon, that made the scorch of sun on earth more bitter, that filled old kingdoms with visions of glory, that exhausted the frames of the people, held back their development, that blinded them to the vastness of the world or to what ideas

145

and dreams of conquest would bring the outside world to our lands; a force that made our kings and rulers think the earth not much greater than their own kingdoms. The blind old man's despair was as deep as the powers he was heir to, a control over the minds of the people that made them unprepared when the invasions came which would change history for ever. His powers wove a pernicious web of rituals and beliefs that froze the minds of kings, deafened their ears to the words of the soothsayers and sages blessed by the jewels of radiant gods, who uttered innumerable prophecies about the invasion by the white peoples. The rituals confused our minds with too many manifestations, too many gods, too many dreams, confusing us in order to rule us, till our history became our own nemesis.

I followed the blind old man in spirit, circling round him as he passed the centres of secular power, the Presidential mansions, the army barracks that would be famed for future coups and secret executions. I followed him knowing that he was reaching the zenith of his power's manifestations. I knew that he knew this. I knew his fear of spontaneously combusting and turning into a malignant force in the air, a potential that can be tapped only by those who reach the unique frequency of his spirit's vibration. And I saw his sadness in having someday to leave this realm behind, for he was a demonic spirit-child of the worst kind, the kind that had developed all its potential for malignity to the highest degree, that had re-connected the old forces which ran in the veins of ancient secret societies and cabals, fuelled by an abundance of spirit energies. I saw his despair, his invisible tears, and his misery beneath his walk of an impeccable gentleman, a diplomat on an evening's stroll.

And as he turned suddenly, aware that I had been following him in spirit, circling his disguise, the door of our room creaked and the wind blew in a black smoke that was hot and acrid with the stench of unmentionable burning things. Then I heard mum say, in the voice of a little girl:

146

'Azaro, don't be afraid. Everything is connected.'

'I'm not afraid any more,' I replied.

'Why not?'

For a moment I was silent. Something else was coming in. I listened. Then I heard the low cry of a small animal outside our door. The wind blew harder, straining the foundations of the house, knocking the door insistently against the bed. Something cracked at the housefront. The horses thundered past. I was about to answer mum's question with an unformulated thought when a strange heat began swirling around in my head. Then something crept into our room, and stopped in front of me, its eyes glowing. It ran further into the room, brushing past the table silently. A moment later I saw two electric green eyes hovering over the centre table.

'Something has come into the room,' I said.

'Shut up,' said dad.

We didn't move. The eyes watched us, unblinking, bright, fierce. Suddenly, dad lit a match. The flare dazzled twice, its harsh phosphorescence startling the two gem-like eyes. The match went out, and the eyes vanished. Dad lit another one and, to our wonderment, we beheld, on our centre table, a three-legged cat.

'A message!' cried dad.

'What does it mean?' asked mum.

The cat regarded us.

'Silence!' hissed dad, his eyes intent, brightened in the lumination of the undeciphered sign.

The cat stared at me, and then at mum. Then it leapt on dad's chair, and sat on its tail, the stump of its bad foot twitching. Dad lit three candles. In silence we studied the cat, oblivious to the noises outside, all of our attention concentrated on the mysterious presence in our room. The cat became bored with our intense sign-reading scrutiny and after a while it curled up and went to sleep, with its tail coiled half way round its fragile form.

It is hard to explain the somnolence and serenity that

came over us as we gazed at the sleeping cat. At some point mum got up and, walking as if under water, blew out the three candles. In the darkness I saw the amazing other form of the cat. A green spectral light was spread around it in the shape of a great lion, filling the room with a mighty animal presence. In the darkness, I became aware of its forest smell of untamed hair, its warmth both damp and comforting. Watching the gigantic leonine aura round the little cat I drifted off into another darkness and into another light and I made several journeys to the shrines favoured by spirit-children all over the world, and when I came back to my body it was daylight.

Mum slept on the floor near me, grinding her teeth. Dad snored on the bed, with his boots on. The warm smell of an affectionate animal was still rich in the room. But the cat itself had disappeared, as if we had all collectively dreamt it into existence during the worst night of the political magicians.

CHAPTER EIGHTEEN

———

The Invention of Chaos

I T WAS THE worst night, but it wasn't the only one. The days afterwards saw us discovering the phenomenal extent of the devastation of our area. It was as if an unrecorded hurricane had swept through our lives, disorienting our reality. The devastation shocked us. When we went out in the morning, it was as if the world had been hurled against a primal rock. Everything was scrambled up and fragmented. The air was darker. The sky was lower, and it seemed to bear down on us with an oppressive menace. Houses had crumbled altogether. Rooftops had been torn off and twisted under the pressure of a malign force. The broken-down political vehicle, which the inhabitants of the street had destroyed in the early days, had been crushed and its parts scattered as if the wind had taken steel fists to it and flung its components all over the area. Some people woke up to find bits of the steering wheel on the beams of their shattered roofs. Others found the vehicle's doors jutting through their windows. Tyres had been hurled into rooms. The vehicle's engine, broken to pieces, was found in buckets, smashed against walls. Some people found pellets lodged in their doors, in their pots of food. It was as if revenge for the vehicle's initial destruction had now been visited on all of us.

We woke up that morning to find the innards of a dog stamped on our door. We wandered down our street and heard that the heads of black cats had been found in living rooms, in communal kitchens. Parts of animal bodies hung from the branches of trees. Houses had been broken into, properties smashed. We saw the corpses of lizards

149

floating on the debris of the streets. There was rubbish everywhere, flung against the clothes we had left out to dry, in our kitchens and toilets and housefronts. The mounds of rubbish were of such volume that only a wind of vicious intent could have blown them at us from other parts of the city. Clothes and shoes, offal and rotting vegetables, slimy feathers and warped tin cans, broken chairs and stinking plantain and mushroom-infested mattresses had been scattered everywhere. Overnight our street had become a fetid rubbish dump. Dead frogs were all over the place. When we stepped on them accidentally, we were horrified by their popping sounds. We wandered the street and saw live fishes wriggling on the rubbish. Toads had been squashed into the ground by metal hooves. The overwhelming smell of fermented palm-wine rose from the earth as if the rain had drenched us in an infernal libation.

Flowers had been crushed everywhere. The bushes had been torn up. Shrubs and low vegetation, clumps of earth, stumps of trees were found in our backyards, on our rooftops, and along the street. Cracks had appeared in houses. Trees had suffered weird deformations. Stalls had been broken up. Water tanks had been turned upside down, with mud and gore inside them. And throughout our area – as if the force that had raged its visitation on us had given birth to multiples of itself in terrifying irregularity – we discovered broken masks, abandoned jujus, twisted masquerades, eyeless heads of wooden carvings, disintegrated statues of minor gods. They were at street corners, nailed against trees, hurled into our rooms. The masks and statues were truly ugly and quite frightening, with big indifferent eyes that stared at our incomprehension in broken silence.

The destruction wreaked on our area stunned us into speechlessness. The mangled dogs, the bloated eyes of goats, the twisted metal and the crumbling houses played havoc with our senses and made us feel that we had stepped out from the reality of dreams and into a bizarre universe. We kept looking at one another with dazed eyes, seeking confirmation that we were not inventing the monstrosities that we saw. The chaos made us brain-shocked: everywhere we looked our stunned brains conjured further devastations. The chaos made us hallucinate. The air had changed. Some people screamed that they saw spirits melting in the air. Some said they saw rainbows turning red. Others that they saw spirits walking about, their mighty heads higher than the tallest trees. A girl cried out in wonder and her mouth hung open as she followed, with her eyes, the flight of seven angels dressed in rainbows, blue lights flashing round their feet. People amazed us by seeing crocodiles swimming in the density of the darkened air. People saw antelopes with aquamarine eyes running through them, as if they were ghosts. Others saw bulls and goat-headed masquerades dancing on rooftops.

It became difficult to separate the actual devastations from the strange effects they had on our minds. People kept disappearing from our midst and reappearing somewhere else. Dad vanished and we found him standing on a rooftop, crying out about the wonders to come. He didn't remember how he got there. We were standing, staring at a partially overturned water tank in which tadpoles swam in serene contemplation, when a child appeared amongst us, crying. A moment later its mother rushed down the street screaming that her child had been blown from her back by a malign wind. We went from place to place, amazed that neighbours whom we assumed were there had vanished from amongst us, and that strangers had taken their places. We suddenly weren't sure who anybody was, or if the people whom we treated as if we knew were in fact the same people we had known all along.

A herbalist amongst us said that we were all dreaming together, simultaneously; that a lesser god had scrambled up our minds; and that we were now floating in the dark sea of our collective confusion, our mingled consciousness, flowing into one another's fears. It became hard to tell if the world was real or if we had collectively invented it. We found, to our terror, that our road had been torn up, gashed, wounded, as if it were a weird snake, or a metal that someone had wrenched with sinister force. The back of the road was humped, the flat grounds had become undulated, the straight places had become twisted, pits had appeared in certain spots and strange waters in which fishes swam had filled them. We came to a particular place where the road had cracked. We looked down into the crack and saw hybrid beings writhing in fiendish torment, fighting to get out. Excruciating noises of tortured creatures rose up on the hallucinogenic smoke.

Strange propensities turned our brains. People were astounded when they lowered their buckets into wells and found that the water had gone. One man, who lived a mile away, said he had woken in the morning to find that a crude well had opened up in his living room. He looked into the hole and saw his centre table floating upside down on the brackish water.

The weird manifestations had stranger consequences. People were reported missing. People hurriedly moved away from the area. The strangers that replaced them had bitter, uncommunicative eyes. I thought I recognised some of them from Madame Koto's bar when I first used to go there. Spies grew in our midst – tall men with trusting faces, short women who seemed generous and affectionate. Even children with mean eyes and thin lips. Those of us that remained in the street woke up each day to see new proliferations of catastrophes. Corpses of yellowing dogs lay at street corners. Decapitated antelopes stared at us from the bushes, their eyes wide open in amazement. We saw fake jewels on the street, glittering their myriad colours amongst the offal and the gore. We were all suspicious of the jewels and no one touched them except a neighbour who had ten children. His house had been devastated and his wife's leg broken by a falling beam. We saw him surreptitiously collecting the fake jewels and two days later we heard him raving in the street, his head on fire, screaming about flying saucers and rainbows which set houses alight. Three houses burned down that night and smoke hung over the area, charring our eyes and noses with its harsh bitter pungency. The next morning we heard the man who had collected the jewels confessing to the burning of the houses, confessing that he had turned into a wicked wizard overnight. He was bound securely with hemp ropes and his relatives carted him away to be treated by a fearful sorcerer deep in the country.

That same day four children died of water poisoning. Everyone complained of dizziness and something akin to seasickness. The world was turning too fast for us. Everywhere we saw signs and inexplicable manifestations. But that evening the most wondrous and the most frightening signs of all were the butterflies.

CHAPTER NINETEEN

――――――

Mystery of the Butterflies

A FTER THE BURNING of the houses we were sitting at our housefronts, when someone cried out that scales were falling in his eyes, obscuring his vision. The scales, he said, were brilliant and yellow. Soon after his cry we all began to see scales in our eyes, scales that fell slowly, with bright yellow wings, delicate and semi-transparent. It was as if his cry had created the condition. It was as if we had all begun to flow into his consciousness. For, suddenly, we began to touch one another. We began to reach out and feel the solid things around us. It wasn't long before we realised that a strange blindness had come upon us all. We stayed up that night, huddled in the street, afraid to open our eyes because we didn't want to see the cascading yellow scales which were like little wings. In the morning, when the invasion had passed, we awoke from our communal blindness and we saw an avalanche of dead butterflies everywhere.

They had fallen on the leaves, on the floor of the forest, had banked up on the rubbish of the street, had piled up on the broken stalls, on the clothes-lines, on the rotting corpses of the animals we had been too scared to touch, and had formed irregular mounds on the rooftops. They were mostly yellow butterflies with vivid striations and batik patterns. Some were yellow with black stains. Others were blue with yellow markings. Some of them were hideously large, almost predatory with their black little claws. A great number of them were deformed, with bodies like little human beings fixed in midway transformation. But many of them were very beautiful and delicate, and the finer ones were joined

154

like twins, with blue radiancies on their partially transparent wings. They had fallen on every visible surface as if they were part of a new weather condition, and they had died as if there had been a secret plague.

They were a frightening mystery to us. We had no way of explaining their presence, nor the sheer abundance of them. More than the destruction of the houses, the rutting of the roads, the unexplained deaths of the inhabitants, the butterflies awoke in us a new colossal helplessness. We wandered the streets concussed by this new demonstration, amazed at the limpid butterflies dead without explanation on our streets and rooftops. The sky was clear that day, but we went around with our faces turned upwards, wondering what the next sign to descend on our lives would be.

Silence came amongst us. The wind was still. The forest was quiet. We wandered in that silvery air of a strange enchantment, as if we had strayed from our true reality into a secret country which exists only in the unpredictable tangents and margins of vision.

We began to doubt our collective sanity. For days afterwards we couldn't sleep. We dreamt with our eyes wide open. We feared sleep because we couldn't be sure what the world would change into while we shut our lives away in our rooms or in our dreams. We stayed outside and communicated to one another in an improvised sign language, mostly using our faces, as if we had developed a new fear of speech. We couldn't be sure that we hadn't somehow talked the new reality into existence during all the careless days of our lives. We were never so close to one another as we were in that time of fearful manifestations. There were those amongst us who believed there was a reason for it all, and for it all happening to us. There were those who believed that after the plague of dead butterflies it was almost certain that the world was soon going to end.

The wind remained still, and there was no rain. During the exhaustion of the long vigil for new signs, I realised with a shock that we could occasionally read one another's thoughts. Hunger came amongst us and the children grew leaner. The faces of the women grew longer. The men became listless and pale. Dad stayed at our housefront most of the time, staring at the street, his energy much reduced, his eyes dull. Mum stayed with the women, who comforted one another in silence. The rest of us merely awaited the final sign which would announce that our lives had come to an end for ever.

We didn't sleep and we didn't speak and we turned our eyes to the skyline, awaiting the annunciation, the great flood, or the flash of lightning which would crack open the sky and unleash eternity upon us. The three-legged cat did not return to concentrate our minds on its wonder. There were no bird or animal cries from the forest. The irrepressible insects were silent. Maybe we didn't hear them. But it dawned on us slowly that the animals had vanished. In the afternoons the sun was relentless. It baked the earth and spread a progressive rust on the leaves. It cracked our faces.

CHAPTER TWENTY

———

Fragments of the Original Way

OUR WILLS BECAME weak. We looked out at the world from listless eyes. We became ill for lack of dreams. The world dissolved slowly under our liquid scrutiny. We began to see holes in reality, in objects, in people, and wherever we happened to look. The sleeplessness increased our mass hallucination. People saw blue flying objects in the air. When one person saw them we all did. Red flares appeared in the clouds. Our houses began to move. The road trembled. The trees changed shape. The world started to succumb to strange distortions. People turned into chickens, goats and iguanas under our gaze. People's features began to alter. Dad took on the soft jaw of the blind old man. Mum's eyes became infected with a yellowish watering. We saw Sami, the betting shop man who had run off with all dad's money. We rushed over to him and when we got there he had turned into a goat. The women began to look like variations of Madame Koto. Someone passed the thought to me that I resembled a baby jackal. Even our mirrors played tricks with our sanity and our perception. When we looked into them we saw ourselves reflected as healthy, fresh and buoyant.

The wind stirred one day and brought rumours and prophecies about the children born on the night of the political magicians. It was hinted that they would be children with rapacious jackal faces, vicious eyes, and teeth fully formed in their mouths. Apparently some of them were born with beards and had the ancient faces of forgotten sorcerers. They were children who scratched their mothers, and dreaded their mother's breasts. It was also said that they would be strong and gifted with longevity and that from birth they had been infected with the darker sides of power. None of it made any sense to me.

It was odd to see how we became altered during the nights when the stars were like brilliant ice-chips in the sky. We began to dream feverishly about water. The street smouldered in the afternoon blaze. Our hunger became so intense that we took to eating mouldy vegetables. We carved up the animals and roasted their flesh and stared into the night-fires, our faces dry and sweaty, our eyes unmoving. The hunger made the world unbearable. We couldn't trust the water and slowly we got drunk on our parched condition. Through the days and nights our thoughts were fixed on water. We stared at the sky, waiting for rain. The sky deceived us often with its cloudbanks.

One night I went into the room and couldn't find dad. I wandered amongst the debris in the street and saw him standing up stiff and straight, his eyes wide open. I was afraid to touch him. That night I left dad where he was and took to wandering around and I was amazed to see the curious state of our neighbours. They were all standing up stiff and straight, eyes wide open, as if turned into stone, transfixed in some mysterious way. Those who were not standing or transfixed were the strangers amongst us. They had bright eyes, nourished skin, were suspicious, and they spied on our every movement. I couldn't find mum anywhere. Many of the women had vanished. I wandered back to our compound and saw three mallams standing, petrified, in the middle of the road. I touched one of them, and he fell. I touched another, and the same thing happened. They fell and registered no pain, made no sound. They lay motionless on the ground, their eyes open, as if they had been murdered in a moment of open-eyed contemplation. Then it occurred to me that we were dying, that people in our midst had died standing up, eyes open, as if all the distortions and manifestations, the bad smells of rotting

158

butterflies, the stench of maggots on dead meat, had finally become too much for us.

Suddenly a great thing heaved in the numbness of my mind. I couldn't get it out. I found myself stuck in one place, frozen, my eyes wide open, unable to move because of the mighty thought that was lodged in my brain. For the first time I became aware of the depth of the darkness in our area. I was entirely oblivious to everything. I stood there and a great darkness, peopled with mighty beings, invaded my mind. I saw the invisible beings and marvelled that giants still existed in our world. The great spirits were innumerable. They had chariots and black beards. They rode on the backs of blue unicorns. They rode through us, through our physical forms, as if they were real and we were ghosts. They rode through us, journeying to a vast meeting place. They were laden with the burden of centuries, the weight of unrecorded illuminations wrought from the history of loving and suffering in the most magical spheres of the universe. I watched them till their momentous procession disappeared into the horizon of blue darkness. After them came the shining representatives of our forgotten gods, our transformative ancestors, robed in dazzling clothes of silver and gold. I noted their lineaments of jewels and cowries, their blazing crowns, their bangles which rattled out forgotten music, their diamond-beaded hair, and their necks borne up with rows of sapphire and cornelian and precious stones whose lights were thoughts given radiant form. I also noted their silver staffs. They passed through our earthly devastation without noticing. The urgency of their journey was suggested in the sage-like and noble gravity of their bearing.

Behind the second procession came the representatives of our spirit world, illustrious ancestors with caravans of wisdom, old souls who had been reborn many times in the magical depths of the continent, and who had lived the undiscovered secrets and mysteries of The African Way – The Way of compassion and fire and serenity: The Way of freedom and power and imaginative life; The Way that keeps the mind open to the existences beyond our earthly sphere, that keeps the spirit pure and primed to all the rich possibilities of living, that makes of their minds gateways through which all the thought-forms of primal creation can wander and take root and flower; The Way through which forgotten experiments in living can re-surface with fuller results even in insulated and innocent communities; The Way that makes it possible for them to understand the language of angels and gods, birds and trees, animals and spirits; The Way that makes them greet phenomena for ever as a brother and a sister in mysterious reality; The Way that develops and keeps its secrets of transformations – hate into love, beast into man, man into illustrious ancestor, ancestor into god; The Way whose centre grows from divine love, whose roads are always open for messages from all the spheres to keep coming through; The Way that preaches attunement with all the higher worlds, that believes in forgiveness and generosity of spirit, always receptive, always listening, always kindling the understanding of signs, like the potencies hidden in snail tracks along forbidden paths; The Way that always, like a river, flows into and flows out of the myriad Ways of the world.

These spirit-masters of the spirit universes brought The Way which had since been corrupted by succeeding generations, by greed and decadence, blindness and stupidity, by vulgar kings and dim-witted chiefs, corrupted and turned into sinister uses in the eternal battle of ascendencies. These invisible masters brought fragments of the Original Way in their silent procession, drawing back to its centre the valuable truths in our stolen heritage, our dispersed legacy, our myths coded with wonderful secrets of living, our splendid feats of memory and science and mysticism, art and learning, poetry and thriving in a universe of enigmas, our accomplishments denied by the dominant history of the short-sighted conquerors of the times.

I saw them with their celestial caravans of the forgotten and undiscovered African Way, and maybe I marvelled. Behind them were the wondrous animals also forgotten to man, whose legends are enshrined in the hieroglyphs on tree trunks, the old mighty trees that retain the stories of the land in their deep roots, always feeding our realities back into the womb of the earth. And then I saw many of the inhabitants of our area amongst the spirits of the great journey. I saw the shoe-maker, the sign-writer, the magician of the bronzes, sorcerers, I saw our neighbours, familiar children. I even saw dad amongst the spirits. He was walking in the air, light and serene, surrounded with blue flames. A silver butterfly circled his head. And when I saw that there were some of us in the procession of spirits who were still alive, the heaving thoughts lodged in my brain came unloose and horror rose in me. I broke out from my slumber of stone and death, from the visions of another world hidden behind ours, and I ran everywhere looking for my mother.

Feeling my way through the cobwebs that had entangled us in the space of my vision, surprised at how thick the webs were, I searched for mum all over the street, and couldn't find her. I ran to the spot where I had last seen dad, but he wasn't there. I searched for a long time, weaving in and out of the labyrinths engendered by the visions, stumbling over the listless bodies at housefronts, avoiding the people who had died standing, and it was only when I noticed a silver butterfly in the air that hope came to me in the only sign which had appeared during those short days when fear obliterated our memory.

I followed the butterfly and it led me to the edge of the forest. I found dad standing in front of a giant tree, with a frozen startled expression on his gaunt face. He was staring wide-eyed at the tree trunk as if he could see into its lighted interior, or as if he were reading a prophetic script on its bark, and as if what he saw had turned his brain to marble. The butterfly circled dad's head and then flew up into the air, disappearing into the darkness, turning into a pulsing star over the trees. I didn't know what to do with dad, so I touched him. When I touched dad he screamed suddenly, jumping back, startling me. He looked around him with bewildered eyes, taking in all the chaos that the upheavals had created. Then he stared at me a long time, tears streaming down his face.

'Why are you crying, dad?' I asked.

'Because, my son, you have woken me up from the most beautiful dream I have ever had.'

I stared at him in silence. Tears still poured down his face.

'And now I can't even remember the dream.'

He looked very miserable.

'How long have I been asleep?' he asked.

'I don't know.'

'I feel as if I have been dreaming for many days.'

He wiped the tears from his parched face and after another long silence he asked me about mum.

'I can't find her,' I said.

'Let's go and search for her,' he said, holding my hand.

We walked over the rubbish and the dead birds. We passed the standing forms of our neighbours. As we passed them dad touched each man sleeping on his feet. And as he touched them they widened their eyes: a confused, astonished, they broke into a babble of voices, and all at once I realised that the people who were standing as if they had been turned to stone were in fact in a deep and unfathomable sleep. And when they woke up they jumped, and fell, and got up, and looked around at the mess and detritus. And they all complained with bitter tears in their eyes that they had been woken from the most profound dreams of their entire lives. One by one the people of the area awoke from their leaden slumber, and one by one the voices rose in the air, speaking of wonders lost to them in their awakening.

As if their sleep had been a chasm which separated them from our reality, they looked upon our wrecked world with stupefied eyes, unable to ascertain whether the dreadful changes had been wrought while they were dreaming.

Without knowing it, dad had broken our silence. Everywhere people spoke abundantly. They talked of unrecorded and forgotten miracles, unremembered signs. And it was only when we found mum profoundly asleep on a bed of rotting vegetables, with yellow butterflies in her hair, that dad screamed again. This time his excitement was almost insane. He shook mum awake on her bed of vegetables, and then he went everywhere, waking people up, waking the old woman curled up near rusted buckets, the young men stretched out on the dry earth, and old men asleep in bushes, with only their feet visible. Dad went around shouting that he had remembered fragments of his dream and the messages given to him during his sleep. He was quite demented. His old energy seemed to have returned, and he went around with the peculiar madness of those who have survived a perilous journey. He was the only one whom sleep had not caught in its labyrinths. And he tramped about, alarming us, shouting that the world was not going to end just yet. Then he gathered us all together and told us he had dreamt, in parts, that the butterflies were weeping for a new life, that the butterflies had to be burned, that they had to die properly for greater spirits to be born. He dreamt also that we were all turning into dead butterflies and that his spirit left him and became a silver butterfly which soared into the adventures of eternity, adventures so extraordinary that if he had remembered them he would have become very great, very happy and very wise. People's voices rose in wonder and I heard them saying that they had more or less dreamt the same thing.

Given our penchant for dwelling too long on the wondrous and the fearful, we began to talk too much, exchanging fragments of dreams. Dad grew impatient. With great vigour, and with the voice of a soldier who had received his mandate from the crisis of the moment, dad hustled and commanded and organised the inhabitants of the area. He got us to bury the corpses of birds and animals. He made us gather the dead butterflies. We worked all through the night, sweeping and carrying the butterflies to the middle of the road. All the children had their hands full of golden and blue-winged butterflies and the women had their basins full and the men had brooms and buckets. We dumped them on to the growing pile and stared with horror at such a mysterious species, wondering aloud about what manner of plague had killed them off.

When the gathering of the butterflies had been accomplished a herbalist amongst us took over the priestly role. He poured libations on the parched earth and made a lengthy prayer. Then dad drenched the obscene heap with kerosine. When he threw a lit match on the heap the whole thing burst into an incandescent blue and yellow combustion, accompanied by an explosion that took us aback. The fire swooped up and burned with strange fizzling noises. As the flames lit up the darkness, flaring erratically, we gasped in terror and amazement at seeing spirits rising into the air on golden plumes of smoke. The brightness of the spirits momentarily blinded us with the sudden sweep of daylight illumination. When the spirits rushed out from the crackling heap, and vanished into the darkness above our heads, the fire suddenly went out, plunging us into profound blackness. For several minutes we stayed still, unable to breathe, unable to speak. And as the silence lengthened, the darkness deepened. The terrible strangeness of our condition returned. Then, one by one, under the cover of a darkness that almost rendered us invisible, and without saying a word to one another, we went back to our rooms. We didn't stay together as a community. For the first time in several nights we went back to our different forms of isolation.

We did not speak after the incident of the fire because we weren't sure of the reality of what we had witnessed. It may also have been that in witnessing a sign that we couldn't interpret we were left with a vaster fear, a fear that had permeated the fabric of our lives.

Mum and dad didn't sleep that night. But I did. I wove in and out of dreams. In the dreams I was riding on the back of the road, and the road became a snake that writhed all over the place, wrecking houses and causing accidents. But when I finally arrived at the destination of the next morning, the world had become a little different.

CHAPTER TWENTY-ONE

How Hope Conquers Lethargy

E VERYWHERE, CROWDS OF people were talking about abnormal miracles. Someone said they saw rainbows flying in the air, with angels riding them as if they were horses. A woman claimed that while walking she had slipped into another world, one which she described as the heaven of birds. She swore that there were many worlds, that there were places where the spirits of dead fishes dwelt, where all the extinct species of the earth roamed, ate and played in the complete freedom of a world without wicked and thoughtless human beings. She also claimed to have entered a universe of shadows and that she had seen all of us there, as if a part of ourselves lived on in another sphere while we slept.

When she had finished, a neighbour gave his own testimony of a wondrous event. While combing his hair the previous evening he had noticed a flash; on looking into the mirror, he saw that his hair was on fire. The fire was yellow, but it did not burn him, and it was only after he had slept and woken up that the fire disappeared. Other people claimed that electric sparks flew off metal stuck in the earth, and that every now and again the air crackled without explanation. A woman said she had dreamt of the blind old man turning into a lizard.

The world, for a moment, seemed new. It was strange to see how our zest had returned, how a mysterious hope was conquering our lethargy. We saw how everything could be different. We dreamt collectively of a new paradise on earth where human beings could live without fear, and so bring about a second golden age of wonder. That day, undirected by anyone, we began to clear up our environment. We gathered the garbage. The carpenters enlisted several men and started to rebuild the broken beams of houses. We burned the garbage and the stinking mattresses, the uprooted bushes. We chopped up the fallen trees. We re-allocated living spaces for the homeless amongst us, making them sleep in our different rooms on a rotational basis. We emptied our fallen water tanks of their poisonous fishes and tadpoles, and washed them out thoroughly. We cooked massive pots of food, and ate as a community.

Two days after the burning of the butterflies, the sky darkened. We stopped in our labours. We looked up, our minds empty, fearing that we were dreaming into existence another frightening phenomenon. Suddenly the sky cracked open, revealing the startled spirits of the air. The crack closed; a forked flash divided the heavens and we all ran into our rooms, screaming that the world had exhausted time, and that the end of all things had finally found us. And then the miracle of rain poured down on the baked earth, on the wounded roads, on the inexplicable chasms that had opened in the remote edges of the forest. The rain lashed down its bizarre blessedness, drenching the houses without rooftops, filling up the empty wells, covering the street with bright waters. As the rain crashed down we saw a rainbow sailing in the sky, as if blown by an abnormal wind. It rained on the piles of garbage, and our efforts at rehabilitation were interrupted. The paths seemed re-organised. We heard the water steaming as it sank into the earth. All along our street the little children were out naked, dancing and bathing in the rain, with the water turning into foam on their dry skin. I ran out and joined them and stayed under the surprisingly warm water, playing and jumping while the adults looked on with nostalgia in their eyes.

When I came out from under the rain, shivering and alive, mum seized me and, laughing, towelled me vigorously. Then she put me to bed and I slept for a long time and had magical dreams which I forgot but which left a glowing lightness in me. When I woke, the world had returned to a curious normality.

It had rained for three days. I had slept most of the time, had woken up and wandered under the eaves of the surviving houses, and had slept again without being able to distinguish my waking from my dreams. On the fourth day the rain stopped. The sky was clear. Insects had returned. Frogs croaked. The weeds and bushes had somehow accelerated in growth, as if the rain had in its waters the essence of all fertilisers. Our devastations remained: the rain had washed away something heavy in us, had cleared the murky spaces, had expanded our sense of wonder, had enlivened our faces, made our eyes sparkle, brought hope to our embattled spirits, had made us dream of a new horizon as vast as the limits of mighty waters, but it had not obliterated the rubble, the rubbish, and the destruction of our possessions. The wounds on the surface of the roads had healed, the cracks and pits had been filled with mud, but the undulations and the writhing shapes remained. The road remembered all, but for the time being its mouth was covered in water.

Through the days and nights, with a mild sun and no moon, we worked on, repairing our houses, disposing of the rubbish, rebuilding sheds and shacks and stalls. The carpenters multiplied. The bricklayers worked solidly. Our landlords came to visit, brought builders and trucks of cement, and reconstructed their properties while we worked on in hunger.

CHAPTER TWENTY-TWO

The Generosity of Sorcerers

WHILE WE WORKED at re-making our lives the blind old man became the perfect gentleman of our area. He wore white suits, dazzling silver-coated sunglasses which reflected everything, and carried a black crocodile-headed walking stick. He had a well-dressed young woman for a guide, and he took an interest in our troubles and in the devastations. He pointed his walking stick at our broken houses, and expressed a greater sense of outrage than we did, speaking excitedly about the necessity of social justice, good housing for the poor, macadam roads, widespread electrification, and tap water for all. He offered his services and staggered about the place trying to help us carry beams and planks, staining his suit, dismissing the solicitations of his guide to be more careful, blindly carrying rubbish to the heaps where it would be burnt, trying to invigorate us with his words of encouragement, offering to contribute money for the treatment of the wounded and the ill, weeping for our poverty and vulnerability, saying how much the lively spirit of the community had changed. It didn't occur to us at the time to mark the fact that his own house had been untouched by the upheavals and the earthquakes. But it must be said that he showed us great generosity, and it was touching to hear him remark how our co-operation in crisis reminded him of his youth in the village when rogue elephants destroyed the farms, felled trees, and smashed the huts.

While we worked he would sit in our midst, with a bottle of ogogoro on a small table next to him, and he would draw out old melodies from his trusted accordion. He played us

169

work songs, folk songs, and songs that accompanied heroes through their tribulations and their momentous journeys. It came as a surprise to us that he could play so beautifully, or that he played any music at all in the midst of our troubles. He played with great feeling. Yellow tears rolled down his face as he squeezed out solemn funereal music that seemed to have travelled across to us from the unrecorded centuries. He stirred old feelings in us, but we did not warm to him. His music threw a bridge from his weird nature to our wrecked lives. From the hidden depths of his feelings, the beating core of music that contained the compressed intimations of struggles without end, we glimpsed something quite disturbing beneath his new guise. He confused us. He had appeared in many manifestations, as a bull with multiple horns, as sorcerer of the elements, but now his features looked softer and gentler. The bitterness that had encased his aged crumpled face seemed to have dissolved. He looked more like us. He looked nice and trustworthy, even normal, even warm. Moved by his own music, which seemed to make him feel more deeply the wretchedness of our lives, he dabbed his yellow tears with a white handkerchief. His harshness was gone. His voice had lost some of its vile cackle. It was as if in unleashing so much evil he had become almost good; as if in expending so much of his dark transformative energies, he had lost the ferocity of his poisons.

CHAPTER TWENTY-THREE

The Kindness of Curfew-makers

E VERYTHING WAS CHANGING, the face of the world seemed an endless series of masks, and we did not know what to believe. We heard that Madame Koto had lost weight, and was now so beautiful that men were leaving their young wives to follow her around slavishly. We didn't know if these were stories manufactured from hallucinations, because for a long time not one of us had set eyes on the fabulous Madame Koto. The only time we saw her was when she invaded our dreams with waves of her mythology.

And then one day, as our labours brought some normality back to the area, she appeared to us. It was a bright afternoon and we saw her resplendent in a red dress, with sequins in her netted hair. Madame Koto seemed like an absentee monarch who had returned suddenly to re-assure her subjects. She appeared to us briefly, full of smiles, beautiful in an oiled ripeness, like the grasshopper in the fire, growing more radiant and stunning as her destruction drew closer. She had indeed lost some weight, but her stomach was still massive with her abnormal pregnancy. Her foot, also, was still swollen. She had a white walking stick and she hobbled amongst us, full of commiserations, promising that her party would do everything in their power to help us in our plight.

She came to our house, and when I saw her I ran inside. She frightened me with her new beauty. Her transformation made me more scared of her than ever before. Her smile revealed an ivory-white set of teeth. The skin had shrunken round her neck. Her face was robust in health, and it seemed to me that her destiny was invading her, filling her with sensual beauty, enriching her skin.

She didn't come into our room. She sent a message instead. Dad went out and talked with her briefly. And when she left all the children followed her in silence, magnetised by her new appearance. And we would have followed her all the way to her bar if a cross-eyed man hadn't emerged from the forest ringing a bell and uttering the direst warnings. He was like a possessed town-crier and when he shouted his warnings Madame Koto hurried on, losing some of her dignity, afraid, it seemed, of the man's stinging prophecies to the community. He had a harsh voice and he came between us and Madame Koto. He was striking in his long white robe, with a red cloth tied round his head. I recognised him as the herbalist who had once prayed over Madame Koto's car and who, in a moment of drunken intuition, had gone on to prophesy that the car would become a coffin. Relentlessly, in his scratched voice, he warned us to beware of those who grow beautiful on the milk of young women, of those who extend their lives in the night. He warned us not to trust any of the parties, saying they would sell us to the world for their own purposes.

'Return to the old ways!' he cried. 'Return to the ways of our ancestors! Take what is good from our own way and adapt it to the new times! Don't follow these witches and wizards. Watch them carefully. Watch these powerful people with all your eyes!' he shouted, ringing his bell, destroying the magnetic pull Madame Koto exerted on us with her sequins and her moonstones.

'WHEN A PERSON'S FAME REACHES ITS GREATEST AND STRANGEST HEIGHT,' he bellowed, 'VACATE THE SCENE BELOW, FOR THERE MIGHT SOON BE A GREAT CRASH!'

On and on he went, breaking into coded prophecies, speaking of rainbows and the dying forest, national confusion and death and war, dire things lying in wait on the roads of our future.

And when Madame Koto neared her bar the herbalist turned to us and, furiously ringing his bell as if it were a magic instrument of fear, he chased us back down the street, hitting us roughly, kicking sand at us, shooing us away as if we were so many chickens. We scattered in every direction, surprised at the herbalist's ferocity. I fled to our room, screaming. I stayed in till I no longer heard his bell, and when I went out tentatively, to see what he would do next, it came as no surprise to me to find that he had vanished.

Soon after Madame Koto's reappearance three trucks came down our street and distributed powdered milk, flour and bags of garri to the different houses. They were from the Party of the Rich. They brought workmen to help with the broken houses, carpenters for the roofs and shacks, axemen to chop up the fallen trees, trucks of sand to fill up the pits in the road. They also distributed leaflets about the forthcoming elections. They presented themselves as the good party, as the organisation that cared for the poor, for communal well-being, and for the country. At first we were suspicious of their loaves of bread, bags of rice, and bundles of dried fish. Some of us were so suspicious that we attacked their vehicles and their drivers. But the party persisted; they made new promises over their loudspeakers; and they continued to bring gifts in spite of our resistance. We were so hungry as a result of the catastrophes, and most families had earned very little during the upheavals, that we began to accept their well-timed gifts. There were those amongst us who urged remembrance of the time of the poisoned milk. But our hunger was more insistent than our memories. One by one we went to the political trucks with outstretched basins.

Dad forbade us having anything to do with the spurious kindness of our former poisoners. He said he would resume work and feed us with his own hands. In the afternoons we watched the re-fragmentation of our community. We noticed that those who accepted the gifts were converted after they had eaten the dried fish and rice and garri. We noticed also that they suffered no after-effects. There were no illnesses and no one complained of poisoning. People began to give the party the benefit of the doubt. Those who did certainly benefited themselves. The lorries returned with more provisions, more help, and they concentrated at first on the new converts. Those of us who doubted watched in silence as the houses of the converts were quickly repaired, as their children received fine clothes. We watched as they ate and drank and regained something of their former well-being. There were times when we felt foolish at having excluded ourselves.

For a while the night-runners were silent. For a while no curfews were unleashed on us in a rash of feverish voices. Masks temporarily stopped invading the night. The Jackal-headed Masquerade didn't ride through our night-spaces on its white horse. We no longer had dreams of Madame Koto pressing down on lives, sucking in our vitality and will. We no longer had visions of the blind old man and his infernal transformations. If anything we began to dream of them as draped in white robes; we saw them as our saviours, our friends. In dreams they smiled at us, they made our lives secure, they policed the realms in which fear and frustration ate up our hopes, they manifested themselves as the powerful ones who could protect us from our worst enemies, and who would fight by our sides in all our battles.

CHAPTER TWENTY-FOUR

What Servants Reveal

O N ANOTHER DAY, Madame Koto appeared to us again. She had seven umbrellas held over her by seven women. It wasn't raining. The sun was bright and the sky was clear. After this brief appearance, which was communicated to all of us by word of mouth, she retreated to her bar and pulled our spirits with a poignant music which was new to our ears. Her appearance seemed designed to make it clear that she was a solid force and that for her a crash would never happen. She seemed destined to rule the fears of men, and to weather all the madness of great heights, like most people of power, to a celebrated old age.

That same afternoon her driver was sent to deliver provisions to us all. He drove up and down the street like a demented clown, his cap askew, dumping fresh fish and rice at our compound-fronts, hurling small bags of crayfish and prawns at us with an unmistakable contempt, the con-tempt which the party leaders tried to conceal. It is odd how servants always reveal the secret intentions and true feelings of their masters. We couldn't read these feelings at the time, but when the driver rode roughly amongst us the mutterings began to grow. And it was only when he knocked over one of the carpenters that a delegation, with dad among them, plucked up the courage to confront Madame Koto with their complaints. They couldn't get an audience. She asked them to pass their message through one of the women in the bar. They did, and she replied that she would scold the driver. He was prevented from using the car for a while. Later, we saw him staggering around the street, drunk, swearing and threatening us for nearly getting him sacked.

CHAPTER TWENTY-FIVE

The Music of Forgetfulness

IT IS HARD to say what made so many of us new converts to Madame Koto's way. The ranks of the Party swelled and people who had suffered together during the long nights of the storms and earthquakes now became hostile to one another. The Party gained an enormous following, and every day the supporters converged outside Madame Koto's bar chanting Party songs. We saw their lives improve visibly.

It may have been the sweet music from the bar which drew us to her. The music spoke of flowers and scented rain, of an ordered life blessed with wealth. The music filled the space where something else had been.

For many weeks after the upheavals dad told no stories, there was no music in our lives, and the forest was silent. At first we didn't notice the silence. Then we were sad at the absence of the sweet female voices that sang so passionately of another way. The silence seemed to last for ever and we no longer heard people talking about white antelopes in the forest, or about jewelled eyes among the trees in the dark. The silence lasted so long and seemed so final that we began, slowly, to forget that the voices had ever been real. They too seemed like things manufactured during our hallucinations. The upheavals and the storming of our minds had the effect of making us doubt our memory. And because we doubted, we forgot. And because we forgot, we were ready for the turning of a new cycle.

The only music in our lives came from Madame Koto's bar. And as it didn't seem malignant – full, as it was, of an indecipherable sweetness – we went there in greater numbers, to drink, to eat, and to celebrate the public birth of a new force in politics.

CHAPTER TWENTY-SIX

The Masquerade Becomes an
Invisible Censor

O N THE AFTERNOON that I set out to the bar with dad, it came as a surprise to find that the Jackal-headed Masquerade had disappeared. In its place was a ladder which had been thrust into the earth and which stood without support. The ladder climbed into the open sky, a sign which hid its own meaning. We were so taken aback with the disappearance of the Masquerade that dad didn't want to go into the bar. Its absence confused everyone.

It was only when night fell, and when the wind whistled over the earth without menace, that a sinister thought occurred to me. The Masquerade had gone, but it had entered a higher level of reality, penetrated our fabric, and permeated the wind. It began to be the only explanation for things which puzzled us and which ultimately controlled our behaviour towards the party and towards one another. The invisible Masquerade became our secret censor; it became the eyes of harmless-looking butterflies; it seemed to invest its spying spirit into lizards and moths; it whispered to us of the right ways of doing things; it made us reasonable in ways that made us more powerless. And without knowing it we surrendered ourselves to its directives. The Masquerade became more powerful and fearful for being invisible, for it now seemed to be everywhere, existing in the corners of our eyes, in the margins of our vision, vanishing when we turned to look at its censoring manifestation.

Those who opposed the party, or who spoke ill of it, and

suffered inexplicable pains, whose children fell to vomiting, who became temporarily blind, seemed to prove to us the greater powers of the invisible Masquerade. Every illness, every fever, every failure in endeavour, the rain flooding our rooms, children who accidentally cut themselves on glass, men who raved for two hours and returned to a stunned normality, convinced us that we were surrounded by an implacable force. And because we could not see what it was to which we attributed so much power, we feared it even more, and built it up into something which could not be defied.

Under the relentless wind of this new fear, dad was silent most of the time, pondering his strange philosophies, breaking occasionally into interpretations of the fragments he had brought back from his dream. But no one listened to him any more. As everyone else seemed to grow more healthy, mum grew listless. Her eyes were dull, her movements sluggish, and she became lean. She performed her tasks with a sleep-walking lassitude. Meanwhile, the area celebrated. The elections drew closer. And the preparations for the endlessly postponed rally resumed greater intensity.

Then one morning we received a message from Madame Koto. She asked mum to come and help with the preparations. She also invited dad to a party she was throwing. And she requested that I resume going to the bar to sit and keep her women company. Dad completely refused our having anything to do with her. He had forgotten his promises to Madame Koto, promises he had made when mum disappeared. We stayed at home, isolated and hungry. One day mum said to dad:

'I must go to her. I have seen what will happen. We are only holding back the future.'

Dad was furious. He was furious because he was confused. He forbade mum going to Madame Koto's bar.

'The future is coming,' mum said. 'In fact it is here already, looking for us.'

179

The next day she fell ill. We didn't know what was wrong. People muttered about invisible powers. Dad tramped up and down the street, challenging the forces of the air that were trying to take his wife from him. Mum was feverish for a whole day, muttering strange words about the future leaking into our lives, about the things which must be. Dad became so scared of her utterances that in the dead of night he gave his consent for me and mum to return to the bar.

The next morning mum recovered completely. Early in the afternoon she went to the bar. It was a fated afternoon. The sun was blinding in the sky and the air was sweet-smelling. In fact it was the day that the future broke into our lives, as if it had been waiting impatiently for all of our artificial obstacles to be cleared out of the way. And in its impatience to become real the future pounced on us in the form of counter-signs – a white snake, an epileptic road, a gentle wind, and vengeance stalking its victim in the form of a boy whose life was about to enter the stream of a spirit-child's uncertain destiny.

CHAPTER TWENTY-SEVEN

The Snake and the Shrine

IT WAS A day without visions, but I heard the road singing as I set out with dad for Madame Koto's bar. The
ladder had gone. Jacarandas and hibiscus had been planted
around the borders of her terrain. The backyard teemed with
elephant grass and cocoyam plants. The bar had been extended. There were white poles outside with banners announcing
the new date of the big rally. It was a hot day. Inside,
the bar was crowded with women, bawling children, and
men drinking palm-wine, their eyes dazed, their faces sweaty.
Dad and I sat in the bar, harassed by flies. We watched the
dance rehearsals going on outside. We were surrounded by
women with spiked, plaited hair and overwhelming per-
fumes. Dad was silent. He didn't drink and didn't smoke.
After a while mum came to us, her face dull, her eyes bright,
and she said:
'There is a knife in the moon.'
Then she went away.
'What did she mean by that?' dad asked me.
'The moon is going to kill someone,' I said.
Dad stared at me. A fly settled on his nose. He blew it away.
'How did the knife get to the moon then?'
'It's a message,' I replied.
He was still puzzled. The heat was solid in the bar.
The music made the heat more intense. A woman came to
us with a tray of food. She put the tray on a little table in
front of us. Dad stared at the jollof rice and the plantain, the
bean cakes and the fried meat. The only cutlery the woman
had given us was two knives.

181

'What meat is this?' dad asked the woman.

'Goat,' she said.

'Antelope,' I said.

She glared at me. Dad stuck the knife into a piece of meat and scrutinised it.

'It's not antelope,' she said.

'White antelope,' I said.

Dad smelt the meat and was about to take a tentative bite when a volcanic wind in my head made me knock the knife from his hand. The woman shouted at me. I watched her. She picked up the piece of meat and, brandishing the knife, began to abuse me.

'If you want to use the knife, use it,' I said.

She stopped abusing me. Then she dropped the knife on the floor and picked it up again and rushed out to the backyard. A moment later we heard a cry from the barfront. We went out and saw a crowd gathered around Madame Koto's car. The commotion had nothing to do with the woman who had served us. Pushing our way through the crowd, we saw that everyone was watching the car intently as if it might suddenly start dancing. The driver was asleep at the wheel, his cap slipping off his head. The crowd wasn't staring at the driver. They were staring at the top of the car, with eyes hypnotised by something amazing. Even dad caught his breath, his eyes wide open, his jaw dropping. I couldn't see what it was that so focused the attention of everyone. I tugged dad's shirt and he lifted me up and I saw a long white snake whose skin gave off iridescent colours. Its head was like a strange red fruit and its diamond eyes held our gaze. The snake was curled into a flattened spiral and its head of an Egyptian icon was straight, poised; and its tongue clicked in a steady rattle, transfixing us. No one spoke. Then the driver slid down on to the passenger's seat, while the snake rattled away above on the roof.

Suddenly, the silence was broken by a cry from the street. Released from the snake's bewitchment, I turned and saw Ade raving, shouting, pouring curses at everyone. I didn't understand. He looked quite insane and he kept trembling under the assault of sunlight. His hair had been shaved, and he looked demonic and bony, as if he had been initiated into a fiendish sect. His clothes were in tatters, his feet bloody, his neck stringy, his hands stiff, and he unleashed a torrent of ominous words at us. Before anyone could react to his disquieting apparition, we were distracted by another cry. The snake had moved. It had turned its Eygptian head in Ade's direction. Then, showering rainbow colours in the air, as if it had been drenched in the liquids of melted precious stones, it uncurled itself slowly. Overcome with fear, some people began to poke sticks at the snake. Others threw stones at it, and missed, and hit the side window of the car, startling the driver. He sat up, looked around, saw a crowd of people throwing stones at him, and panicked. He started the car frantically, shot forward (barely disturbing the snake), reversed violently, and sent everyone scattering. Then he drove forward again, ran into the white pole, and brought down the banner announcing the rally, which draped itself across the windscreen. The driver, confused even further, rammed the car into the bushes, and then stopped suddenly. The snake serenely uncoiled itself above, its head elegant and primeval, its eyes like illuminated beads.

Before anyone could make a movement, Madame Koto strode towards her vehicle. She was wearing a yellow robe, with a little mirror on a chain round her neck. Without looking at any of us, having taken in the whole situation in the space of a glance, she strode to the car and grabbed the snake by the neck. The snake stung her once on the wrist, and she let out a piercing cry. She staggered backwards, her face contorted by the agony of her bad foot in its plaster cast. She was still holding on to the snake, but it bit her again, swiftly, bursting a vein. Blood dripped down her arm and evaporated on the hot earth. There was a deep silence. Something curious happened to time, for, in the space of a

183

frozen moment, Madame Koto looked magnificent, she efflo-
resced, her hair twinkled with sheen, her face glowed with
well-being, and even her massive stomach had a sculptural
grandeur. The moment passed swiftly and the next thing I
saw was Madame Koto pouring out incantations, uttering
strange sounds and a string of commandments at the snake.
To our astonishment, the snake seemed to listen. Its head
was still. Then, as we watched, a fantastic battle of wills
ensued, and the snake coiled its tail round Madame Koto's
neck, slowly. Then, just as slowly, the grip was tightened.
The wind blew in a mild frenzy. The snake, replying to
Madame Koto's incantations with a rattling language of its
own, stung her a third time.

We expected to see her drop. Instead, her shadow became
more voluminous. She didn't even wince. The third bite
seemed to empower her spirit, for she suddenly expanded,
swelling out before our startled gaze. Her face darkened, her
eyes became darker and deeper, and a wild energy obliterated
her beauty, till she stood before us revealed in the full
splendour of her ritual power. For a moment, unveiled, she
seemed like someone else, like a secret self that we had
never suspected was there, something quite monstrous, part-
bull, part-woman, with black lips, sagging double chin, hot
staring eyes, a stocky figure, and a neck trembling with
insane rage. Uttering a word of unspeakable vileness and
potency, a word capable of bringing on blindness or madness, she bashed the snake's head on the top of the car,
pulping its brain, as if infusing the painted metal with the
powers of the snake's poison, antidote to curses and bad-
wishes. Then, turning all of us into soft stone with the
withering heat of her eyes, she strode off with splendid
dignity, taking the dead snake indoors to her tumultuous
secret shrine.

CHAPTER TWENTY-EIGHT

———

Dark Stream of a Hidden Life

WHEN MADAME KOTO disappeared into her room, it took a while before we recovered from the hypnotism of the event. The crowd poured into the bar, to slake the thirst of their curiosity. Dad went with them. I didn't go into the bar. I went over to Ade, who stood alone in the middle of the street, trembling, muttering dark words, his eyes rolling. I wasn't sure if he recognised me, but when I got near him he laughed, and stopped, and held me, shaking. His shaven head was covered with cuts and bruises, his face with sores and welts. His eyes seemed deranged, his lips were chapped, and saliva dribbled from his mouth. His spirit was like a dizzying vortex bristling with inexplicable cries. In a weird, rattling voice, he said:

'The day has come.'

'What day?' I asked.

'The day the elephant dies on its feet.'

'I don't understand you.'

'Crocodiles do not fly,' he said, feverishly. 'The moon does not sing. Everything you see now is going to be washed away. The forest is going mad. All my hidden lives are calling me. Madness is maybe too many lives overlapping in a single mind, it is only the mind locked in its own cupboard, with the key lost. The heart looks out of the keyhole and sees strange human beings turning the world to ashes and deserts. The stream flows into the river, but the river that doesn't flow turns human bones to diamond. Nothing can stop an old wound from breaking out in your brain if the wound hasn't healed. The road is singing and no one hears because the future speaks to us clearly in all the things that are here, right in front of our eyes. The future holds a bold signboard which no one can read because our minds are locked in an old cupboard. On the third moon of a remote century they fed me and my family to an incestuous pair of Egyptian crocodiles and the high priestess was a woman who buries moonstones. All the songs in this world cannot stop the rush of a mighty ocean.'

Suddenly he stopped speaking. He fell to the ground and began to tremble. I hadn't understood a word of what he had said. Writhing and jerking on the ground as though he had been bitten by a poisonous snake, foaming slightly at the mouth, Ade had taken on a demonic glow. He looked ugly, deformed. I held him tightly and his tremulousness began to affect me, seizing my brain, distorting my sight. After a while a bigger spasm took over. His limbs contorted and he gave out a cry that momentarily deafened me. And then he was still. After a few moments he stood up, his face pale, his lips bleeding, and he stared at me with unfamiliar eyes.

'What am I doing here?' he asked, puzzled.

I got up. He looked genuinely confused. His eyes were red. It occurred to me that he had again been overwhelmed by the dark streams of his other lives, the spirit-child's underworld.

'You've been saying things,' I said.

'Me? I haven't been saying anything.'

He looked at me as if I were a liar. Then he looked about him. Some people were staring at us.

'Are you all right?' I asked.

He didn't answer. He dusted himself and ran away. I followed him. When we got to his house I began to understand a little of what had been happening to him. The house had been altogether destroyed. A tree had crashed on to the roof. The walls had disintegrated. His parents weren't around. All about the house I could see their scattered belongings. The floor of his father's workshop was covered in foul water. Dead fishes lay on the carpenter's work-bench, spiders crept out from the kit of rusted nails and hammers, the freshly cut wood was stained with mucus, the walls were festooned with moss and algae, ferns sprouted from the floor.

Ade sat at the housefront, twisting sporadically. The house had become a haven of strange birds. Yellow eggs had been laid on matrimonial mattresses. Chickens strutted about the room in which the entire family used to live. A goat chewed on yam peelings near the cupboard in the makeshift kitchen.

'What happened to the house?' I asked Ade.

'That witch destroyed it,' he said. 'Now we have no home. My father has gone mad. My mother is dying in a hospital where no one will treat her. My brothers and sisters have been taken to the village.'

I didn't believe him. He sensed it.

'There is a snake in my head. Did you know that elephants sleep on their feet, standing up? My father looks at the sky and sees Madame Koto pissing on him.'

'Come home with me,' I said.

He laughed hysterically.

'There is only one home I want to go to,' he said in his fiendish voice.

'Where?'

He burst into his cackling laughter again and said:

'Look!'

He pointed at the sky. A flock of red birds, wings outstretched, sailed beneath the sun. When I turned back to him, he had gone.

CHAPTER TWENTY-NINE

The Secret Truth in Hallucinations

LATER I DISCOVERED that all he said was true. The political storm had rendered them homeless. His father had become deranged. He had gone from herbalist to herbalist, asking them to pluck out his eyes so he could stop seeing Madame Koto everywhere he looked. Then one morning he snatched up his biggest hammer and was seen running through the streets, towards Madame Koto's bar. The thugs held him, bound him, and carted him off to a hospital on the mainland. Ade's mother had been taken ill during the devastations, and one night she was seen raving in the street, with her arms stretched out, apparently blinded by the horrors of the storm. The blindness was temporary. They had since moved away from their ruined house and people said that every day they saw Ade sitting at the housefront, like a spirit bound to a place of suffering. He was always seen playing with a knife.

Everyone had concluded that suffering had unhinged the minds of the entire family. They also said that Ade had been bound twice for treatment. Small as he was, he had burst free from the ropes and taken to roaming the wild forest and the hot streets, his feet bleeding, sores on his shaven head, raving and shouting out curses, and frightening the birds and animals with his madness.

CHAPTER THIRTY

Pavane for a Spirit-child

I COULDN'T SLEEP THAT night. Neither could dad. The air was poisoned with forebodings. There was no wind and the street was silent as if the area had been evacuated. Dad sat on his three-legged chair, thinking, nodding his head constantly. Mum slept soundly on the bed. She had retreated curiously from the drama in our lives. She said nothing about her first day back at Madame Koto's bar. But she occasionally made bizarre pronouncements, in a tone of almost fatalistic acceptance, which left echoing spaces in our minds.

In the morning it rained. Dad went off early to earn some money carrying loads at the garage. I no longer went to school. Our building had been blown away by the storm. Most of our teachers had left the area and they hadn't been replaced. The pupils often went back to what was left of the school and played in the afternoons and recited their disrupted lessons.

That morning I went with mum to Madame Koto's bar. The earth was soft. I noticed a wan rainbow in the sky; it was incomplete, and it didn't touch the earth. Suspended, the rainbow looked sad. When we got closer to the bar we saw another crowd. The signs were beginning to multiply. The crowd was gathered round Madame Koto's car, which had been rescued from the bushes. Everyone was staring at a rash of little blue snails which had attached themselves to the car. They were all over the windscreen, the doors, the bonnet, and even the wheels. The driver had been trying to wash them off with water, but they wouldn't budge.

While we watched the frustrated driver trying to get rid

of the snails, Madame Koto came out of the bar. Behind her
were three women, two of whom carried a large chair, and
the third bore an umbrella. Behind them was a man with a
fan of ostrich feathers. Madame Koto herself had a flywhisk
in one hand. The women put the chair down near the car.
Madame Koto examined the blue snails, surveyed the crowd
and, in a powerful voice, said:

'Whoever sent these snails to my car should remove
them now!'

No one moved. She made the statement two more times.
The wind rose, fluttering her wrapper. She gave swift orders
to her women. Then she went to the backyard and returned
with a bucketful of hot water. She poured the fortified water
on the car, uttering spell-breaking incantations that made
us come out in goose-pimples. As we watched we saw the
snails writhing, the blue colour dissolving off them, turning
a golden-red, then black. The melted snails flowed down the
car in ugly colours, and the crowd let out a disturbed cry.
Madame Koto, enormous as a moon on strange nights, sat
down on the chair with a grim expression on her face. She
paid the closest attention to us, studying our reactions to
the demonstration of her powers, as if she expected us to be-
tray ourselves and confess to having tried to bewitch her car.

'You people are not serious!' she said, as the women
fanned her.

Touching the moonstones round her neck, which glowed
pink under the radiant sky, while the rainbow faded into a
lilac mist, she said:

'What does it take to make you people fear me, eh?
Heaven knows that I am good to you. When you are in
trouble I send you provisions, I get our party to bring you
help, I give you food, I take care of your damages, I protect
you, and yet you people still want to poison me, to kill me.
Well, I am too strong for you all. My father was an iroko
tree. My mother was a rock. The tree grew on the rock. It
still stands deep in the country. The rock itself has grown.

Now it is a hill where people worship at the shrine of the great mother. My enemies sent thunder, but the rock swallowed the thunder. They sent lightning, but the rock seized the lightning. Now, when the people of the shrine touch the hill with iron, electric sparks fly in the air. Our enemies sent rain, but the water made the rock grow even bigger. Now, flowers and plants that cure blindness and cancer can be found on the rock. Then our enemies tried to cut down the iroko tree, but their instruments were destroyed. And when they tried to blow up the rock the explosives failed and the rock started to bleed. Then one by one our enemies died, or went mad. And when the worshippers of the shrine saw the blood they made a great sacrifice and the oracle told them that the blood of the rock saves lives, cures palsy and madness, it cures leukaemia, epilepsy and impotence. Some people even say that when you rub the blood on your skin a knife can't cut you. A new god will be born for our age from the blood of the rock and the trunk of the great tree. I am only a servant. Friends of mine are friends of great forces. My enemies will turn to stone, will go mad, go blind, lose their legs and hands, forget who they are. They will tremble from dawn to dusk, their wives will give birth to children who will torment them, and some will give birth to goats and rats and snakes. The rock is my power. The sea never dies. Anyone who tries to kill me will kill someone else in my place, will kill their best friends, their child, an innocent bystander, a servant, but they won't touch me. I am only a servant of the people who want me. So don't stand there looking at me. Either you come into my bar and drink and celebrate with us or go away and carry your trouble with you!'

There was a long silence when she had finished. No one breathed. The sun rode higher in the sky. The earth began to warm. The scent of jacarandas and hibiscus floated over our skins. The driver began to wash the melted snails off the car. Some people drifted into the bar. Some hung around. Others wandered off reluctantly. I didn't see mum.

Then quite suddenly an agitated wind materialised beside me. I turned and saw Ade, with flowers round his neck, snot in his nose, standing next to me. His eyes were clear and fierce. He stank of an unbreakable deathwish. His spirit swirled around him, creating the eddies of agitation. He seemed utterly possessed by a deranged understream. A tidal fury roared about him and his eyes shone like polished steel. An old rage, bursting through the bounds of his young body, through the doors of his spirit, frightened me and made me tremble in his presence of a boy at the gates of an unfathomable destiny, a destiny like a poison in his brain waging war on his urge to live. Suddenly I could see his future as an unconquerable foe of lies and corruption, a martyr, a madman gifted with prophecies of stone; but now he was compact in the spirit of vengeance, like an inscrutable force. A heroic mission was taking over his dreams, borrowing his body, turning him violently away from the road lined with broken glass that runs up through seven mountains, each higher than the one before, leading either to the kingdom of rainbows or to the realm of mad religions.

And then, with the force of a new cycle that has waited too long to be manifest, he pushed me aside and stood in front of Madame Koto – the child challenging the rock, the boy daring the iroko tree that has survived centuries of turbulent history. With a rough voice, blasting the air with more power than a sorcerer could command, he said:

'Where are your crocodiles now?'

Storming the gates of our cowardice, he shouted:

'Where are your crocodiles? Where is your kingdom? Where are your servants? Where are your slaves? You fed me to crocodiles because I wouldn't follow your religion. You watched the crocodiles eat me up. My head was the last to go. I died with the face of your spirit lodged in my destiny. I have returned. I am a spirit-child and I have returned to your womb, you ugly daughter of rock. I have returned and

192

I am chained to your neck just as the abiku-children in your womb are chained to your death. One way or another we will get you. Where are your crocodiles now?'

The silence that followed made the trees creak. They were straining against the wind to hear our hearts beating in the presence of such fierce mystery.

'What crocodiles? What crocodiles?' Madame Koto asked. 'This boy is mad! Seize him! Hold him!'

Then I saw the knife on the moon. It quivered, flashing its fantastic lights in Ade's hand. Awkwardly, like a child withdrawing from the brain's confusion at sacrificing a chicken; awkwardly, as if he had never held a knife before, Ade thrust the sharp instrument towards Madame Koto's stomach. She turned and, falling with the chair, saved her life. Ade missed her stomach, but managed to plant the knife into her massive arm. The flowers fell from around his neck. Then he blew his nose and his snot landed on her moonstones. The women fell on him. He disappeared under the weight of their bodies. I heard the earth singing. I heard Madame Koto, the knife still in her arm, shouting:

'Seize him! Hold him! Don't beat him! He's mad! A witch has entered his brain!'

And when the gathered people howled and the driver gave out a cry of horror, something shifted in my eyes and I saw Ade's spirit. It was large and brilliant, distinct in the effulgent shape of a diamond lion. I saw the size of his spirit, but I couldn't see him. I heard the growl of his spirit energies before I saw him burst out from under the weight of the women. He stood there, with all the women thrown from him. He stood renewed. Then, screaming weird biblical prophecies, he fled up the street. He ran like the wind which precedes a hurricane. Madame Koto commanded her minions to go after him.

'He's mad! Seize him! He has bad blood! We must treat him! Hold him, but don't hurt him! Catch him!'

Galvanised by the terror and the confusion, by Madame

Koto's screaming, and by the general pandaemonium, the crowd, the women, the thugs bounded after Ade. The driver jumped into the car and, with an unthinking concentrated expression on his face, reversed furiously, and swung into the street. It was a blazing afternoon. While we pursued the deranged figure of Ade the diseased goats and chickens, suffering from dropsy, stared at us. The driver shot past in the car. Blasting his horn, nearly running us over, nearly mowing us down, he sped up the street, driving as if fleeing from the furies. Then, to our horror, in the heat of that unforgettable afternoon, Ade stopped. He stopped and turned to face the oncoming car. The car hurtled towards him. He even seemed to go towards it. The horn went on blasting, turning us momentarily into wood, and I could have sworn I saw an ecstatic glow on Ade's face. For a long second I thought the joke would stop. The driver had done this to us before, rehearsing the moment when his life would change for ever, and it changed that moment when his brakes failed him. We watched in dread and in silence as the car crashed into Ade's fragile pathetic frame. The gates of the road opened. A red light poured out. A single spirit with the head of a lion emerged. And when we saw the red light bleeding on the road we screamed, ran to the car, which had stopped too late, and found Ade quivering in an agonised spasm underneath, blood on his tattered shirt, his arm pulped, his forehead cracked, his eyes fierce. The world was full of strange sounds as we pulled him out. I leant over his broken form, crying, shaking uncontrollably. Ade, in the voice of a child, said:

'Shut up!'

I couldn't. Something kept tearing at my entrails. Vicious lights burned at my heart. I trembled in unbearable sympathy with his spasms. And then I noticed that he had a sweet ghoulish smile on his face. He motioned me to lean closer. All around me women were wailing, rocking my soul. I saw Madame Koto hobbling in a great frustrated hurry up the

194

street. Her plaster-cast foot made her look ridiculous. Ade held my head with his good hand and pulled my ears down to his mouth. In our private language, in whispers full of heat, his breath stinging my eardrums, his words scratching my spirit, he said:

'I failed.'

He said it simply, without a sigh. Then his voice became ghostly, remote, old, as if someone else were speaking through him. I glimpsed other selves, subterranean personalities, lurking beneath his present incarnation.

'I failed,' he continued. 'I knew I would fail. My destiny was not to be an assassin, but a catalyst. The tears of a child dying of hunger in a remote part of the country can start a civil war. I am the tears of a child. I am the country crying for what is going to happen in the future. My new life is calling me. I will always be your friend and helper, but you won't recognise me.'

He paused, his spasms returned, his eyes faded. Then, with blood pouring from his nose, he coughed, and his eyes brightened in what seemed like a final enlightenment. Around me the adults were in confusion. The driver had stumbled out of the car and was wailing, tearing his hair, throwing himself on the ground, demented at the thought that just as his life was entering a higher level he now had the death of a child on his hands for ever. The crowd tried to restrain him, but his grief overran, and from his kicking and wailing it became clear that the mad fevers of the road had entered his brain.

Madame Koto was still making her painful journey towards us, waving her white crocodile-headed walking stick in the air, walking clumsily on her plaster-cast foot. Ade pulled my head down again, and after a low harsh laughter, he said:

'Everyone has been assigned a spirit that will come for them when their time has arrived. You have a frightening spirit coming for you: I can see her stirring. The spirit with four hands is coming for me. I am not afraid. My destiny has been hidden from me and it was because of all the poverty, all the suffering in the world, the wickedness and the lies, it was because of all these that I didn't want to live. But now I know I was born to love the world as I find it. And to change it if I can. I will get a better chance. But before then we will meet again and play in the fountain of rainbows and in the golden sea of music.'

He shut his eyes. There was a contorted smile on his face. I looked up and saw the spirit of rainbows and golden ghosts gathering around his broken body. I heard crying and shouting; but from the spirits, with their sad eyes, and their four hands brilliant like the topaz and ruby lights radiating from the sky when the sun is fading, from the spirits I heard in my heart the unnatural pavane for a spirit-child's death, the poignancy relieved only by the soaring notes which were the promises of his eventual return.

When Madame Koto got to where Ade lay she brought the urgency of a great mother, hitting her minions with her stick, shouting at the women, lashing the driver till he bled from his ears, commanding her servants to carry the body to her bar for first-aid treatment and then to organise a car to rush him to the best hospital in the city. It was only when she waved her good arm about, hitting people, stunning them into a sense of responsibility, that I noticed she still had the knife stuck in her other arm. She was so engaged in organising her disorderly minions that perhaps she hadn't noticed. When the women came and pushed me aside and lifted Ade's body, Madame Koto saw the knife in her fleshy arm, registered its presence, and the blood burst out like a little red fountain when she yanked it from her. She showed no pain. Her blood stained the after-noon with its dense odour of an ancient animal. Ignoring the blood pouring down her arm, her gestures empowered, she urged the women to hurry with Ade's body. She dispatched a servant to go and fetch a party van. One of the women hurriedly bandaged her wound. The other women carried Ade to the bar and laid him down on three tables joined together. They bathed his broken head and they washed his pulped arm. Yellow liquid flowed out of his mouth. It had a bitter smell that would never leave the air of the bar, branding the signature of his death on the spaces of Madame Koto's earthly kingdom. The women fussed about him, wailing, singing funereal songs in cracked voices. Amidst their fragmented threnodies Madame Koto stood over Ade, her mighty breasts heaving above his face. He lay still. His eyes were shut. His breathing was almost non-existent. Madame Koto looked down at him with her eyes dark as almonds and she didn't notice the other presences around his body. She didn't notice the spirit of rainbows with wonderful colours swirling about it, or the golden ghosts with ruby eyes and blue mouths. These other presences floated over him, breathing consolations into the terrible suffering of his spirit, soothing his restless and terrified soul, assuring him that all was well, that the world would not end, that he had serenity and music and joy ahead of him, that his parents would be all right after their own fashion, that everything keeps turning and changing, and that there was nothing to fear because he was entering the world where love flows from all things and where the spirit is a music that never stops playing and which invents itself all the time, expanding the good spaces in all the worlds.

The women in the bar were silent. All the banners of the party had been furled and lay on the floor. I noticed mum sitting apart from everyone in a corner. She held her head low and I could see her lips quivering.

For the second time in all the years I had known her, Madame Koto wept. Her tears dropped on Ade's face and turned yellow, as if they were bleaching his skin. Ade opened his eyes, moved his head sideways to avoid the dripping tears, and shut his eyes again. I could see the spirit-lights everywhere becoming more intense. The intensity made the silence deeper. And the silence ended when Madame Koto's servant bounded into the bar, out of breath, saying the van had arrived but was stuck at the other end of the road because of a tree that had fallen during the storms. Ade had to be carried again, down the street, alongside the forest, to the waiting vehicle. I knew one more journey would be too much for him. Mum lifted up her head to the ceiling, toward the heavens, a painful expression on her face. Madame Koto dispatched another of her servants to find Ade's father and tell him of the hospital where his son was being taken. The servant rushed out, raising dust with his slippers. The women came and carried Ade once again.

'Be gentle!' Madame Koto admonished them.

The women lifted him up gently and Madame Koto, following them, kept dabbing Ade's face with a hot compress, rich with the healing steam of roots and herbs.

That evening they took his body away and I trailed behind them down the street, weeping for the loss of a special companion, my only true companion, a fellow spirit-child, who knew the things that I knew about death and life, about the worlds beyond, about the fountains and the fauns, about the original river and the original fire, and about the seven mountains of our mysterious destinies. I followed the women who bore the small body of my friend, feeling that his dying was altering my relationship with the living for ever. I felt more alone in the undeciphered spaces of the earth than ever before. Now I had no one with whom to speak the private language and share the secret philosophies of those who, though appearing normal, are in fact wondering strangers on this earth.

Mum walked beside me, her eyes bright, and her silence like the light of diamonds. She may have been looking at the spirits and the bright ghosts that also accompanied Ade's body, but I doubt it because when their lights dimmed, when the radiant four hands of his guardian spirit began slowly to diminish, when the shimmering ghosts faded into a barely perceptible lilac mist floating over his body and up beyond the trees, mum still looked on ahead, her eyes unchanging in their sad brightness.

And then, suddenly, as if a voice which had existed in other regions of the universe had burst into our world, Ade began to shout his name over and over again, till it echoed in the forest, rebounding from the bark of ancient and absorbent trees, soaring in the empty spaces where only the wind stirs and the birds flutter in their kingdom of perpetual dreams. And when Ade stopped crying out his name, as if his unique identity would either save him or help his passage through the narrow gates of death – the gate which gets tighter as you get closer to the beneficence and glory of the life in between – when he stopped altogether, leaving only his echo wandering lost and homeless in the forest spaces and the secret roads, a voice seeking its origin, a soul seeking its true home, I knew that Ade had died and that the air and even the trees would remember his story and record it on the coded scripts of their silent trunks. I broke into deep wailing and ran toward his body hanging in the air. The women bearing him froze. Madame Koto's face collapsed into its true visage of a woman hundreds of years old. But before I got to him mum caught me and held me back, seizing my arms. She held me to her as I fought her suffering incarnation. She embraced me very tightly, absorbing in her flesh the full fury of my grief. As I fought the boundaries of her lean and loving body my grief overcame me. And she took me back home, limp on her shoulder, while the women resumed their procession, and Madame Koto her burden. And as mum took me home I still heard Ade's name faintly ringing in the forest. And it still echoes to this day when you knock on the doors of certain trees.

Book Three

———

CHAPTER ONE

A Transferred Death

TIME QUICKENED. WHEN we got home we didn't sleep and we were silent. We sat on the floor, with a single candle burning on the table. The door was wide open. The wind brought in the advancing smells of too much perfume, beneath which lurked the faint odour of dung, though it could only have been the intensity of a secret desperation. When dad returned we knew our hunger had driven him into a shameful line of work that we noticed in retrospect and never mentioned. There was no shame on his face as he came in drunk and spread on the table the amount of money he had earned doing something that eroded his spirit years in advance. He was quite drunk, his boots stank of mud and disinfectant, and he had an abstracted look on his face. He kept creaking his neck as if he had been carrying loads more infernal than they were heavy. He struggled to smile, to display an exuberant lack of care, but our silence made him awkward. He was drunk and couldn't seem to light his cigarette. He was drunk on a secret shame. We were silent and unmoving and we didn't register any impression of his return or of his dubious exuberance. After three attempts he lit his cigarette and smoked as we stared at the solitary candle. Dad misinterpréted our silence. He thought that we knew what he was trying to keep secret. His pride stirred his anger.

'A man comes in after doing a dog's work . . .' he said, and mum got up from the floor.

Dad didn't finish his sentence. He stubbed out his cigarette and took notice.

Mum sat on the bed, taking his hand in hers, and told

him what had happened, without any pathos in her voice. When she had finished, dad sighed. He lit another cigarette and then put it out. All three of us sat in the advancing darkness, staring at the flame of the candle.

We slept badly that night, entering into one another's dreams. In the morning we heard about the driver's fate. We heard that all night he had been seen wandering the streets, talking aloud to everyone, recognising no one, saluting and prostrating to goats, knocking away invisible flies from around his mouth. People said that from the moment of the accident he had aged immeasurably. He seemed to live his life in advance, as all his secret and public ages caught up with him. His face became wrinkled, his jaws became slack, he became cross-eyed, and he kept blinking. He would fall on the road and scream that it was trying to pull him in. When he fell he fought as if several invisible hands were holding him down, dragging him under. When he freed himself from the imaginary hands, he talked of flying. He kept jumping up into the air, and was amazed when he fell back down. He helped old ladies across the roads and forgot to cross over himself. He directed the traffic, and caused untold chaos. He pursued chickens, calling them by the names of Madame Koto's thugs and minions. People said he had gone mad. But others said that he had entered the world which those who have committed murder wander into – a world of spirits and silences, where chickens become familiar people, where cats are antagonists; a world of unidentified voices, where nightmares drift past the eyes as they stare at the ordinary faces of the earth; a place in which several spheres and realities are all scrambled up. The driver was wandering in the serenity of one sphere – and at the same time raving up and down the main road – when a lorry ran over him. The lorry ground his body into the road and sped on, apparently unaware of what had been done; and it may be that Madame Koto's distraught driver, having entered another reality, weaving in and out of materialisation, was knocked over when he was invisible.

People said the strangest things about the driver's death. But the notion that struck me most was something an old woman said. She told us that the driver was a stand-in death for Madame Koto, that he had died in her place. When she first voiced the notion people moved away from her. The idea had an infectious terror. But over and over again that day, before the new cycle of fighting broke out, we heard people whispering that Madame Koto, with her enormous and temporal powers, had transferred her own death to her poor driver. She had in fact postponed her own death, and was now desperate for something we couldn't remotely imagine – an intangible elixir, perhaps. We heard people warning others to keep their children indoors, that the night-runners would soon begin their curfew-making, their reign of horrors.

And before the fighting started, each new event draining significance from Ade's death, the people of our area learned a lesson from the driver's fate which they did not put into practice: his fate was a warning that one mustn't get too close to powerful people. The world, for me, became instantly full of transferences – people transferring their illnesses, their troubles, their nightmares, their fates to those who happened to be around, to those perceived of as being dispensable.

Again we began to suspect one another of strange powers. And again we were wholly unprepared when the new fighting began which would eventually launch our lives into the time of the relentless flood. It began with the innocent sign of men wearing the faces of white antelopes. They appeared from the bushes, singing snatches of songs which we had entirely forgotten.

CHAPTER TWO

The Battle of Mythologies

T HE ANTELOPES CAME first. And then the crocodiles tried to eat them. We saw men with the faces of crocodiles, yellow paint blazing on their bodies, their machetes giving off electric sparks in the dry air. A new spirit entered our lives. It was a hungry spirit and it rose from the marshes and moors, spreading the larvae of mosquitoes everywhere. It breathed out fire and its footsteps were thunderous and it had all the powers of transference. It made us transfer our fears to one another. We became distrustful, suspecting others of having poisoned us with fevers that induced sleep-walking in the afternoons. It made us think that the demons with the abnormal mouths of blood-hungry crocodiles were hallucinations planted in our eyes by our neighbours.

Everywhere the thugs of the two parties clashed in their endless war of mythologies. Everywhere machetes brought sparks, chantings became frenzied, and people spoke of war as if it were a human being. The new spirit multiplied itself over the city. It spread its instant offspring to every street, every municipal county, to every house where tenants lay in fermenting numbers in small sweltering rooms. The spirit accelerated its dominion over our lives and made our nights longer.

Then, infected with its presence, we saw the wars of mythologies everywhere. The night fought the day. The moon extended its sphere into the dominion of the sun. The rain lashed the earth, lacerating its surface, creating gullies, washing away poorly rooted trees. The air whipped the waters, creating unusual disturbances on streams and rivers, creating new waterways that rushed through old villages. The disagreement between men and women became aggravated by the new elemental crisis. People from different tribes quarrelled with one another, disputing their myths of supremacy and their legends of the origin of all things. Neighbours quarrelled with neighbours, craftsmen with artists, praise-singers were chastised by satirists, children disobeyed their mothers, the colour brown conquered the colour green, historians argued bitterly with mythologists, journalists mocked griots, politicians attacked the forests, the government declared war on poverty and made us more wretched, the corrupt business men waged a relentless campaign against the crusaders for social justice, storytellers were hounded by the secret police, poets were harassed by propagandists, musicians were dogged by spies, photographers were beaten up by soldiers, the whites locked up the blacks, the blacks rioted against the whites, mottoes warred against mottoes, proverbs discredited proverbs, christians preached against moslems, and moslems against christians, both of them denounced the animists, normal children turned against the abikus and the dadas (who were children born with hair, and whose hair was never touched by razor or comb), and all over the country dissension grew fat while a new curfew extended its control over the evenings.

There were isolated strikes in the city. The producers of food, the distributors and retailers, managed to make all of us hungry. Fighting was general in many spheres. It even infected the animals. Cats pounced on chickens. Lizards harassed snails. Dogs barked at birds. Through all this the supporters of both parties enlisted new members, and hurled charms and chants at one another. The air became bad. Children fell ill. The air smelt of a corrosive poison. Sulphurous odours hung everywhere. And the spirit of dissension became an *ignis fatuus*, exploding in brilliant lights of blood, impossible to pin down, so that each attempt at a truce led to bigger misunderstandings, and nothing could be neutral.

It was a weird and compressed era. Two buckets clanging, while fetching water from a well, could make two families into bitter enemies. Words took on more meanings than ever before. A simple greeting could be read as a lethal insult. Every fever diagnosed directed suspicion at an unspecified neighbour. Innocence fled from our community, and to smile was no longer an expression of joy, but of some hidden triumph over others.

Masks multiplied into our nights. We saw crocodile faces turning red. Antelope faces changed into the expressions of hyenas. We ceased to be aware of the numbers of the dead. We began to live with ghosts and spirits. Our night-spaces began to crawl with other presences. The world was changing very fast. Then one day Madame Koto announced that she was going to bury her car. She bought a new one, exactly like the old. On another day someone slaughtered her sacred peacock. It was hinted that Ade's father, the fierce-eyed carpenter, was responsible. They also said he had taken to the bushes and had become something of a prophet and something of a terrorist against the Party of the Rich. Not long after the death of the sacred peacock, a house belonging to a staunch supporter of the Party of the Poor was set alight. It burned into the morning. No one died. The wars of mythologies escalated and after three days the fighting managed to reap its first significant harvest.

CHAPTER THREE

The Red Harvest

FRUSTRATED BY THE limitations imposed on his movement by all the fighting, dad ventured out into the disrupted world. He took me with him to Madame Koto's bar, the heartland of dissension. Dad went straight in and ordered a calabash of palm-wine. He was thirsty for confrontation and his eyes were rather crazed with undirected fury. He took the calabash outside, along with two chairs, and he drank steadily, itching for a fight. He kept trying to provoke people by the way he stared at them. His big hands trembled as he drank.

Dad's reputation as a slayer of giants and a conqueror of boxers from the spirit world made it hard to get the thugs to disagree with him. No one took up his baits. He tripped thugs over with his outstretched foot, he shouldered them, he insulted everyone, but got no results. His frustration grew worse. He drank heavily till his eyeballs were fairly floating in palm-wine.

'Nothing creates more controversy than the truth,' dad said, glaring at me with diverging eyes. 'So I am going to tell these people some very troublesome truths indeed.'

He got up suddenly, weaving, staggering. He trod on the instep of a particularly hideous-looking thug. The thug apologised. Dad called him a coward. He said nothing. The women of the party, seeing that dad was raising trouble, hurried over to defuse the tension. Dad called the thugs animals in disguise. They merely backed away from him. Finding no one to respond to his provocations, dad went slightly berserk.

'Monsters!' he shouted. 'You are all draining our people of sleep. You are stealing our powers, taking over our lives. I am not afraid of you. My name is Black Tyger and I eat stones first thing in the morning. I eat rocks last thing at night. My hands are made of tree trunks. You can only conquer people who are afraid of you. I fear only two people, my wife and my son. You monsters with crocodile faces, I shit on you!'

Still there was no response. So dad went on and on.

'The only thing you stupid people like is War. Trouble. Confusion. You will destroy this country before we are even free.'

Dad was extremely drunk. His wild gestures had burst open his shirt. He began to shout animatedly about the kind of ruler he would be if people voted for him. He said that in the country he rules anyone who proposes war as a solution to any problem must first enlist their wives, their children, their parents, and all their relations into the army and they must all be given front-line positions before the war can begin. He was launching into another speech when the battle of mythologies started to rage at the barfront.

At first all we saw was a prophet in a white robe, with leaves in his hair, kaoline on his face, and a hammer in his hand. He had emerged from the forest and was threatening vengeance to all those who murdered a rare son of the earth. Mixed in with his wild threats were prophecies delivered in a high-pitched insane voice about the great flood that was coming, about the congregation of spirits from all over the continent, about the dreadful consequences that would be visited on those who had been killing the white antelopes. He spoke in waves of incoherent passion, cursing the rock that would be broken by women, the iroko tree that would be felled by a single drop of black water.

'All of you who killed my son — Beware!' cried the insane prophet. 'BEWARE! BEWARE, because the giant of the night is dying on the road. Grass and weeds have covered its GREAT body. BEWARE, a tree is growing on his heart, and a THOUSAND people are trying to move it. BEWARE, because this GREAT giant was killed by a small bird with

210

blue wings, and the fall of this GIANT will create a hole so DEEP that people will think it is a VALLEY. All of you who think you will avoid judgement, BEWARE. Strange animals with eyes of fire will come out of the forest, animals with the feet of men who never die. BEWARE, because the SACRED PEACOCK has been eaten by fearless men who listen to the songs of the forest!'

It was only during his pause that I recognised the demented prophet to be none other than Ade's father, the fierce carpenter. His voice was mighty, but his presence was diminished, as if a great part of his stature had been eaten away by his insanity. The hammer shone in his hand like a holy instrument. Suddenly, brandishing the hammer, waving it about in the air like an illuminated sword of war, he shouted:

'MY SON IS NOT DEAD! MY SON LIVES IN MY HAMMER!'

And then he charged at the startled guests, the astonished thugs, the mesmerised women, the indifferent drunkards. He charged at the supporters of the party, uttering a terrifying war cry, and everyone fled except dad. Ade's father, waving his hammer like a primeval god of thunder, rushed into the bar and proceeded to destroy everything, shouting:

'TEAR DOWN THIS TEMPLE!'

He broke the tables and the chairs, he smashed the calabashes and the charms and the images of the new religion and the earthenware pots, he tore down the banners and the political posters and the cultic almanacs. He hammered the doors into broken splinters, he pulverised the plates and the glasses and the walls and the mirrors. He ran out to the backyard and the women fled screaming. He bounded back to the barfront and chased everyone all over the place, but he left me and dad alone. In and out of the bar he went, breaking things and swearing, shouting and destroying. But by the time he came rushing to the barfront again, swirling his hammer like a blood-crazed ancient warrior, the thugs had organised themselves. Fortified with hatchets, leather

211

shields and spears, they calmly waited for his raging presence to re-emerge.

There was a moment during the pandaemonium when I thought I saw Madame Koto inside the bar, looking out. Enormous as the night, her neck quivering, her eyes severe, a yellow light surrounded her, burning her sequined lace clothing without consuming it. She seemed so fat, so enormous, and yet she seemed to be floating, hovering above the ground like a dream-image, with a great peacock in her hand. The moonstones were turning red round her neck. Servants were fanning her as if in a liquid dream.

I was still trying to make out whether she was real or a simulacrum, when I heard a piercing cry. I turned and saw Ade's father holding his hammer up in the air, holding it high, as if summoning the mighty powers of the heavens to charge him with their divine thunder. I thought I heard the road screaming. A car horn blasted. An eagle with the face of a jackal swooped down on Ade's father's head. He froze. His hammer remained poised. A swift wind jolted me. The eagle vanished and a fountain of blood, thin and clear, burst from a vein in Ade's father's neck as one of the men stabbed him in the throat. Then another man stabbed him in the navel. His white robe sprouted patches of thick blood. The smell of the evening changed and I heard the laughter of the blind old man on the wind. Ade's father cried out long and loud and a third man struck him in the forehead with the sharp point of a knife. He became stiff as stone and when he fell the earth didn't move. Ade's father died with an expression of obscene shock on his face.

There was a yellow silence. The wind blew the darkness from the forest and into the open spaces. Then suddenly, from all around, from the distances, from the isolated huts, from the forest, and in the air, great wailings began to grow, to accumulate, voices awakening other voices, till we were surrounded with cries so frightening and omnipresent that for a moment it seemed there were only outraged spirits left in the world.

The thugs and supporters and guests vanished from the barfront. The wind occasionally blew the darkness away, revealing Ade's father floating in the dense pool of his own blood. His eyes were wide open, almost bursting at the shock of his end. The blood that spilled out from the hole in his forehead filled out the hollows of his face.

Madame Koto's holographic form remained in the bar. The electric lights weren't on, but there was a solitary lamp on a table. The lamp shone upwards, making her face bigger and more unreal, covering her loneliness in deep shadows. She looked out, but she didn't move. The silence was universal, the wind was cold, and dad stared at the dead body of Ade's father without comprehension. Then he looked at the lonely figure of Madame Koto. He was confused. His drunkenness, obliterating his memory, bewildered him. He didn't seem to know where he was. He made a futile movement and I felt the agitation of his thoughts and his muscles.

'There is a war going on,' he said, rather pointlessly. 'We are on a battleground.'

The wailing started again.

'Isn't that a dead man there on the ground?' dad asked, stupidly.

I couldn't speak. The night suffocated me with an ancient smell of blood. We were alone outside with the dead body and when the lamp went out in the bar a greater darkness fell on us. Then, as if awoken from a nightmare, from a dream of stone, dad began to scream. He screamed for the world to come and do something about the dead man. He cried for help. He wanted to get Ade's father to a hospital. The universal silence answered him. The wailing had stopped. In the icy silence I felt the swift wind of the eagle again and dad cried out that something had knocked him on the head. He turned, venturing into the darkness, and something hit him again. The darkness became full of the Masquerade's censoring presences. Hot wind blew into our faces. The blast of a furnace opened above my head. A bucket of ice-cold water landed on us. I felt the lash of a metallic whip across my back, and dad screamed. Something scratched my face, just missing my eyes. I ran, howling, towards the street. Dad was behind me, stumbling, staggering, tripping. Then I saw him wandering down the street towards me, his hands outstretched, as if he had suddenly been struck blind. He wandered into the forest, walking into trees, getting entangled in climbers. I caught his hand, disentangled him, and led him back to our room. My head was feverish with excruciating colours. Mum was waiting for us. And when we came in, with dad blind as if the night had entered his eyes, mum wasn't even surprised.

CHAPTER FOUR

———

City of the Blind

THAT NIGHT, AND for many nights afterwards, Madame Koto's enormous presence encompassed us in the room. She did nothing about the dead man at her barfront. What could she do? She couldn't bring him back to life, so she began to oppress us who were witnesses with more weight than ever before.

The next day, when people of the area gathered near her bar, watching every movement of her supporters, Madame Koto took to hiding from the world. The corpse remained at her doorstep, restricting her activities, attracting blue flies. That afternoon she ordered her men to move the body. They dragged it to the street, and left it near the bushes.

At first we thought that dad's blindness had something to do with shock. He doggedly refused any treatment. For two days we waited patiently for his sight to clear. He sat in his chair most of the time, cocking his ears to every sound, his eyes open, staring straight ahead, his expression fraught. I stayed with him, watching over him, while mum went out hawking again, to bring in money.

Dad would get up from his chair, would bang into the centre table, walk into the walls, his hands outstretched, his mouth open, trying bravely to fight his blindness. Against my pleas, he insisted on going out, and I would be forced to lead him by the hand, as if we were a pair of beggars. He made me take him to the toilet, to the compound-front, so that he could get some sunlight on his eyes. His frustration made him want to go out further into the street, and he would tread through obstacles with a bizarre obstinacy. He made

215

me take him to Madame Koto's bar, because he wanted to give her a good piece of his mind. And when I refused he set off by himself, stumbling into stalls, tripping over empty milk cans, walking into patches of mud. Then, suddenly, he would stand in the middle of the street, swearing that he saw spirits moving through him as if they were light passing through glass. With his hands always stretched out, he was assaulted by all the sounds of the world that he had never paid much attention to, and the children baited him as if he were an animal. But nothing deterred him. He wandered through ghosts wearing yellow eye-patches. He began feverishly describing the city of the blind, with its seaport and its fishes swimming in the air, its one-armed musicians playing blue accordions and asking him for money, its beggars with one eye in the middle of their foreheads, its large tortoises with red-rimmed glasses. He staggered to Madame Koto's bar through a universe in which old warriors rehearsed battle movements in yellow fields. I went with him, guiding him when I could, and often he pushed me away, mistaking me for a legless beggar. When he got to Madame Koto's barfront, he began to rain imprecations down on everyone, thrashing his arms about. He confused me with his rage, for while he stood at Madame Koto's barfront he actually thought he was before the palace of a diseased and hidden king. He saw masks riddled with holes everywhere and statues ravaged by woodworm. He abused the minions of the queen. He called attention to her rotting womb, in which children shrank from being born. He shouted about a pool of blood in front of the monstrous palace which the sun couldn't dry. He said strange maggots had started to grow on the blood and crawl about the place, maggots which seemed indestructible, for when you cut them both halves took on their own lives, and when you burned them new maggot eggs would start to move about in the ash. Dad poured out such abuses and terrifying notions that even the thugs who had previously feared his reputation – whose minds were being over-

216

whelmed with the cries of the dead man, the smell of his blood, the pool of his blood which seemed to attract secret earth-liquids to itself, the pool which had become a vast red patch, thick on the surface, with minute fishes and worms making its outward cohesion bristle – even the thugs who were becoming frightened of the dead man could not restrain themselves under the assault of dad's words. And when they realised that dad had been struck blind, when they saw him casting about, his face lined with agitation and agony, they set upon him with sticks and metal and proceeded to give him a savage beating.

But dad's blindness only multiplied his energies and his rage. He threw them off. A punch sent one of the men flying into the pool of blood. When the man got up blood dripped from his hair and he began to scream that the maggots were eating up his face. Ignoring the firewood landing on his head, the blows falling on his wooden face, dad pursued the scream-ing man, caught him, and pounded him into unconsciousness. The others should have known that dad gets more powerful the more his disadvantages increase, but they didn't. They jumped on him, and he swung them round and flung one of them right through the front door of the bar, and hurled another against Madame Koto's new car, his head smashing the side window. They came at him again, and dad released a thunderous cry, and for a moment it made them pause. But others rushed in with machetes and long poles and dad would most certainly have become one of the unnumbered dead if the people of the street hadn't come to his rescue, throwing stones and bricks at the thugs, forcing most of them to beat an undignified retreat. Meanwhile, dad flailed about, his voice fearless, shouting of the glories of battle. And when a solid punch from an ex-boxer connected with dad's chin, he was momentarily immobilised. He was stock-still. His eyes swam, his mouth drooled and, risking my head being chopped off in the confusion of battle, I rushed to him. When I caught his hand, he awoke from his immobility, and said:

217

'My son, we are in the most wonderful city.'

'We are in trouble, dad,' I said.

'Everything is covered in gold,' he replied.

'Like where?'

He pointed up to the sky, to an empty space where the clouds were thin beneath the fiery sun.

'There!' he cried. 'There the trees bear fruits of precious stones.'

Someone cracked me on the head from behind, crushing me to the floor. Dad was still pointing at different places of the sky and earth, the battle raging around him.

'There!' he cried again. 'There is a man eating a rainbow. And there is a woman just like Madame Koto with worms crawling out of her ears. She has jade eyes.'

He was turning around, naming the mysterious golden city of the blind, when a man brought a thick piece of firewood down on his head. I cried out too late. Dad crumpled at my feet. When he touched the ground, he jumped up again suddenly, as if the earth had somehow regenerated him. He went running and growling in all directions, flailing, swearing. Then he stumbled over the corpse. He got up and the people of our street rushed over and held him and hustled him away before the full fury of the political mob fell on him and deprived us of his mad energies. While he was being whisked away, mum appeared amongst us. I don't know how. And as dad went, tripping, cursing, refusing to be treated like a blind man, walking off into the bushes, submitting himself to mum's voice, I heard him swearing that he would never go to Madame Koto's place again, that the pact with her involving us had been broken for ever. And now he wanted the whole world to broadcast the fact that Madame Koto, Queen of the ghetto, Ruler of a new religion, had just acquired her most terrible adversary. He shouted the fact so loudly, knocking the heads of his protectors with his blind misdirected rage, that those who were helping left his side, and it fell to mum to guide her

218

uncontrollable storm of a husband back to our compound.

Dad astonished us that day. He swore that our room was the great atrium of a fabulous palace. The walls were draped with rich cloth. There were bloodstones in the eyes of warrior statues. The ceiling was glorious with royal chandeliers. Twinkling glass was everywhere, and even his three-legged chair was a mighty velvet sofa. And as he described the great atrium of his blindness, marvelling at how much and how miraculously our lives had improved, how our true royal condition had finally caught up with our poverty, mum looked at me with an expression that seemed to wonder if it wasn't better in some ways that dad retained his blindness and his enchanted palace rather than live again in the dreariness that sight would bring.

CHAPTER FIVE

———

The Secret Agony of Tygers

D AD BECAME HUMBLE in the presence of his mysterious kingdom. Everywhere he turned he saw his subjects. Mythic
warrior-kings, long dead, paid visits to his court. They came
with ritual beads thick round their necks, their crowns so
weighty that they couldn't walk without the help of their
royal entourage. Dad made us realise that there was much
in common between kings and the blind. In his kingdom,
dad was a prince. He spoke of our obscure royal birth, of
mum being a princess of a small kingdom in the country. He
spoke of his father as being one of the heirs to the throne in
his home town. Everywhere dad saw animals with crowns on
their heads. He saw tigers and leopards, lions and jaguars. He
saw hunters who went out into the forests and who returned
with boars that had tusks of bronze, ostriches with lapis lazuli
eyes, unicorns with horns of topaz. There were many beautiful women in his court, and they were his handmaidens. They
bathed him with milk and saffron oil. They were so beautiful
that dad became suspicious of them. Sitting in his three-legged
chair, he followed them in his mind as they went out for the
afternoon. He noticed that as soon as they entered the forest
they turned into wonderful antelopes. Dad spoke of the
rich gift of songs they brought back to him from their other
kingdom.

Sometimes his eyes hurt so much that he said there were
butterflies in his head trying to get out. Sometimes the world
drifted in a great bowl of milk. He swore that Ade came to him
and begged him to bury his father. Then he began to speak
of something growing in his eyes. He kept trying to get

220

it out and we had to restrain him. Eventually, for his own good, we got some of the compound men to tie his hands behind his back. Dad would sit silently, surveying the peaceful splendour of his kingdom. Apparently, he had fifteen children and three wives and he kept getting their names confused. Mum watched him, marvelling. And I watched him knowing that something had struck his head and had burst open a strange door that opened him to fragments of another life.

Sometimes when he was quiet we were afraid for him. His silence became deep and unfathomable. His breathing became shallow. We never knew if he slept at night. He would sit there in his chair, his eyes open, and he would spend hours talking to his father who he said was right there in the room. They had long conversations in a language that even dad couldn't properly understand. Sometimes dad spoke about a stream with the moon as a canoe which his father was paddling. Sometimes he sat still, his facial muscles all bunched up, his sweat dampening the air. He would sit up deep into the night, re-dreaming the world, and I would be unable to follow him on his crepuscular journeys to the remote places of his vision.

We were very sad for him. He didn't eat, didn't drink, and even the mosquito coil began to enrage him. Through all this, mum carried on with the hawking of her meagre provisions, treading the endless winding roads that led to new settlements, her feet blistering on the heated sand and stones, her face darkening under the onslaught of sun-strokes. And when she returned exhausted she would sometimes suffer the bizarre transferences of dad's blindness, and for twenty minutes she would see holes in objects and walls and in me.

Dad stayed silent and often I tried to console him by reading aloud from books on precious stones and Egyptian astrology. At no point during all this did he want the door shut.

221

Sometimes he amazed us by saying that he could see the wind.

'The wind has many colours,' he would say. 'When the weather is cool, the wind is red. When it is hot, the wind is blue. But the colours keep flowing and they can be very beautiful. And when a bad neighbour is passing our door-front, the colour of the wind changes a little.'

Then after a long silence he would cry out and say:

'Everything is alive.'

We would wait for him to continue. After two hours, when we had completely forgotten the original statement, he would say:

'The table has been listening to us. The walls have senses. The ceiling has eyes. The bed breathes and suffers all our tossing and all our dreams. The secret stories of our lives are stored in all these pots and pans and spoons. My boots know more about me than I do.'

Then he would be silent. After another five minutes he would say:

'This chair I am sitting on has been talking to me, releasing its stories. It used to belong to an Englishman who died in this country. He died of malaria. He had a child by one of our women and he disowned the poor boy. His wife didn't enjoy sex. The chair then travelled from the expatriate quarters of the city and passed through two families and was nearly burned when a house caught fire. Then it was stolen, then sold, and I don't know how it got here.'

There was another pause. Fearing it would go on for ever, I asked:

'What about your kingdom?'

'What kingdom?' he said.

I stayed silent. The evening darkened the room. Dad forbade us to light a candle, saying it made the darkness in his eyes worse. We ate in the darkness, listening to the corpse of Ade's father getting more bloated with the night. Later, as the wind blew its strange colours into our room, I saw the form of Madame Koto standing on dad's head.

'I am carrying a mountain,' dad said.

He became sober. He shrank into himself. His neck disappeared. Nothing I did could budge Madame Koto's form from dad's head. And as the night grew deeper dad began to cry, but he disguised the pain in a weird kind of laughter which made mum's jaws ache. Her eyes burned in the darkness, and mum saw more as dad saw less. The uncanny transferences began to operate again. The weight pressed down on dad, and we found it hard to move: my limbs became heavy, as if I were a boy in an elephant's body; and mum walked with an unbearable lassitude, as if she were two years pregnant with twins. The weight on dad made me sweat all the time. At night I heard him grinding his teeth and we had to keep waking him up because we feared his teeth might crumble in his mouth. Our sleep became oppressed. In our dreams we were unable to move or speak. It seemed as if the house was actually on top of us all through the night. In the morning it came as a shock to find that dad's hair was flattened and his scalp bleeding. There had been nothing visibly on him. Dad complained of excruciating headaches and as it grew worse he spoke of being in an unrecognisable country where people were thrown in fires or thrown to crocodiles, in a city where the poor lived in caves. He said our room was a catacomb and that there were worms on the walls. He rejected the plate of fried bushmeat we gave him, saying that it was a live animal, and the rice we fed him made him cry out again, saying:

'EVERYTHING IS ALIVE!'

He spoke of tormentors everywhere. He said a wizard was whipping him with a lash made of crocodile hide. We didn't believe him at first, but when we looked at his back we were horrified to find it covered in fresh welts. Other times he said the wizard was making razor incisions on his flesh and we noticed that he came out in strange cuts and blisters.

'Fight them!' I said. 'Fight them, Black Tyger!'

'I am a blind Tyger,' he replied gravely.

I saw dad's spirit shrink, and his other form became smaller as Madame Koto's form became greater on his head.

'I see blood everywhere,' said dad.

His eyes had turned red. I stared into them intently.

'A seven-headed spirit is staring at me,' he said.

I began to cry.

'Shut up,' he said. 'That noise makes the weight on my head heavier.'

I fell silent, swallowing my tears. After a while mum began to sing in a low voice. She sang sweetly and her voice made me sad. I didn't understand her song.

'Don't sing for me,' dad growled. 'There is blood in my ears.'

Mum stopped singing. We didn't look in his ears to see if what he said was true. We were very afraid. Dad began to moan. He held his head. As the pain grew worse, he said:

'The wizard is hammering a nail into my ear-drums.'

Mum opened her mouth in alarm. Dad continued:

'My head is full of pressures. I am breathing the air of diamonds.'

We stared at him, wondering what he was going to say next. His silence expanded the spaces in our heads. I became quite terrified of dad's blindness.

Sometimes, as I stared at him intensely, his blindness would enter me for a moment, and I would make out the solitary form of an angel hovering just below our ceiling. Dad would suddenly cry:

'I can see!'

At that precise moment the angel's form would dissolve. Already, dad had jumped up, his face brightening with a diamond joy. My eyes cleared. Then dad would sit down again, disconsolately, and in a scared voice he would say:

'It's gone. The darkness has returned. All I see now is the wind stirring just beneath the ceiling.'

It became so bad that mum began to talk of getting a herbalist to treat dad. She mentioned a few names, outlining the awesomeness of their reputations. Dad refused such treatment. He swore. He accused mum of trying to get herbalists of dubious politics to make his blindness permanent. He went on and on, ranting about how we were making faces at him, mocking his blindness, sticking feathers in his hair, tickling his nose, shadow-boxing round him, and blowing hot air into his eyes. We were dumbfounded by his accusations. And when we failed to deny them he took them for the truth. He wouldn't let us touch him. He became suspicious of the food. He demanded that we tell him our exact positions at any given moment. This went on for a whole day. When he slept, snoring heavily, he would wake up all of a sudden, calling my name, saying that an angel was offering him precious stones. He wouldn't take them. And when the angel left, Madame Koto started to dance on his head.

'Take me outside,' he cried. 'This room is full of demons!'

I led him out into the street. Neighbours greeted us, offering profuse condolences, and dad growled at them.

'Who was that?' dad asked, after a particular neighbour had gone.

I told him.

'I never knew how ugly he was till I couldn't see him,' dad said.

Then as I led him down the street he asked me to describe things to him. He wanted the minutest details about objects and the world. I did my best, and dad kept saying:

'It's not the same place. Nothing is the same. What colour is the sky?'

I tried to describe its mixture of lilac and brutish gold.

'Even the sky has changed. I see it as green. What about the road? Describe it.'

I tried again and he shook his head as if everything were betraying him, and he said:

'The road is like a river. It won't keep still. It keeps moving. Where is it going, eh?'

'I don't know.'

'Take me to the front of Madame Koto's bar and tell me what is happening.'

I didn't want to take him there. For the past three days a terrible smell had been drifting over from the area in front of the bar. We had heard that at night strange forms had been converging above the bushes where I had last seen the corpse. Nightmares went there to get fat and, like birds with monstrous wings, they circled around Madame Koto's bar and widened their flight to the rest of the street. We no longer went near the bushes at night, but the place became the centre of our discontent and unease. In the evenings, when the forest began to speak in nocturnal murmurs, people with ragged clothes and bad dreams raw in their eyes gathered there. They waited, and watched, and were silent. None of those who went while there was still some light in the sky, none of those who were unaccountably magnetised by the rumours of the dark converging forms, not one of them noticed the bad smell. Apparently, it got less the closer you were to its source. No one noticed the smell any more, and no one spoke. They were like a brooding Greek chorus that had been deprived of speech.

I took dad to three different places, deceiving him that he was in front of Madame Koto's bar, and each time with increasing anger he said that he couldn't see the palace of his enemy. When we finally got there he became agitated, pointing at trees that bore garnet fruits, pointing at the palace gates with their beautiful bronze statue of a half man, half crocodile. He kept asking me to describe what I saw and when I did he marvelled at how different it was from what he perceived. He kept asking me questions about colours, angles, textures, shadow forms. He saw ghosts

226

where I saw bushes. He saw a fountain of yellow light where I saw the pool of stagnant blood. Plants with streaks of lilac had flowered in the pool. I described everything dutifully – everything except the corpse, which I never looked at, and never saw. But by its shadow, which was a form surrounding it – solid in the muted orange lights of the dust-peppered evening – by its shadow I knew that the corpse was bloating and growing fat with all the fevers and bad dreams of the road.

Dad asked me about the corpse, which he had heard about, and couldn't remember.

'Is it there?'

'It has walked away,' I said.

'Where to?'

'To another city.'

'What city?'

'A city of gold.'

Dad hit me on the head.

'Look!' he said. 'Tell me if it is there.'

I looked. I couldn't see it. I told him so.

'I can smell a corpse,' he said. 'It must be there.'

'It's not. I can't see anything,' I said.

Dad cocked his ears.

'I can hear something singing. The song is coming from the ground.'

'It's the wind.'

'I know the songs of the wind. This one is different.'

He pointed in the direction of the shadows.

'It's only the flies,' I said.

'Can flies sing?'

'Yes.'

'In one voice?'

'Yes.'

'Like a human being?'

'Yes.'

He was silent. He listened again.

227

'Whatever is singing is asking me not to forget him. Is someone there?'

'No.'

'Are you sure?'

'Yes.'

'What do you see then?'

'Only the road and the flies.'

'Describe the flies.'

'They are big and blue and they have strange eyes.'

'What is strange about their eyes?'

'I don't know.'

'Are the flies looking at me?'

'A lizard is looking at you.'

'Describe it.'

'It has a red tail and a yellow mark on its head.'

'Can you catch it?'

'Why?'

'It is talking to me.'

'I can't catch it.'

'Why not?'

'The darkness is coming and I don't want to leave you alone.'

Dad was silent. Behind us, around us, the sullen brooding crowd were themselves becoming shadows. They seemed to be dissolving. Their faces were like the lineaments of ancient soapstone statues. Their eyes were dull.

'Something is going to happen,' dad said. 'I can smell it.'

'Let's go home,' I said. 'The clouds are coming down. It's going to rain.'

'I can't smell rain.'

I tried to drag dad home, but he was immovable. He had acquired immense weight. As I was pulling him he suddenly snatched his hand from mine and, staggering towards Madame Koto's bar, began to bellow out his challenges. He defied her to send the worst of her demons and wizards, he shouted that he was ready for anything she could hurl at

228

him, and that not everyone would keep silent for ever. He went quite berserk, stamping one way, staggering another, shouting and foaming. It took all the silent gathered people to hold him, and it took mum whispering something in his ears to restrain him. The moment dad stopped raging, he cried out that the weight on his head had multiplied. Everyone thought he had gone completely mad. Dad had challenged Madame Koto in public, but she had replied to him in secret, and in silence.

Dad carried Madame Koto's weight home, carried it in his sleep, and woke up to it. But that evening, as we led him home, he could barely move. His eyes bulged as if his secret agony would make them burst out of their sockets. The veins in his eyes were blue and green.

I never saw dad more sober than he looked that evening. The shadow-minions of Madame Koto surrounded us, followed us home, filling our footsteps, measuring the psychic vibrations of our souls. Dad was very sober and he walked as if he were a midget in a world of monoliths. He cowered from the empty spaces. Noises antagonised him. The wind made him tremble. He was even scared of the leaves that were blown into his face.

The weight on him made him humble for a whole day. He never went out. He never spoke. His agony began to affect us and mum complained of a black rock in her brain. But like a lamb, dad did everything we told him to do. He retreated from our world. His shadow grew smaller.

Meanwhile, the season was changing, and the preparations for the great rally were moving steadily towards their climax. And a new cycle of time was beginning. It announced itself with another inexplicable plague and a smell of sulphur in the air.

CHAPTER SIX

A Plague of Blindness

I T WASN'T ONLY dad who was overcome with the fear of shadows. We had all become afraid of the corpse. We were afraid of breathing in its air and its silence. We feared that it was spreading death in the atmosphere, sowing it in our eyes, reaping it in our dreams. And because we were so afraid and so cowardly, we stopped looking at the corpse.

The activities for the rally became hectic at the barfront. Fire-eaters, somersaulters, soft-limbed dancers performed in bright-coloured dresses to the beating of drums, while Madame Koto's stomach grew bigger, while her bad foot split the plaster-cast, and while the dead man rotted on our street. None of us looked at the body as we hurried past the bushes, and a great infernal stink settled over our houses. Not even the winds that made the trees bend could move the smell. We made no reference to the body and we stopped using the word death.

Then one day we heard that the body had gone. The first person to say this publicly went blind that very night. The smell of sulphur increased the darkness in the evenings. Those who went past the bushes and came back to tell us that the body had disappeared were struck with blindness. It wasn't long before the ordinary inhabitants of our area began to go about the place with their hands outstretched, feeling the empty air, saying that everything had changed, and that minor spirits with large heads and kwashiorkor stomachs were passing through our buildings as if they were transparent.

We woke up one morning to find that a mysterious plague

of blindness had struck our community after we had stopped seeing the dead body. In the mornings or in the afternoons, in the midst of daily tasks, we heard people crying out that they couldn't see. No one went to their aid because of the fear of its transference. The blindness spread like the night, invading the carpenters, the street traders, the hawkers and the butchers. We heard stories of children who were born blind. We heard stories of hawkers who went down the streets, selling their wares, with children leading them. The blind multiplied in our street. Then the nightmares which grew fat over the bushes began to appear amongst us with quickened wings, swooping into our midst, flying over our houses, entering our rooms, dwelling with us, eating our food before we did, drinking our wells dry, spreading the pungent sulphurous smell into our living spaces. The nightmares became our companions. They came with red eyes and weird vegetable growths on their disgusting bodies. We could no longer bear our rooms. In the evenings the inhabitants began to go out into the street. No one spoke of the plague or the unbearable smell.

Dad was silent through it all. He sat in his chair, in a royal solitude, weaving in and out of his new kingdom, suffering his agony with a curious timidity, asking no questions, and doing everything we asked. His body began to lose its forceful presence.

'The dead are more alive than the living are,' he said one night.

His pain had opened a door in his spirit. He spoke of strange animals with diamonds round their necks. They wandered around in our room. That night mum went out and didn't return till we were fast asleep. In the morning I noticed that she too had changed. Her acceptance made her sadder. That evening she went out again, and when she came back I could smell the forest on her clothes. There was a new moon out and when it was brightest in the night sky the corpse began to sing.

CHAPTER SEVEN

The Light of the Dead

I TOLD DAD ABOUT the corpse singing. He listened intently through his pain, and said:

'That is the road singing. Everyone should be careful.'

As the night grew darker the song of the corpse became more intense, and sweeter. It made the room hot. I found it difficult to sleep. As I listened to the solitary voice of the abandoned corpse I began to feel quite ill. That night the room glowed with a little green light in the dark. The light had nothing to do with dad, who sat in his chair, disappearing under the invisible weight. It had nothing to do with mum, who became more compact in her inexplicable stillness. Something was being born in our living spaces. The little light kept flitting about the room. It shot past my face and I saw it as a phosphorescent fire which didn't hurt.

'The moon is burning our room,' I said.

'It's not the moon,' mum said. 'It's the fire of sorcerers.'

The light hovered over the centre table.

'I can see it!' dad cried. 'It is a wandering spirit, a soul that has lost its body. My father always told me that when I see this light I should know that there is a person who is dead and who is trying to be buried.'

'A child trying to be born,' mum added.

Then, suddenly, the light went out through the open door.

'I can still see it,' dad said again. 'A spirit is trying to tell us something.'

After a while mum got up and, saying words we couldn't hear, went out into the passageway. I followed her. She went to the housefront. The street was covered in rubbish again.

The inhabitants, under the spell of blindness, had begun to dump their refuse everywhere. In the backyard, near the well, two men, recently blind, were talking while the moon cast a spectral bewitchment on their faces. Mum went down the street. In front of her I saw the phosphorescent little light flitting over the road, darting all over the place, while the solitary voice sang from the bushes. Nightmares deepened the shadows in the air. The moonlight brightened the road as if it were a river of silver reflections. Mum followed the erratic light, and I followed her.

The world was silent except for the corpse singing and the jackals baying somewhere at the other end of the forest. Mum went past Madame Koto's place and alongside the forest till she came to the marshes where a crocodile lay dead on a fallen tree. Mum didn't see the dead crocodile. Maybe I'm the only one who did. When the erratic light reached the marshes it became two, and the two lights became three, and they darted everywhere, sometimes colliding. Mum stopped near the invisible crocodile and watched the lights. Then she turned and went into the forest.

I followed her till I came to a black rock which not even the moon could illuminate. The rock gave off the living smell of a great human body and when I touched it I was amazed to find that it was sweating. I drew back and noticed that curious-looking flowers were growing on the rock. The horror of it knocked me backwards and I banged my head against a tree. Almost immediately afterwards, I heard voices inside the dark stony mass; and I went round it three times, but I saw nothing. Then I drew closer, and put my ear up against it, and listened. When I heard my heart beating inside the rock, I gave a startled cry, and jumped back. And when I recovered, alarmed by the certainty that the rock was alive, I fled from its monstrous freakishness.

The forest was silent. The trees watched me with blind eyes. The wind was quiet. I couldn't find mum. After running for a few moments, I stopped. I stayed still and let the world re-align itself about me. I watched spiders weaving their webs from threads of moonlight. A bird swooped over me and when it had gone I noticed the little green light flitting across the forest floor. I followed it silently, tripping over climbers. The leaves of medicinal plants cut me with their serrated edges.

The corpse had stopped singing and the moonlight made me sweat. The green light danced among the leaves and eventually led me back to the crocodile with its head on the tree trunk. Jumping everywhere like a compact and luminous butterfly, the light wandered to the marshes and skated over the shadow of bushes, dimming when under the power of the moon, brightening when under the power of the earth. Away from the forest, further up the street, it gathered more light to itself. Then it hovered over a dense whale-like form under the bushes, and suddenly stopped. I noticed that there were more lights around. They were bigger than fireflies, and more intense. They kept moving round the hidden form like eyes without faces.

The moonlight made the forest shimmer, made the air limpid, and it shone on the rooftops with a hallucinatory sheen. The moonlight made all metallic objects sharp with points of unmoving lights, it made the eyes of cats and dogs a little deranged, it made all things weave, but not even the moon with its omnipotent democracy could light up the solid whale-like form beneath the bushes.

Surrounded by errant green lights, I looked around. The area seemed transformed. There was a white heat in my eyes. I couldn't seem to blink. My eyes were stuck fast, wide open, unable to shut, and my brain was momentarily paralysed. Incomprehension flooded me. The delirium of lights was all about me, luminous without heat, alive without bodies, intense without intention. Then something very peculiar happened to me as I stood there under the bewilderment of an intoxicated moon. I couldn't move. I was rooted to the quivering road. Everything began to sizzle. The wind was still.

Suddenly, two green lights, the size of needle points, flew into my eyes, burning my eyeballs. It was as if bitterwood ash had been blown into my brain. Tears flowed down my face. The world was silent. The moon, fertilising me with incandescent hallucinations, planted strange words in my head, words that hinted at the near impossibility of seeing clearly.

I have no idea how long I was rooted to the road, but when I heard something gliding on the ground near me, I was surprised to find that I could turn my head. And to my horror I saw the black form glowing in the dark. There was a white snake stretched out over its length. The snake had eyes of liquid diamonds, and it was staring at me. I jumped in fright and fell and hit my head on the ground. But before I could cry out, I heard the road raging, and I heard the dissonant wailing of the forest spirits, angry at the loss of their companions.

The air turned sinister. The moon spread the incredible stench of a body in advanced decomposition. And when I got up, my head reeling from the fury of the sulphurous smells, I saw the corpse for the first time in seven days.

The night was a forest of disembodied eyes. My head was full of grating noises. While my teeth chattered the snake slid off the corpse and drew itself across the road and disappeared into the forest undergrowth. The corpse was bright under the moonlight. It was a mystery how it always seemed hidden. The dead man had bloated and his feet had split his shoes. His trousers and shirt had burst at the seams. His eyes, still open, were large like two diseased mangoes. And a mush-room, bright yellow, had sprouted from his navel. All sorts of obscene flowers sprouted in my brain. All sorts of harsh voices gnashed in my ears. A strange peppery heat fanned my face.

Everywhere I looked I saw the dead man's eyes. And with the boiling rage of the road crashing in my head, the fevers of forest spirits goading my thoughts, and with isolated cries all around me, I ran home as fast as I could, stumbling, but not falling, over the debris in the dark. The errant lights were now everywhere. Insects crawled on my living flesh. The moon made the air shimmer with a new clarity.

CHAPTER EIGHT

A Good Man Has to Be
Blind Before He Can See

WHEN I GOT home I found dad staggering around the room with his hands outstretched, talking to the green lights that weren't there, talking and laughing like a madman. The room looked as if a malign storm had paid a visit. The table and chair were upturned, the mattress had been hurled from the bed, the bed had been wrenched from its position, the cupboard was tipped over. Dad charged round the room, kicking things, throwing clothes and pots about the place, muttering under the influence of an incoherent fever. I held him round the waist and he dragged me all over the room as if he were a deranged bull and I kept telling him that the corpse of Ade's father was still there but he wouldn't listen to me because of his new obsession with the fires of sorcerers and the wandering souls. I was very afraid of dad that night because the world was changing and the moon was beginning to brand itself on everything. And it was only when I let go of his waist and sank to the ground, weeping and wailing, that dad heard me and came to me and felt for my eyes and wiped the tears from my face. Then he lifted me up and held me to him so tight it was as if he wanted us to become one person. When his obsession had cooled, and I knew that he was listening, I said:

'Dad, the dead body is still there.'

He put me down. He felt for his chair, and couldn't find it. I found it for him. When he sat down, he said:

'But you told me it had walked away.'

237

'It has come back.'

He was silent. I lit a candle. I straightened the centre table. Dad looked doubtful.

'Did you see it walk back?'

'No.'

'Then how do you know it came back?'

'Because I saw it.'

'With what?'

I didn't understand. His question confused me. Then he said:

'What happened to the light?'

'What light?'

'The fire of sorcerers. The light that was flying about the room like a sign.'

'I don't know.'

'It was a wonderful light,' he said. 'A homeless miraculous light. Did you see it?'

'Yes.'

'Where did it go?'

'It went away.'

'Where to?'

'To the dead man.'

'What dead man?'

'Ade's father.'

'Is he dead?'

'Yes. You know he is dead. You saw him die.'

'Did I?'

'Yes.'

'Very strange. I don't remember.'

'But you were there.'

'Is that so?'

'Yes.'

'And the light went to him.'

'Yes.'

'To do what?'

'I don't know.'

Dad sighed. He seemed very confused indeed. And he seemed quite aged when he said:

'When the light comes back, tell me. I am very tired. I feel as if I have been dreaming for three years.'

Then he fell silent for a long time. The candle kept spitting. I watched dad. He had begun to snore with his eyes open.

I put out the candle and listened to the wind blowing hard. I listened to the silence beneath the wind, wondering what had happened to mum. Everything was dark. I shut my eyes. Time must have passed. When I opened my eyes again, the darkness was still there. I didn't move. Then I heard mum's footsteps coming down the passageway. When she entered the room I smelt a strong aroma of leaves and bark, medicinal herbs and the sleeping earth. She noticed the chaos in the room, the mattress flung on the floor, the scattered clothes, but she said nothing. Her hair was wet. She still had the moonlight on her face. A radiant lilac brilliance faintly shone round her cheeks. She came over to me, and crouched. Overwhelming me with the nocturnal aroma of forest vegetation, and speaking in a soothing voice which lifted the heat of ashes and fevers from my brain, she said:

'Look!'

In her open palms, glowing like incandescent moonstones, like disembodied eyes alight with rainbow sheen, were two errant fires of sorcerers that she had captured.

'How did you catch them?' I asked.

'They came to me.'

'Where?'

'In the forest.'

Dad moved on the chair. We both looked at him. I could see his face in the half-darkness. His eyes were still open. His mouth was also open, but he wasn't drooling.

'What are you going to do with them?'

'Put them in your father's eyes.'

239

'Why?'

'To help him see again.'

'Won't they burn him?'

'They will burn out his blindness.'

'Are you going to put them in now?'

Mum looked at dad again, and then back at me. Mum had become a fire. Her whole being was alive. She seemed like a secret priestess of the moon. The intensity of her presence made me feel as if I were floating on limpid air.

'Yes, but we have to wake him up first.'

We were silent. Then, suddenly, in the dark, his eyes still open, dad said:

'What are you two conspirators talking about, eh?'

'Nothing,' I said.

Mum lit the candle. Dad was sweating profusely.

'I am covered in witch's piss,' he said.

'We are going to cure you,' I ventured.

'Of what?'

'Your eyes.'

While dad thought about it, mum suddenly started to become transformed. She became more erect. An intense energy emanated from her, brightening her face. When she stood up she looked very serene. Then, as if she were in a secret space, enacting a secret ritual, she began muttering words to herself, the same words. Her movements became both fluid and definite. I couldn't make out the words, but she uttered them rapidly, altering her own energies. The words made the candle flare. And then, in a dream-like voice, mum said:

'I was in the forest. There was a rock inside my head. I saw an old woman who had fallen on her back and couldn't get up. She was very old and she was crying. When she saw me she asked me to help her. I was very scared . . .'

'What were you doing in the forest?' dad interrupted.

Mum continued, without answering his question.

'The old woman stank like a dead body. She was very

ugly and she had the face of a rotting owl. But something made me want to help her. As I bent down to help her up, she seized my neck with her bony hands. She didn't let go of me till I had taken her to a hut deep in the forest. There were birds asleep on the roof. Everywhere on the ground outside the hut there were white eggs. On her wooden bed there were black eggs. When I helped her on to the bed she began to cough. When she stopped coughing she began to laugh. She had sores all over her body and it occurred to me that she was blind. Her mouth stank like a vulture. She said: "You people are all blind because you don't use your eyes." I was surprised. "What about you?" I asked her. She didn't answer. Looking at me with eyes like those of a strange bird, she said, pointing at me: "I know your husband. He likes to fight. Sometimes I watch him training here in the forest. He thinks I am an eagle. He is a good man, but he is also a fool. That's why he is blind. A good man first has to be blind before he can see." Then she laughed again. Then she said: "I have got a message for your husband. One day a great animal will visit him. Tell him to take care of it. The animal will show him some of the wonders of the earth." Then she gave me two lights of sorcerers. "Put these in his eyes. Tell him to bathe with alum and kaoline. He has a strange destiny and he is the only one who can stop the plague of blindness." Not long afterwards the old woman became different. She started to shout at me as if I were her worst enemy: "Leave my house now!" she said. "Leave now, before I turn you into a goat!" I ran away from her hut, and didn't stop till I got home.'

When mum finished there was a long silence. Without any ceremony, dad rose from his chair and asked us to fetch him alum and kaoline. Mum had already purchased some. Dad went out with his towel and after a while he came back. He couldn't find his way. I led him to the bathroom and waited for him to finish bathing and led him back to the room.

'The world is full of new lights. There are more colours

on this earth than the eyes can see,' he said. 'When you see too much you become blind.'

We waited for dad to oil himself and dress. And when he had settled back in his chair, mum began the ritual of his unblinding. After uttering her strange words seven times, after she had prayed to the angel of women, mum pressed the two lights into dad's eyes. He screamed. Then he shouted that we were burning his eyeballs with bitterwood ash. The lights stung him. They made his eyes red, then yellowish, then greenish. While he groaned me and mum tidied the mess that his storm had created in the room.

All through the night green liquids poured out of dad's eyes. He couldn't sleep and it was a wonder that he stayed silent, rocking his head, while his eyes flamed, while the invisible weight pressed down on him, and while the cuts became sores on his face.

In the morning he went around flailing, screaming that he had flames in his eyes, that the fire of sorcerers was burning his brain, turning his old thoughts into green ash. Apart from the pain, the lights had no effect on dad's eyes. He was as blind as ever. We were bitterly disappointed. Mum stayed silent. Every now and again, she looked at us sheepishly. She had returned to her normal personality. When dad screamed about rocks in his eyes, fire in his brain, all we could do was stare at him. He was in utter agony for three days.

CHAPTER NINE

A Day of Half-miracles

T HAT MORNING, HOWEVER, the whole street was talking about the lights they had seen flying about in their rooms. Clusters of blind neighbours, with crude walking sticks in their hands, stood at housefronts, gesticulating excitedly, speculating about the marvellous lights. Some of them had seen yellow balls of fire, some had seen blue flames, others said they watched green lights wandering in the mist of their blindness. They all agreed, however, that the lights vanished after midnight.

Driven by the fever of the new day, I went from one group to another, telling them that the corpse had returned. The ones that hadn't yet been struck by the plague shouted at me. Others knocked me on the head and drove me away. But wherever I went, repeating the words that had grown roots in my brain, people began to leave. It was as if I was the bringer of a new plague. I carried on saying the words and when no one listened I began to cry. Some of our neighbours jumped on me from behind and sealed my mouth with strips of cloth and tied my hands behind my back. Mum eventually freed me and when I told her what had happened she admonished me, saying:

'There are some things people don't want to hear. Why don't you learn to shut your mouth, eh?'

I tried to explain to her that the words seemed to come out of their own accord, that it wasn't really me who was speaking them, but she wouldn't listen. Mum was very strange that morning and I wasn't sure if her odd behaviour didn't have something to do with her failed attempt to cure dad's blindness.

It wasn't only mum who was strange. The whole world was somewhat bad-tempered that day. Shopkeepers put up the prices of their goods. Landlords sent word round that the rents were going to be increased. People were brusque with one another, and arguments broke out all over the place. The presence of the corpse became more monumental in our lives, and not even the wonder of the errant lights lasted till the afternoon.

It was also a day of half-miracles. Women in white filed silently down our street and disappeared into the forest. Someone shouted that they had seen a one-eyed boar in their backyard. We rushed there, and found nothing. A woman said that she had heard knocks on her door the previous night, and when she opened it she beheld a man with bloated eyes. She had screamed, people came rushing with lamps, they saw nothing, and put it down to a vivid dream which she had confused with reality. And when another man, recently blind, said that he had seen a ghost, people merely laughed and asked where he bought his ogogoro.

Looking back on the previous night it seemed to me that there had been two real miracles. The first was that Madame Koto, fatigued by her swelling foot and the widening domain of her power, entirely left our night-spaces to the spells of the moon. And the second miracle was that no one had seen the nightmares flying about in our lives like birds with primeval wings.

The heat was mild that afternoon. No one gathered outside the fabulous bar where men with masks of bulls and crocodiles performed their mock wrestling matches or their somersaulting dances. People spoke of the taste of ash in their mouths. Children were invaded by visions of spirits in caravans, with veils glittering in a silvery sheen over the faces of dead women. Eggs were found to have worms in them and the blind old man appeared amongst us saying that he had swallowed a diamond. The smell of the decomposing corpse had become part of our air and at dusk we had a complete shock when the wind blew over to us the shrill noise of the corpse singing.

The moon was out early and parts of the sky seemed to bleed with the fierceness of the evening. The clouds were stained with a brilliance of red. And when the corpse started singing the people of our area woke up temporarily from their long and impenetrable sleep.

The half-miracles became omens that drew the blind together, and for the first time they acknowledged the existence of the corpse and the necessity of its burial. No one referred to the corpse directly, but we all understood. And as the evening made the face of the moon brighter the community of the blind gathered to have meetings about the corpse. They argued for a long time. We could hear them from ten houses away. And when the offspring of dissension went amongst them, sowing confusion, they argued with bitter vehemence. It was strange to hear how ferociously and with what certainty the blind disagree.

CHAPTER TEN

The Perverse Justice of the Poor

T HAT EVENING DAD began to rave again. His eyes itched furiously and he couldn't stop scratching them. He screamed that we had stolen his kingdom from him and poisoned his mind with ash. He swore that the ash had compacted into a rock, and that now he saw only the rock when previously he had seen magic trees with fruits that were precious stones.

He became uncontrollable in his hallucinated rage, swearing and stamping up and down the room, punching the walls. We were afraid that something horrible was eating up his brain and mum had to get ten strong men before we could hold dad down and tie him up with cow-hide ropes. When we placed him in his chair he sat bolt upright, with green liquids rolling down from his eyes. His rage had temporarily cooled and he was silent. Mum began all the prayers she knew, appealing to all the different gods that human beings have wept to and worshipped, while the heat intensified in our room, and hunger made me light and airy. We stayed up late, listening to our stomachs groan, listening to the community of the blind arguing bitterly about a corpse they had never seen.

Dad's own blindness had grown worse. He saw only the colour green. The weight on him had become heavier. He refused to eat what he couldn't see. And we felt so ashamed at eating while he listened and salivated that we took to cutting down our food. And to make matters worse, the night-runners started again.

They came on waves of fire. They brandished blazing

firewood in the air. They poured unfamiliar chants at the houses, uttering deep cries, ominous threats, in voices dark with menace. It was only when we made out their words that we understood what was happening. The Party of the Poor had started their own brand of terror. They banged on doors, disturbing the air with the noise of glasses breaking, talking drums stammering, and cowhorns blasting the wind. And to our greatest astonishment they brought a new and perverse message. In voices with ancestral accents, frightening and pitiless, they told us that no one in the area or in the whole wide world must bury the corpse of the carpenter unless they were the murderers. In effect they were saying that anyone who buried the dead carpenter was admitting to having murdered him.

A new curfew had begun. The war of mythologies had entered a bloody-minded dimension. In some ways it wasn't surprising that the Party of the Poor tried to intimidate us back into the fold, but it was surprising that they tried to use the methods of the other party to frighten us into remaining loyal. In fact it seemed that their new strategy was to out-terrorise the Party of the Rich. They had seen just how many converts the other party had won through sheer terror and it was a measure of their desperation that they were now using the same methods to protect their natural constituencies. But the real shock of it was that they used those methods against us. And beyond that was the astounding intransigence of using the dead body of the carpenter as a weapon in the battle of political ascendencies.

That night the stench of the decomposing corpse was stronger on the wind. The night-runners and thugs and masquerades ran up and down our streets, through our compounds, with feet of stampeding elephants. We sat in the room, in the dark, listening to the domination of the night-runners. As they sounded more terrifying, drawing closer to our compound, dad began to stir from his inscrutable silence. Then the masquerades and thugs ran

247

past, howling and ululating, hurling firebrands everywhere. Dad moved. He creaked his neck. I could feel an elemental rage growing in him. And when the night-runners came back again, stamping, beating their drums, warning us not to bury the dead carpenter unless we had murdered him, dad suddenly shouted something about protecting his kingdom and with a demonic, unnatural scream he burst free of the cow-hide ropes, and went charging into the street.

I ran out with him, clinging on to the back of his trousers, trying to restrain him, afraid of what might happen to him in his blindness. But he threw me off, and when I landed on the ground I saw the air lit up with blazing firebrands. The humidity made it hard to breathe; the moon seemed to have lowered and its light made everything hotter. The night-runners of the poor people's party wailed their eerie message. They floated on moonlight, their faces like grim ancestral carvings. The antimony on their features was set on silvery fire by the intensity of the moon. And their bodies, solid and quivering and half-naked, were like ancient memories of a mystical time without boundaries when it was possible to enter the consciousness of a cornseed and foretell the harvest to come. But the terror they spread, their breaking of windows, the people that they beat up who were returning home late, and the vehemence of their counter-mythology was a distortion of that mystical time, and it made the night alien. There was the smell of woodsmoke on the air and in the midst of the bristling masquerades dad was turning round blindly and shouting like a heroic dervish:

'Coup-plotters! Bandits! Destroyers of my kingdom!'

The night-runners surrounded him like shadows and when they began to hit him with sticks and whips dad raged, saying:

'I have a mountain on my head, I have fire in my brain, and I am as blind as a king, so why should I be afraid of you?'

And he lashed out with his mighty fists and pounded two men so hard that I heard their masks splinter.

'Men of wood, bandits of stone,' dad cried, 'you have undammed the fury of the sleeping Tyger!'

The night-runners pressed on him and he swung at them, unleashing thunderous blows, disconnecting the fearsome jaws of the masquerades. He broke their wood with his bare fists. He pulverised them. He fought them with a white-hot animal rage and in complete innocence of his own danger. And while he lashed out, throwing vicious punches in lightning arcs, he kept shouting. His voice had taken on an enormous pressured ferocity. He charged in every direction, howling as if he were mad. And when he laid out his antagonists it was almost completely by accident. Or instinct. Blindness somehow made him a more terrifying fighter. Someone struck him on the head with burning firewood and dad laughed, and muttered something about the fire of witches, the weight of sorcerers. And then he charged at the man who had dared to strike him. He grabbed the man round the waist, lifted him up, and hurled him into the darkness. Such was his fury that he harvested confusion everywhere. I had never seen him so demented, never witnessed him release such elemental energies. His cyclonic rage mesmerised them. He battled them, unaware of their knives, their broken glass, their whips and their clubs. And all the time that he battled against them he thought that they were enemy warriors besieging his kingdom.

'My kingdom must be protected!' he kept shouting.

And while he was rushing from one direction to another, he tripped over a man he had laid out. He fell on a thick piece of wood, snatched it up, and swung wildly, furiously, like a deranged swordsman. He laid out the antagonists, one after another, not knowing how much success he was having. He kept swinging at them, and the night-runners – frightened by the violence of a man who met their terror-mongering with unrestrained madness – retreated swiftly into the darkness, dragging their fallen companions with them. Dad went on swinging at the empty air. He lashed out at antagonists who weren't there.

'They've gone!' I shouted.

But dad, in his madness, not recognising my voice, charged in my direction, swinging the ugly piece of wood. I fled into the dark, and watched his insanity from a safe distance.

'But there is no one there!' I cried again.

And dad went on battling against imaginary dragons, slaying beasts with human faces, knocking down the invisible warriors with their copper raiment, whose faces were like severe wood-carvings. He fought them tirelessly, kicking, bellowing and shouting into the vacant spaces. As I watched him, and as the moon cast its lights on the sleeping road, weaving a white diaphanous spell over everything, a strange epiphany insinuated itself into the solvent darkness. A shroud of mist came over the night air and I suddenly noticed the other forms, the multiplying ghosts, the tall and great spirits like pre-historic giants, the unbowed colossi, the negative ghommids, the swooping nightmares like vengeful earthbound birds; and dad fought them all. He battled with their lions and plumed tigers, he pounced on their foot-soldiers and attacked their brave warlords. He battled them even as he couldn't see them, and even as they went through him, disdaining to engage him in his furious combat. It was strange to see dad so demented while being surrounded by spirits of air and night bound for their own unalterable destination.

Dad's fury became more intense as the serene spirits and the chaotic nightmares concentrated around him. The area of his rage seemed to be the conjunction of different dimensions, the transient meeting-point of the negative and the semi-divine. His blindness served him well; his undammed energies routed the political night-runners and left them stunned in the tornado presence of a wild human force. But his powers were not infinite, and when a little errant

250

light went through the back of his head and disappeared into the fever of his brain, dad released a mighty cry of a warrior conquered by an insignificant thing, and sank suddenly to the floor. He had won three different battles, and hadn't known it: he had driven away the thugs; he had triumphed over forms visible to him in his blindness, but which I couldn't see; and he had earned the respect of the spirit-warriors and hierophants who were in their enigmatic procession.

He lay on the ground with his legs twitching as though he were still fighting in his unconsciousness. I crawled over to him apprehensively, afraid that he might jump up suddenly and knock me out with a blindly flailing fist. But when I touched him on the face with the palm of my hand, he sat bolt upright and said:

'It's cold. Where am I?'

'You have defended your kingdom,' I replied.

He lay back on the earth and complained that a horse had kicked the base of his skull.

'What horse?' I asked.

'Didn't you see them?'

'No.'

'You must be blinder than I am, my son,' he said.

I was silent.

'There were one hundred and seven horses, and all the horses had white and black and red bandits. They had spears and cleavers and shields of gold. Some of their faces were made of marble. Their master, the devil, sent rocks in the shape of human beings to destroy me, but I answered them with bone.'

Dad's fists were raw and bleeding, he had cuts and bruises on his head and face, his hair had been singed, his neck had come out in burns, and all he could say was:

'If it hadn't been for that horse I would have defeated all of them.'

'But they've gone. They fled. You defeated them,' I told him.

'They've gone?'

'Yes.'

'They ran away?'

'Yes.'

'How did they run?'

'I don't understand.'

'Did they run like rats?'

'Like chickens,' I said.

He seemed pleased.

'Help me to stand up. I think I've twisted my ankle.'

I couldn't help him to get up. He was too heavy. We sat there in silence. He breathed deeply the rarefied air of his blind conquest. The moon was low and the road fairly quivered under its ambiguous light. Ghosts flew over the forest like glimmering ancient birds.

'Describe the world to me,' dad said.

'I'm tired,' I replied.

He was silent. His dim sight stared into the intensifying night. Insects made dissonant music around us. The moon-swept wind brought the smell of the corpse and the aromatic dreams of sleeping vegetation. Then suddenly, from the ghostly distance, from beyond the dense shadow of trees, beyond the houses, and seemingly from all around us, we heard a voice speaking through a loudhailer, saying:

'NOBODY MUST BURY THE CORPSE OF THE CARPENTER. ONLY THE MAN OR WOMAN WHO KILLED HIM CAN BURY HIM.'

There was a pause. And then:

'IF YOU DON'T WANT TROUBLE, AND IF YOU DIDN'T KILL THE CARPENTER, THEN DON'T TOUCH HIS CORPSE.'

Another frightening silence. Then the voice rose again, swirling in the air, changing its accentuation, deepening the threatened dread in its voice:

'ONLY THE MURDERER MUST BURY THE BODY AND MAKE A PUBLIC CONFESSION. ANYONE WHO BURIES THE BODY IS THE MURDERER! DON'T SAY YOU HAVEN'T BEEN WARNED!'

On and on the voice went, weaving menace and terror, threatening the burning of the house and the destruction of the family of anyone who dared to go against their edict. It surprised me that dad couldn't make out what was being said.

'What corpse?' he asked.

I was exhausted. I got up, went in, and came back out with mum, whose face seemed altered by her prayers. Together we managed to get dad into the room. But as we entered the compound I noticed that the errant lights, spirits of the dead who speak with fulgent eyes, had all returned. The lights, unburning fires of invisible sorcerers, flitted about with the intensity of their numbered days. When we got to the room I was surprised that none of them came in with us.

Without complaining, mum treated dad's wounds. She even managed to get him to the bathroom where he washed himself. When they came back we were all silent. The room was sad in the candle light and the air stank of dad's blood. His furious spirit, uncalmed by his bath, crowded us. He breathed heavily and his blind eyes were suspicious. He held his head at an angle, his ears cocked to pick up the slightest sound. When the candle spat he asked:

'What was that?'

'The candle,' I said.

'It sounded like a cutlass on our gate.'

'It isn't.'

'Have our enemies returned?'

'No.'

'Are you sure?'

'Yes.'

'How do you know?'

'Because you drove them away.'

He was still restless for action, for combat, for deeds

253

of courage. I felt his spirit rising at the prospect of a good war against our antagonists. He was very alert and his presence became very large in the room. His shadow was a giant behind him, filling the wall, moving constantly, afraid of the candle's brightness. When mum finished with his wounds, and bandaged his forehead, she took great pains in preparing the bed. Then she went out to bathe.

When she returned she combed her hair, anointed her skin, and perfumed herself lightly. She seemed to be preparing for an important event, as if she were going to be presented to an august personage. I was surprised, however, when she urged me to get some sleep and unceremoniously blew out the candle. For the first time in many weeks she allowed dad to sleep with her on the bed. And when the springs began to creak, mounting in suppressed vigour, in the hunger of remembered movements, I slipped out of the room, out into the adventures of darkness and dreams.

In the freedom of the night, with the great velvet universe breathing all about me, I followed the brightest errant light there was, the little star of the dead, which burned with a satin purple fire, and which bounced over the rubbish, and wandered across the bushes, and disappeared into its own dreaming, and re-appeared into its awakening. And as I followed the erratic movements of the little light, allowing it to lead me where it would, I nearly fainted when out of the great mysterious silence of the earth the dead body suddenly started to scream.

CHAPTER ELEVEN

Into the Dead Man's Dream

A LL THE LIGHTS in the houses along our street were off but I knew that no one was asleep. I knew it because there were no dreams floating about in that moon-dominated air. Usually dreams floated from their dreamers and entered the minds of other sleeping forms. Sometimes dreams were transferred from one person to another. I remember once entering the dream of the carpenter's wife, who was encoiled round the solid post of her husband, and who was dreaming the dreams of the tailor across the road who found himself in a land of birds and who had been asked to sew the cloth of leaves into one vast garment that could make the earth more beautiful.

While the corpse screamed, the moon did all the dreaming that night. I had been following the flitting light and it had led me on a confusing journey. The road was wide awake. Cats occasionally cried from the bushes with the voices of abandoned babies. Enchanted by the erratic light, I had passed Madame Koto's bar without knowing it. And when the light vanished completely, leaving me isolated in the darkness of the watchful road, I saw ghosts floating beneath the clouds. The road held its breath while the wind cleansed the air with moonlight. I looked behind me and was surprised to see that someone had left a solitary lamp near the corpse.

There were the ghost forms of dogs over the body. Spirit-jackals came and tore off the corpse's thighs before time would. Invisible vultures had hollowed its eyes. I became terrified. There was no way I could get home without going past the dead body. It occurred to me to run. But the air had

255

turned mysteriously static. I picked up a stone, threw it at the jackals, and missed. The jackals fled into the forest without a sound. My stone had knocked over the lamp. The oil, pouring from the fallen lamp, made the earth burn. Feeling something hot on the nape of my neck, I tried creeping past the corpse. But something rooted me to the ground. The air became an invisible wall. The earth around the lamp flared and when I noticed that a yellow flower had grown from the dead man's forehead, the space around me exploded.

I turned and ran without thinking. I scampered into the bushes and stumbled on sleeping dogs. The sky suddenly went dark. I screamed and flailed, I walked into trees and tripped over their roots, I waved my arms about, fearing that blindness had come upon me. There was no wind, but the air had become dense. The smell of sleeping weeds, the somnolent thoughts of wild flowers hung in the air like a thickly scented pall. I couldn't move for the sheer density of the smells. My arms outstretched, I pushed through the unmoving air, with blackness all around me. I had been struck blind by the sight of a flower.

The rich humus of the dreaming earth suffused me and the warm aromas of herbs and lilies floated on heavy wings of purple all about me. Everything was silent except for the persistent dialogue of those insects which give off a bitter perfume when crushed. The darkness intensified. I looked up and saw that the moon had dimmed. Veils of moondust clung to everything. In my panic my sight kept clearing and darkening. The wind blew leaves into my face. Creepers seemed to twist themselves around me. And as I stumbled about in my new blinding, casting around, screaming for mother, I noticed that the forest was full of the ghosts of trees that were no longer there.

I had steadied myself and had launched out into the purple darkness, when I saw the dead man tramping around, muttering feverishly to himself. Flailing in the dark, I fled in another direction, unable to distinguish the night from the bushes. I ran right into the black rock and cracked my head and when I recovered I saw the dead man again. His hair was matted with blood, and he was pursuing me. I ran deeper into the forest, screaming, and not hearing my own voice; tripping, and not entirely falling down; completely lost, and not being able to see a single thing – except for the ghosts, who watched me with neutral eyes.

A strange fever had seized my brain. I stopped running and rested against a tree, and held on to it with all my might. The forest spoke in many harsh voices. And as I stood there, my heart pounding in my brain, a cold wind blew the back of my neck. And when I turned round I saw the dead man, with his empty eye sockets and his mad breath, right behind me. I tried to scream but he grabbed me with his bony rotten hands and he forced me to the ground and began to press me into the earth. He pressed me down with a demented roughness, as if he wanted to bury me alive. He held me so hard that the night suddenly became populous with errant lights spinning around in my eyes. The dead man gave off such a foul stench of putrefaction that I could hardly breathe. He went on shaking me, hitting me against the earth, deafening me with his high-pitched agonised silence. And then, as the wind changed, he stopped. Slowly, as if to emphasise the importance of what he was about to tell me in his dreadful silence, he brought his monstrous decaying face closer to mine. The empty sockets of his eyes glowed with bristling yellow things. Worms crawled out of his nostrils. And when he opened the gaping hole of his mouth I saw earthworms slowly uncoiling themselves. And when he spoke in the harsh unnatural voice of the dead, when his dead breath hit my face, begging me to tell the world to bury him, banging my head violently against the roots of a tree, something burst open in my mind, something cracked asunder – and I heard the great howling funereal wail of the unnumbered dead, heard their complaints, their cries, their lamentations, their regrets, their simultaneous speeches, their threats, their

257

broken promises, their perpetual dreams, their furious lists of all the ways they would have lived their lives differently, more luminously, with wise silence and effective courage; I heard the voices of the unhappy dead, the unburied dead, those whose deaths were unacknowledged, those to whom justice hadn't been done, whose restless sleep was spiked with the lies and silences of the living; I heard their voices, full of messages and signs, lessons to be learnt, histories that mustn't be forgotten, stories that must be told, melodies that must be created, possibilities that must be discovered, lives that must be redeemed, sufferings that must be transformed into wonders, and all the thousand permutations of love that must be incarnated and kept whole and regenerated every day of our lives. I heard all these things and saw the forms of the dead all around me. I saw my spirit-companions with them, serene in the white boiling agony of my entrapment, joyful even that I had been caught in the middle space between the living and the dead, the shining purgatory brimful of negation and signs. And through all this, the dead man was begging me to tell the world to remember him; and all that time he didn't stop banging my head against the twisted roots of a living tree. And then something happened. My agony became too much for me, and I passed through many spheres full of radiant voices. Streams of blue pulsating light poured over me, and then quite suddenly it all went dark.

When I opened my eyes the spectre of a big stubbled face looming above me and huge clammy hands feeling my face made me scream and jump. I leapt up and scampered around in a forest of tables and chairs and clothes hanging from a line and ran into a wall that seemed like a rock and rebounded to the table and nearly set myself alight on the steady magnified flame of the candle. I found myself running round the room, shouting and raving, as dad, with arms outstretched, came towards me. Then mum caught me from behind and held me tight and said:

'Why are you so afraid of your father?'

But I went on raving, unable to control the words pouring out of me. With great gentleness mum covered my mouth with her palm and lay me down on the bed, stroking my hair, and speaking to me softly. I raved on as she spoke in the voice of one whose secret powers had somehow grown fainter. And when she asked, 'What were you doing in the forest at this time of night?' all I could think of saying, through the confused heat of my brain, was:

'The dead carpenter asked me to bury him.'

No one said anything. Dad, sitting in his chair, kept nodding. Mum stared at me for a long time. Then she took off a layer of wrapper from around her waist and spread it over me. The warm comforting smell of her body surrounded me and I fell asleep, and woke up in Madame Koto's dream. She was dreaming that all her enemies were turning into trees and that the trees were growing on the island of her body, fastening her flesh into the earth with their relentless roots.

CHAPTER TWELVE

_____

Manifestations of the Hidden

M Y RAVINGS WERE worse the next day. No one could
cure me of the raving. My eyes were twitching hot and
I talked about the dead carpenter wandering around at night,
reciting the names of all the people he knew, all of whom
refused to recognise him, or even acknowledge his existence. I
talked about the people for whom he had made beds and tables
and chairs, people whose cupboards he had fixed, who ate off
the tables he had shaped, slept on the beds he had fashioned,
and sat on the chairs he had constructed. I raved on about the
women who spat when they went past him, about the men who
had somehow become blind to his presence, about the nasty
treatment the dogs and birds dealt him, about how his own
party had betrayed him, and how his thoughts were turning
into a yellow flower whose roots were made of steel. I couldn't
seem to stop talking about the horrible earthbound hell of his
unburied existence, how his spirit tramped the nights, banging
on doors, trying to get through the greater doors beyond
which lie the adventures of infinity. How could I stop muttering about his rage and bitterness, his promise of vengeance,
the swirling molten heat of his unfinished condition? How
could I stop, when it seemed as if the dead man was speaking
through me, taking over my mouth and thoughts, growing
inside my flesh in an unhappy occupation of my being?

Dad listened to my ravings intently. He listened without
moving from his chair. He listened, it seemed, without hearing me. Mum spent the whole day going from one herbalist
to another, praying loudly along the street. None of the herbalists appeared to be able to do anything. They all said that

260

the chains tying us down must first be broken by us before they can be of any help. By the evening my energy ran out. My jaws ached. And horses stampeded over the flowers and visions that seared my brain. The curious thing is that when I stopped raving I saw butterflies everywhere, fluttering amid the vibrations of which objects are composed. Then I saw a clear field with a white tree in the middle of it, on which the dead carpenter lay asleep in the topmost branches. And sometimes when I ceased raving Ade would come into the room and sit beside me with a sweet smile on his face. On one occasion he said:

'Your father is right.'

'About what?' I asked.

'What?' dad said.

'Everything is alive,' Ade continued. 'There are some things that can make a stone cry.'

'Like what?'

'What?' dad asked again.

'Many things,' Ade ventured. 'A dry wind, a dying bird, the death of a nation, the birth of a witch, the laughter of angels, the songs of the devil, the dreams of a toad, the piss of a goat, the serenity of a tyrant, the destruction of a people's history, the triumph of the wrong, the thoughts of a butterfly, the dreams of the dead.'

'How come I've never seen a stone cry?' I asked.

'Because you don't use your eyes.'

'Why should a stone cry?' asked dad, sitting up and turning his blind eyes towards me.

'How should I use my eyes?'

'By not using your head first.'

'But how?'

'Azaro, what's wrong with you?'

'Nothing.'

'It's not the eyes that see.'

'Then what does?'

'It's the light in the eyes that sees.'

'What light?'
'Are those lights back?' asked dad.
'No.'
'The light that makes everything alive.'
'So how do I use the light?'
'You have to discover it first.'
'How do I discover it?'
'Azaro, who are you talking to, eh?'
'No one,' I said.
'I better go,' said Ade.
'Don't go.'
'Your grandfather is worried about all of you,'
'How do you know?'
'Have you seen the rainbows?'
'No.'
'Have you seen the trees turning into ghosts?'
'Yes.'
'Have you seen my father?'
I was silent. Dad knocked me on the head. He was quite frustrated. He got up and began feeling the space around me.
'Are you talking to yourself again?'
'No.'
'So you haven't seen my father?' Ade pressed on.
'He nearly killed me last night.'
'Why?'
'He asked me to bury him.'
For a moment Ade vanished. Then, after a few seconds, he re-appeared behind me.
'I have a message for you.'
'From who?'
'Your spirit-companions.'
'What is the message?'
Dad lifted me up and held me tightly to him. He was crying. He was crying that his son had gone mad. He irritated me with his heavings.

'You will find out what the message is when my father has been buried.'

Then Ade was silent. Then, with the smile becoming even sweeter on his face, he said:

'I'm going now.'

'Wait!'

'What?'

Dad covered my mouth with his palm. I bit him.

'What?'

'Are you still my friend?'

'I am your father,' dad said, sadly.

Ade vanished altogether. When he vanished the bed and the table, the walls and the ceiling, the cupboard and the jumble of clothes and the rafters and the air in the room burst into great flutterings of butterfly lights and I cried:

'EVERYTHING IS ALIVE! EVERYTHING MOVES!'

And dad put me down on the bed and sat on his chair of golden butterfly lights. I saw him rocking on air, with his feet on the centre table that was ablaze with dense motion. An emerald wind blew into the room, bringing mum's footsteps closer. And I saw that the darkness is nothing more than vibrations moving more slowly, and light nothing more than vibrations moving more swiftly. I noticed also that there is darkness in light, and light in darkness. Everything in the room shimmered and the glow of things made my head swell. I stared with amazement at the radiance of solid things and at the hidden glimmer of the air. Then mum came into the room, surrounded with a barely perceptible aura of emerald lights, bearing aloes and oregano herbs which she sprinkled on my head. She also had a piece of kaoline in her hand, and it had an absorbent quality made to soak up all the bad vibrations around me. With the kaoline firmly grasped, she circled my head thrice with her hand, uttering incantations and prayers, and then, taking the bad things around me with her, she went and threw the kaoline out on to the road. When she left my head cooled and the shimmering of things ceased and the radiance of the air returned to its hidden condition, but I saw the spirits of aborted babies crawling about and voices from realms both distant and near called my secret names, weaving them in sweet threnodies, and the forms of the dead appeared to me in flashes of darkness, and my head caught fire, and I began to rave again.

When the night became very dark dad ordered mum to sit beside me. He left the door open. He lit no candles. I could still see him rocking on air, could hear his jaws working, could feel him reaching for the place of spells and silences within, spells with which to cast a gentle enchantment over my ravings, silences with which to quieten the excessive motion of my being. I could even perceive the film of butterfly wings growing thicker over his eyes as he stared into a dim yellow paradise, full of doves and crystals and rubies and beings whose hearts gave off a brilliant diamond light. He stared into the yellow paradise, which was drawing closer, which would enter him briefly and leave huge unoccupied spaces inside him, spaces potent with yearning and dreams of a higher, hidden reality. And when the raving began to pour from me again, dad cleared his throat, creaked his neck twice, and started to speak. He spoke as if words were spells, as if words were a kind of magical wind that could blow away the bad vapours of the spirit.

'Last night,' he said, 'I dreamt that I was in a world of rainbows. There were beautiful trees everywhere and they knew the hidden cures for all human diseases. The trees could talk and they were telling me their life stories when a tall man with no eyes in his head came up to me and said: "Do you remember me?" "No," I replied. Then he smiled and went away. A long time passed as I watched him go. Then people appeared and began to cut down the trees. The rainbows started to fade. The world became darker. That was when I realised that I had a sun in my head. But it was going out slowly. I was worried, so I looked up at the sky. Then an alligator pepper seed fell on my head, knocking me down, and when I got up the tall man came back again. This time he had one big eye. The other socket was empty. "Do you remember me now?" he asked. "No," I replied. "Look around you," he said. I looked. All the rainbows had gone. All the beautiful colours of the world had gone. All the lovely lights and the sweet music had gone. The trees were turning into stumps. Some of them were bleeding. Many of them were ghosts. The air was dry. "Where have the rainbows gone?" I asked the man. "People like you have been destroying them," he replied. "How?" "With your eyes," he said. Then I realised that I could see in my dream. "Who are you?" I asked him. "Some people think I am an animal," he answered. "People like who?" "People like you," he said. "Are you an animal?" I asked. The man laughed. He laughed for a long time. His laughter frightened and confused me. When he stopped he looked at me and said: "If I am an animal, what kind of an animal am I? An antelope, or a leopard?" That was all he said. I didn't understand him at all.'

Dad paused for a moment. His silence baffled me as much as his dream did.

'Then what happened?'

Dad turned his face in my direction and, in a low voice, said:

'Nothing. I woke up.'

'Is that all?'

'Yes.'

The room fairly quivered with the unfinished riddle of his dream. We were silent. The darkness and my incomprehension were beginning to re-awaken the raving in me when dad cleared his throat again, and said:

'Let me tell you a story.'

'Yes, tell us a story,' I said.

'Once upon a time,' he began, 'there was a hunter. He was a great hunter and he could imitate all the different sounds and noises of animals. He understood their language. He also had a beautiful voice and when he sang even the

265

fiercest animals would stop what they were doing and listen. He was so successful as a hunter that there wasn't a day when he didn't bring home a dead deer or duiker or a wild boar. It so happened that one day his luck changed. He tried hard, but he couldn't kill anything. He didn't even catch a single rabbit in any of his traps. The animals had begun to understand his tricks. This went on for seven days. All through that time he remained in the forest, swearing that he wouldn't return home till he had caught something. On the seventh day he was so tired with trying that he fell asleep at the foot of a tree. In his sleep he heard the forest talking about him, planning the dreadful things they would do to him for killing off all the beautiful animals who hadn't harmed him in any way. He was in a deep sleep when a strange light flashed past him. He woke up suddenly, and saw a woman standing in front of a mighty anthill. The woman looked left and right to make sure no one was watching her. And then she turned into an antelope and went into the anthill. The man was astonished.'

'How can an antelope enter an anthill?' I asked.

'It seemed like an anthill,' dad said, 'but it was really a palace.'

'How is that?'

'It was a palace that only certain beings can see.'

Dad paused.

'Your story isn't going anywhere,' mum said, in the dark.

'A story is not a car,' dad replied. 'It is a road, and before that it was a river, a river that never ends.'

'And then what happened?' I asked.

'The next day, the man returned to the same spot, at the same time, and pretended to be asleep against the same tree. He heard the forest talking about him again, planning something cunning and terrible to do to him. Then the light flashed past a second time. He opened his eyes and saw the most beautiful woman in the world standing at the door of

266

the great anthill. She was naked and her skin shone like polished bronze and she was covered in golden bangles round her neck and ankles and up her arms. Beads of precious stones gave off wonderful lights about her slender waist. The man fell in love with her instantly. The woman looked left and right and then turned into an antelope and disappeared into the secret palace of the anthill. The man went home. He could not sleep. He could not eat. All he could think of was the beautiful woman. He fell so completely in love with her that he swore he would marry her even if it was the last thing he did on earth.'

Dad stopped abruptly, alarming us.

'Fetch me some water,' he said. 'This story is making me thirsty.'

I rushed out to get some water and when I came back mum was sitting at dad's feet, stroking his ankle. Dad drank the water and resumed his story, clearing his throat, while outside a mysterious new wind was blowing.

'The next day the man went to the same spot very early. He pretended again to be asleep against the tree. This time the forest was silent. He kept his eyes shut and waited for the strange light to flash past him. He waited for a long time. Evening turned to night. The forest began to laugh. The man still went on pretending. Then when it was so dark that all he could see was the darkness itself a big light flashed past him. The light was so big that he jumped up, with his heart beating very fast . . .'

At that precise moment of the story the wind outside blew suddenly into our room, banging the door against the bed. Then I heard a deep growling noise that made me jump. Dad caught his breath. When I recovered, the room was silent. Then I noticed that dad was staring with an uncanny intensity at something near the door. I turned and looked, and saw nothing. Then the wind blew harder, blowing in the emerald form of a majestic and mighty leopard. A powerful light, swarming with the green vibrations of butterflies, surrounded the great invisible beast. It had eyes of diamonds and it sat there, on its tail, like a giant cat. Its wild and feral presence filled the little room with the vast smells of unknown forests. None of us moved.

'What are you two looking at?' mum asked, mesmerised by our concentration.

I couldn't speak for the unearthly wonder of the emerald manifestation. And for a long moment dad was silent. Then, just as the sign of the leopard had gatecrashed its way into our lives, dad let it enter the spell of his narration. Rarely taking his face away from the radiant form, dad continued with his story, his voice quivering.

'As I was saying, the light flashed past the hunter and it was so great that he jumped up, his heart pounding as if an earthquake had taken place inside him. In the darkness he could see the woman, because she shone. Her skin gave off light. Her golden bangles glittered around her in the moonlight of her mystery. But before the woman could change into an antelope, the hunter started to sing. He sang to her in the most enchanting voice he had ever managed. He sang to her with his heart full of weeping. And with his sweet voice he begged her to accept him as a husband, swearing that if she refused he would kill himself at the very door of the anthill.'

'Typical man!' mum said.

'At first, the woman was shy, and tried to hide her nakedness. But he went on singing, he sang with all his soul, all his love, and he went down on his knees. The woman was moved by his singing and his gesture. Then, relenting a bit, she asked him how long he had been watching her. Still singing, the hunter told her the truth. Maybe it was because he told her the truth that she smiled. Then she said that she would marry him on one condition. The hunter swore by the many names of the great God that he would honour the condition to the day he died. And her condition was that he must keep what she is a secret for ever, he must never reveal to anyone or anything the mystery of her origin. He swore that he wouldn't, and that if he did he deserved just punishment.'

'Then what happened?'

'The next day he lead her into town and married her in the most lavish style . . .'

'Unlike me,' mum said.

'Anyway, after they were married they had six children. The woman brought him incredible good luck. He stopped hunting, and became a successful trader. Everything he touched turned to money. He was blessed with good health, lovely children, and the respect of the world. He became wealthy and famous. They made him a chief in seven towns. Rich men gave him their daughters to marry. He had five wives, but his first wife remained special. He built a mighty mansion for her which she had all to herself. But as he got famous, he got proud. As he got wealthier, he got arrogant. And even his great happiness helped him forget the secret origins of his success. He boasted a lot and drank too much.

'Then, one day, the king made an announcement that a black antelope with a special jewel in its forehead had been seen in the forest and that the person who killed the antelope and brought it to the palace would marry his beautiful young daughter and inherit the kingdom. The man, who used to be a great hunter, let it be known that he was going out into the forest to kill the animal. That night he had a terrible quarrel with his first wife. He was drunk and as they quarrelled he said, in a loud voice: "Is it because you are an antelope yourself that you don't want me to go, eh?" The wife became silent. The man went to his room. In the morning he woke up to hear his other wives singing about his first wife, mocking her for being an antelope. Then he realised what he had done. He rushed to his first wife's house and found that she had gone. He also found that she had taken their six children with her. Quickly he changed into his hunter's clothes and went back to the forest to lie against the same tree. He pretended to be asleep, he listened to the forest talking about him, but he didn't understand the riddle of their speech. Deep in the night the strange light flashed past for the last time. It was his wife. He began to sing in his most sorrowful voice, begging her forgiveness. But she stopped him, and said: "The black antelope you want to kill is my mother. The jewel in her head is God's gift to her, and her crown. She is a queen, I am a princess, and what you think is an anthill is really my hidden kingdom. You betrayed my secret. What do you think I should do?" "Forgive me," the man said. His wife laughed. Her laughter started a mighty sound in the sky. The hunter, terrified, looked up. When he looked down again he saw that his wife had changed, not into an antelope, but into a leopard.'

Dad paused again.

'All things are linked,' said mum.

'Then, with a great roar of anger, the leopard pounced on the man, tore him to pieces, and ate him up. And till this day . . .'

I followed dad's gaze, which had become more intense, as his words trailed off into silence. Up till that point of the story the emerald form of the leopard had been still, unmoving, as if it too were held captive by dad's fable. But when I followed dad's gaze I saw nothing there except a faint green light, like a mist, with butterflies tingling the air, and I smelt nothing but the haunting essence of the dying forest.

'It's gone!' I cried.

'What?' mum asked.

'It's still there,' dad announced, in a voice that suggested he had finally understood the meaning of the sign.

Then he rose from his chair. He rose like one who was lifting himself into a higher destiny. Such was the certainty and power of his rising that we were riveted and confused, unable to react. We watched him as if his new knowledge had cast a jewelled spell on us. Then, with the swiftness of one accustomed to sleep-running, dad bounded out of the

room, and out into the dark street, following the sign of
the emerald leopard.

It didn't take that long for us to rouse ourselves from
our astonishment, but when we got outside we couldn't
find dad anywhere. The moon was low in the sky. The
night was warm. The unbearable stench of the dead carpenter encompassed our world. And butterflies vibrated in the
secret heart of all things. It was a night of intense dreams.
Everywhere I turned I encountered the bad dreams of our
community. The dreams merged into one another and took
on frightening and concentrated forms. The forms filled me
with terror.

'Let's go back home,' I said to mum.

'But your father is blind. What if he falls into a well?'

I was silent. But the twisted forms of our bad dreams,
bristling in the night air, also made mum scared. With great
caution, and without daring to go near Madame Koto's place,
we searched for dad up and down the street. The negative
potencies in the air almost made me ill. After we had failed
to find dad, we hurried back to our room, and waited for
him to return. We waited a long time. We waited through
all the dreaming phases of the new moon.

Book Four

CHAPTER ONE

Deliverance

A DREAM CAN BE the highest point of a life; action can be its purest manifestation.

That night, as I waited for dad in the anguish of my spirit, I rediscovered the secret of flight. With the effortlessness of my hidden inheritance, I flew in and out of the dreams of the living and the dead. While mum sat on dad's chair, praying in a voice weakened by hunger and the accumulated weight of her days, I took off into the air, leaving my body behind, and I followed dad as he railed against his own blindness, stumbling with new feet, naming the world with new words. I was in the air with him as he trailed the apparition, his spirit bursting the bounds of his agony, his voice raging out against the invisible censoring forces of our earthly sphere, calling on the winds to drive him on into greater powers, calling on the hidden God to liberate him from the fears that kept him poor, kept him in a corner, kept him from discovering his true resplendent identity. Dad was a tempest of energies that night and we felt his passion in our squalid room where all our stories are stored.

Dad went on following the sign of the leopard. He stumbled over the debris in the street, but he walked on boldly as if his feet had an instinctive sight of their own. He dared the road to trip him, to keep him down; he dared trees to fall across his path; he dared the night to keep him from seeing; he dared the forces of the air to blow him away or dissolve his being altogether – and through all this he persistently followed the emerald hallucination of the leopard.

While he raged, voices of our area joined him, one by

one. Dad unblocked the spirit of the community with his daring. He challenged the sorcerers of the air and mind, the negative spirits of the lower spheres. Dad didn't know it, but his incandescent daring concentrated the spirits of the dead and the unborn around him. They followed him, marvelling at a man so blind – and so fragile, as forces in the universe go – who could muster so much rage when it was easier to lie down and die.

His voice rang out over the rooftops, penetrating the ears of dreamers who lay on beds bristling with the invisible broken glass of poverty; his voice was clear and harsh, resonating through the bald patch of trees, magnified by moonlight. And as he cried out for justice and more vision and transformation, cried out that the gods unveil to him his destiny, he unknowingly broke the seven chains that tied our dreams down, that kept our vision of more light disconnected from our reality. One by one we began to wake from a layer of sleep so deep that our lives had seemed to exist only in a somnolent unfolding of time – and that is why we had to resort to legends and myths to explain why time seemed to pass so slowly while momentous events exploded so rapidly and with such simultaneity in our dreams.

As dad's voice lifted the sky higher above our heads, I realised that the whole community was dreaming him on towards our universal deliverance, urging him on towards our restoration, each within the indignities, humiliations, privations, fears, meanness and the great hidden goodness of their secret lives. We willed him on within our dreams, praying for him to succeed in countering the negative gravity of our spaces, the bad smells of our days, the dreadful weight of our cowardice and powerlessness, to neutralise the spells and enchantments of powerful witches who had been done injustices all their lives and who took out their vengeance by sealing us within the poisoned cage of limitations and hunger. We dreamt him on, calling on the road to guide his feet, and when he tripped over the extinguished lamp and fell on the bloated body of the dead man in an unholy embrace, when the body – stewing with bile and nauseous gases and suppurating gore – exploded its resentments, its foul purple liquids, its rotting flesh on dad, surrounding him with its noxious odour of death, we could not help him, he was alone, and we retreated swiftly from the void which was his incomprehension, and left him to disentangle himself from the wilful embrace of the neglected corpse.

At first dad was not sure what had happened. He had fallen and had found himself swimming in soft inner tissue and strange liquids. The stench invaded his eyes with a deeper darkness that made the sign of the leopard disappear. His raging ceased instantly. Dad got up, and staggered, and felt the liquid alive on him, and he screamed. He screamed as if he were trying to dislodge a rock from his brain. The rock left him, the weight on his head also left him, and he became heavier. He had stumbled into a zone of unearthly gravity. And when he stopped screaming, when he looked up and saw the moon mighty and white just above his head, a new madness possessed him. His voice changed, it took on the timbre and weight of the earth, as if a new being were speaking through the mouth of a void. Then he began the naming of the things of the world as if everything were nothing but a quivering incantation. He named the different trees, the obeches, irokos, baobabs, sacred trees whose great presences exuded the monumental serenity of hidden deities, and who were old with history and unheard stories; he named the night birds who were never what they seemed, the ones with the eyes of wise old men, the owl that was a benign old witch; he named the plants, the secret herbs, the poisonous vegetations which themselves cured other poisons, the wild roses of the forest, the tranquil agapanthis, the flaming lilies, the hidden honeysuckles, which give off their fragrance only in praise of the new moon, the cocoyam plants whose leaves are drumskins on which the rain quickens the heartbeat of the land, the banana plants whose leaves are umbrellas for the poor, the dongoyaro root and its untapped cure for malaria, the matted grass which accelerates its growth over the narratives of the continent; he named the cowardly jackals, forerunners of disaster, the ambiguous antelopes and their twilight enchantments, the lions that roar from the muffled depths of our sleep, the leopards that prowl the untested boundaries of our will, the tygers and their unconquerable enigmatic hearts. He named the spirits from higher realms that restore balances, the wise and royal spirits on their migration to the great meeting-place of human justice, he named them in his private language; he named the houses, the mud huts, the zinc abodes, the thatch buildings; he named the wind of good fortune, the wind of bad health, the wind of equality; he named the stars, each one lambent with its own new light, he named the great luminous crab of the African sky, the transformative fish of the watery heavens, the dragon-star of powerful hopes, the horsestar of swift realisations, the tygerstar of courage, the lionstar of bold dreams. Bewitched by the shining mythologies of the immortal sky, he launched into a fever of incantations, crying out a new logarithm of stars, the star of sacrifice and of vision, the star of war and of joy, the star of suffering and of redemption, the star of creativity and of transformation, and the great invisible star of love. Out of the motherland of the heart, quivering under the mysterious omnipotence of the sky, he named all the planets in a new language, inventing one for the bursting elevation of his spirit; he hailed the comets, he sang of the meteors that fall back into the phoenix ash of earth, and he praised the mirror of disasters and redemptions that is the sky. He glorified the nebulae of the gods and spoke of them as signs and ciphers in the book of fate that is the visible face of the heavens; he spoke of stars and comets as letters of a divine alphabet, letters all scattered and scrambled up in an eternal riddle or enigma – scrambled up so that each man and woman has to re-order the words they perceive and transmute their own chaos, creating light out of the

278

terrible conundrum of their lives. He sang powerfully about the cities of the Heavens, where the Blessed souls sing to us from beyond the hidden realities of our sleep-walking days – WAKE UP, AND BE JOYFUL, they sing – WAKE UP, AND CHANGE YOUR DREAMS. Drunk on the wine of his new unblinded mythology, dad sang of the ecstasy of the cities of the hidden heavens which we never connect because of the innumerable piled-up problems in our eyes.

With the liquid of the dead man still writhing on his flesh, mixing his horror with exaltation, he named the rivers, creeks, streams, and even the waves of the great ocean that perfumed the air of that island. He named the gods of the ghetto: the god of poverty, distant relation to the god of rainbows, the god of fear and of transferences, the god of timidity and suspicion, the god of self-imposed limitations and fatalism, the god of quacks and diseases, the god of pullulating superstitions and negativity, the god of blindness and fear of what other people think, the god of illiteracy and refusal to think. Then he named their counter-gods: the god of Consolation and Solidarity, the god of Music and Beauty, the god of Good Visions and Quiet Consistency, the god of Mystery and Wisdom, the god of Work and Health, the god of Art and Courage, the god of Democratic Kindness and Humility, the god of Clarity and Strong Thinking, the god of Time and Creativity, the god of Light and Universal Love.

His voice changing pitch, moving away from his glorious contrapuntal recitation, dad began chanting out the secret names of those that dwelled within the sundry abodes, the baker who lay dreaming of a garden of diamonds, whose name meant REVEAL TO US OUR GLORIES; the sign-writer, who dreamt of a river of magic words, each in brilliant colour, whose name meant OUR DESTINY IS IN OUR HANDS; his wife, the seamstress, who lay in a huge cave where yellow fauns and white antelopes played on flutes and drums while she made clothes for the patient rocks, whose name meant NOTHING CAN KEEP A GOOD SOUL DOWN; the petty trader, enchanted in a blue landscape with happy iridescent snakes, whose name meant TIME IS ALWAYS ON OUR SIDE; the butcher, who was being lectured by a unicorn on the theme of forgiveness, whose name meant SAVE US FROM EVIL; the carrier of monstrous loads, three streets away, who was dreaming of being in flight amongst silent angels, whose name meant WHATEVER HAPPENS TO US WILL MAKE US STRONGER. Yes, dad named them all, he named the owners of stalls, the hawkers, the marketwomen, who battled flies and moths and thugs; the ghetto musicians, who never stopped believing that one day the whole world will fall in love with their melodies plucked from the flaming heart of suffering; he named the children, who never celebrated birthdays, who were born chained to poverty, whose names meant GIVE US LIGHT or KEEP US ON THE GOOD ROAD or GOD IS OUR GUIDE, who would die in wars or in famine or by food poisoning or the accumulated stench of corpses or as world heroes of mysterious origins, who are condemned to having to transform their lives and dream a new beautiful future for the world, from misery and love; dad named the supremely heroic mothers, and praised their subtle and obdurate goddesses, their innumerable angels; and he named the byways, paths, streets and roads, not forgetting to celebrate the father of roads, the great river, grandson of Time, who leads everything to its concealed destiny; and he astonished me that night when, in the midst of his scary exultation, he gave me a new name, a long one for a long life, which meant KEEP RE-DREAMING THE WORLD WITH MORE LIGHT. Dad named everything with a booming quivering voice which made us all afraid that sight was a kind of transcendant madness, an undiscovered chaos, a hallucinatory window into the mysteries lurking behind ordinary reality.

And when he named the flies, the blue ones, the green ones, the big and the small, when he named the mosquitoes, and praised them for helping to prevent the colonialists from entirely taking over our lands, when he named the ants and woodworms and applauded the service they rendered in the dissolution of old gods so new ones can be created, when he named the termites, the cockroaches, and all the rodents, all the busy occupants of the continent's undergrowth, all the curiously valuable lower forms that destroyed wood, carvings, statues, our paper, our histories, making it necessary for us to invent a science best suited for our continent, making it imperative that we be perpetually creative, constantly inventive, worshippers at shrines of beauty, self-inventors who have to re-dream the world anew because it is always passing away, workers in the vineyard of new life, a people who have to create paper which the termites won't eat, narratives that the ants somehow recreate in their devouring, histories that don't become fixed only into written or spoken words, stories that are re-invented in each new generation, myths that always live because they are always allowed to die, melodies that spring from the same unchanging source of the redemptive heart, philosophies hidden in rituals, hidden in stories, hidden in moods, concealed in places where time and change cannot get to them, when dad noticed the flies again and acclaimed their polyphonic existence, when he named the smells, the stenches, the debris, the gutters, and all the forms of our deaths — he had come full circle, he had travelled a sublime arc, made a parabolic journey, starting with his eyes, proceeding to the cosmos, and ending where he really began. And when he found himself naming the dead body, the dead carpenter, he instantly unravelled all his hallucinations, his dreams, his fevers, and all the messages that had been invading him in so many signs and riddles. As he named the dead carpenter, he saw the corpse, and speech and exultation deserted him.

It was his silence that told us he was seeing the world with terrible new eyes. It was his silence that began our liberation, for it went on a very long time as he underwent the agonising process of deciphering what he was seeing, and as he separated what he actually saw from all the feverish narratives he had been living during the period that he had been blind.

CHAPTER TWO

The Freeing of One Vision Is the Freeing of All

HIS VOICE MADE us realise that we were still alive, but his silence made us aware that we had all been dreaming. Some say it was the weight and majesty of the moon which unblinded him, but I think it was death. His silence was his dialogue with the dead man. And he spoke and listened for a long time as his brain, going right back to the moment when the carpenter was murdered, unscrambled itself from the coil of his hallucinations. But when, in silence, dad began to move the dead body, something quite extraordinary woke up in the air. It brought me down from my circlings and I sat up and then I ran outside. Mum came with me. A blue cord had encircled the moon. And when we got to the housefront, the night had begun to speak; voices were rising within darkened rooms; a strange storm was gathering. The voices were indistinct, a dark mystery. As dad carried the body into the forest, with a feverish emerald mist swirling around him, we heard an unbounded voice shouting, over and over again, as if a miracle had been made incarnate:

'I CAN SEE! I CAN SEE! SIGHT IS WONDERFUL! THE WORLD IS HOLY! EVERYTHING IS GLOWING!'

Then the night became populous with cries, astonished cries, as at a universal revelation. Other voices joined in, lights came on in different rooms, and people poured out of their houses, into the street, throwing their canes up towards the moon, jumping about in drunken jubilation, proclaiming the miracle and restoration of sight. It seemed as if all the people who had been recently blinded, who had been tossing on their beds, willing dad on, had been simultaneously liberated into new vision. They chanted and sang in their passionate rejoicing, as if the freeing of one vision had freed all the others.

And while dad carried the dead man through the forest, treading on the prickly undergrowth, kicking stones and making them crack, the recently unblinded people gathered themselves together into one vast group. I went and joined them, and told them that dad had followed the sign of a leopard, and though no one had ever seen a leopard in our area before, they believed me. They rushed off to their rooms to get axes, machetes, pikes and dane guns – while dad laid the body down on the forest floor and began to dig a temporary grave with whatever he could find. He dug the soft earth with his bare hands till they bled at the fingernails; he dug with sticks and branches; then he found a broken shovel and dug frenziedly as if he were trying to create a hole big enough to bury all our bad dreams, our cowardice and our fears; he dug like a madman, without the help of moonlight, disturbing the spirits of the forest, cleaving the sleeping earthworms, and while he dug the homeless spirits of that realm watched him with sad silver eyes. And as he began burying the body, laying it in the hole that would not be its home for long, tramping about the vegetation plucking wild flowers which he strewed over the body with incantations and prayers to appease the fury of the dead carpenter, the community of the unblinded marched down the street with their pickaxes, sticks, machetes and dane guns, like a night army, and stopped at the front of Madame Koto's silent bar. But when I shouted that the dead body had vanished again, they all broke into a run, bounding into the forest, calling dad's name till it rang out through all the mouths of the trees and the wind. We ran deeper into the forest, astonished to find that it had grown smaller, amazed that while we had been living within the closed circle of our lives the forest

284

was being turned into a graveyard of trees. And when we came upon dad, his hair wild and tangled with cobwebs and earth, his hands bleeding, his shirt torn, gore on his chest, the burying accomplished, we found him pushing the great black rock, moving it by inches, and we were astounded into silence. He was shifting by slow degrees the black rock of enigmas whose infernal density was the home of inexplicable voices. We were astounded because none of us could understand how he could move the black rock infested with so many fearful legends, which was heavy and monumental like a compressed planet. But dad moved the rock, grunting, completely ignoring us, until it lay at the head of the grave of the insurgent corpse which had been a plague in our lives.

When dad had marked the grave with the fiendish and semi-sacred rock, he turned to us, his bleeding hands in the air, his eyes vibrant with a sulphurous divine madness, his chest heaving, the moon glowing unveiled over the trees, and he greeted us with a great terrifying cry, saying:

'MY PEOPLE, THE EARTH IS ALIVE!'

And then he collapsed on the ground.

———

CHAPTER THREE

Astonishing Lives in the Mirror

D AD LAY ON a bed of leaves and he was out for a long time while the cold wind blew about us. He lay very still, his arms stretched out as if the earth were his cross, and nothing the community of the unblinded could do managed to bring him round. In the silence of our double confusion a woman with a voice of ghostly beauty started to sing. She sang about the ancient heroes of our forgotten dreams who journeyed through the underworlds and carved a new road to our futures. When she finished singing the men lifted dad up and began carrying him home, but mum asked them to put him down again. It was mum who managed the curious feat of reviving him. She bent over his inert form and whispered strange words into his ears. She whispered them for a long time. Then, slowly, he began to stir. When he eventually got up he was subdued. He refused to speak. Then he started to weep. He wept so hard that he drew weeping from the secret wells of our hearts and we all wept with him for the dead man whom we had all refused to see. And then the woman with the ghostly voice changed our weeping into a funereal lament, singing piercingly, her voice ringing all the way to the realms of the dead. The other women joined her and when they finished an old man began impromptu obsequies, a prayer for the dead, for all the unjustly treated dead, a prayer of appeasement, begging God to forgive us for having failed a fellow human being. We stood around the grave till the night deepened around us, with the moon obscured by dense clouds. When the wind blew hard amongst us dad, holding me by the hand, started to leave. The community followed. As we neared our place dad said:

'I killed him a second time, because when he was dead I refused to see him.'

'We all killed him twice,' someone behind him said.

Dad was silent. Maybe he was thinking about the threats of the Party of the Poor.

'What will happen?' I asked.

'Whatever it is will make us stronger,' dad said.

He paused. And then he told me something quite strange. He said that while he was unconscious the forest had told him a secret which he would reveal only when he had seen the right sign. And then he said:

'The earth is growing.'

'Bigger or smaller?' I asked.

'Not bigger or smaller. It's becoming more.'

I didn't understand.

'The night is growing,' he continued. 'The earth is growing like the night. One day there will be a new earth and a new night.'

'What about the day?'

'The night is older than the day, and greater.'

'Is that the secret the forest told you?'

'No.'

He fell silent again. And then, for no reason, he spoke.

'The light comes out of the darkness,' he said.

After that he didn't say another word till we got home. Neither did anyone else. And it was only as we went back silently that I noticed the silence of the unblinded. A new mood had come upon us. One by one, without any parting gestures, the community went back to their different houses. The moonlight, quivering against the houses, made it seem as if the people were stepping into distorted mirrors. With their sticks, their machetes, and dane guns on their backs they looked like soldiers from a lost kingdom. They did not speak about their regained sight. They had become weighed down by the air of the forest, the air of sorcerers, and fears of a reprisal. That night belonged to the dead carpenter; he

287

commanded our silence. And there were no festivities to mark our passage into a second sight, because now that we could see we were all ashamed. We were ashamed of what we had allowed our lives to become. And even the moon, casting its white transfiguration over everything, did not prevent us feeling that there could be more astonishing lives beyond the mirror.

CHAPTER FOUR

To See Anew Is Not Enough –
We Must Also Create

S HIVERING IN HIS three-legged chair, after his cold bath, dad began talking semi-exultantly about the astonishing lives beyond the mirror. He talked about the continents of our hidden possibilities, about the parts of us facing inwards in the direction of infinity, and about how we should bring those realms into our visible world and so create a kingdom of serenity and beauty on earth. He spoke for a long time about the intimations that had come to him when he was blind and when he was unconscious on the floor of the forest. I partly understood him to be conjecturing about the dreams of the dead and the unborn; but he declared over and over again that the most astonishing lives we lead are the lives beyond the mirror. We listened to him in silence as he spoke of the relationship between the infinite and the abyss. He swore that there are corpses in the consciousness of all peoples, all histories and all individuals, dead things that need to be acknowledged and buried, dead habits, dead ways of seeing, dead ways of living, things that weigh us down and drag us towards death and prevent us from growing, choking out the sunlight. How many of us carry neglected and unseen corpses in our minds and in our histories, he asked. Without answering the question, he said:

'I earned my blindness because I refused to see.'

Then, without noticing the hunger in our silence, and in the radiant animation of those who have stumbled into a realm of blind prophecy, he spoke about forgotten heroes, those who win our liberation and light for us before we do; and that because of them we should live our lives with fire and love and wise hope. Dad was definitely drunk on something that night – for, without seeing our diminished presence, he sang about the luminous jugglers of dreams and those who manage to be escape-artists from the hell of our accumulated negative perceptions. He sang about the wisdom of those who always remain dancers in their spirit, and about the joy of those who break out from their own darkness and soar into the exclamation of their own secret light. He sang about those who, in breaking from the chains of fear and centuries, help us break our chains in advance; and those who, in bursting out from the dark sea caves and from time's terrible enchantments, help us burst from ours. But they do it in advance, he said, with thorns on their head in the darkness which later for us becomes a crown of illumination.

Then, quite suddenly, his voice changed and became a little ghostly as he told us about some of the things he had seen when he collapsed on the floor of the forest. He saw clearly, for the first time, signs of our hidden realities. He saw worlds behind our world, a mere sleep, or a mere thought away; he saw parallel worlds, simultaneous realities, inverted universes, where the roots of trees were branches, and where plants released the essence of their flowers into the spaces in the earth. He saw the hidden realities of our thoughts and actions, and their immediate consequences which lurked beside us, waiting for the confluences of time when they would become real and irrevocable. He saw how we created our lives with our thoughts, how our thoughts created our realities, and how we carry around with us the great invisible weight of all our thoughts and actions and secrets. He saw a world co-existent with ours where all our secret selves were real and visible.

It was at this point that he fell silent. He had talked himself into slowly noticing his own condition. Maybe he suddenly realised that the fabulous weight had left his head and that Madame Koto's monumental form was no longer sitting on him. Maybe he noticed for the first time how light he felt. He had been talking semi-exultantly while me and mum had remained silent, merely staring at him. It was his turn to stare at us. The silence in the room widened and became quite unnerving. Dad was suddenly uneasy and an unhappy expression appeared on his face as he looked around our room, his eyes watering. I couldn't enter his spirit but I knew that he was seeing the true wretchedness of our condition with new eyes. He made us see it more poignantly. He looked at the floor, bare and rough and pitted. He looked at the centre table and the bed and my mat. He looked at the grim walls and the ceiling with all its holes. He stared at mum's bony face with its hollow shadows of forbearance, and then he stared at me. He was very miserable at what he saw. I think that, for a while, in the midst of his agonies and exultations, he had thought that the hard world was really a place of fables and magic lights. There were no magic lights in our room and even the candle-flame seemed quite famished. We had not eaten decently for many weeks. Mum didn't cry that night, but her silence was deeper than tears. And while dad stared at our abode, at the bald facts of our lives, and at the narrow spaces we had been living in all this time, mum retired to bed with the heavy sigh of one for whom it had all been foretold.

I watched dad's incomprehension. His misery was as deep as his exultation had been high. I could almost feel him thinking that to see anew is not enough. We must also create our new lives, everyday, with will and light and love. The endlessness of effort unto death frightened him because he was probably a man who would like a single great act, a heroic act, to be sufficient — for ever and ever. I suppose he was overwhelmed by the conundrum of living always while alive. He sat in his three-legged chair with the look of a man who had been cheated of his most precious possession. He had re-entered the kingdom of sight, but had lost the other enchanted kingdom of which he was sole ruler and defender. He had lost his magic servants, his invisible wives, and the splendid lights of that world. He had lost them all, and had found us, lean, famished, and patiently awaiting his return from his forest of dreams. While he dreamt, while he was blind, we suffered. I had never seen him look so defenceless, or so ashamed.

CHAPTER FIVE

The Invisible Radiance

DAD'S SHAME WAS so pungent that I crept out of the room and went and sat on the cement platform at the housefront. The night was still and the air was alive with white enchantments. The dead man was still stirring, refusing to die. Reprisals were on their way. I was not afraid. The inhabitants of the area were asleep, and dreaming about the dead carpenter. And the moonlight, mysterious and benevolent, cast a revelatory spell over the sleeping world.

My spirit-companions had tried to scare me from life by making me more susceptible to the darker phases of things, and by making reality appear more monstrous and grotesque. But so far, they had failed. And they had failed because they had forgotten that for the living life is a story and a song, but for the dead life is a dream. I had been living the story, the song, and the dream.

While I sat there on the cement platform, within the magic circle of the moon's enchantment, breathing in the mysteries of that diaphanous air, I suddenly became aware of the brilliant manifestation of a hidden personage next to me. My skin fairly bristled at the proximity of the manifestation. When I turned my head I nearly fainted at the sight of Ade sitting beside me on the platform. He was splendid in a white suit that the moonlight made almost effulgent. An unnatural serenity shone from him in the form of silver lights, as if he were aglow in a tremulous mirror. His airy presence made me quiver.

'What is the message you promised to tell me?' I asked.
'Has my father been buried?'

'Yes.'

'Are you sure?"

'Yes.'

He was silent. It was a silence that was capable of inducing madness, or profound understanding.

'Things are never what they seem,' he said after a while.

'What do you mean?'

He shrugged, and was silent. Then:

'The five-headed spirit is still coming for you.'

'I am not afraid,' I said.

He looked at me out of cryptic eyes.

'Your spirit-companions said to tell you that after the rainbows, there will be the riots. After the riots will come the butterflies. And after the butterflies, the flood.'

'What does that mean?'

'I can't tell you.'

It was my turn to be silent. I may have been thinking, or I may have suddenly gone beyond the mirror. The wondrous moods of the land of spirits bloomed in me.

'Tell me something that will help me,' I said.

He stared at me again with glowing eyes. His stare concentrated my spirit.

'One great thought can change the dreams of the world.'

'I think I know that one already. Tell me another.'

An imperceptible smile rose to his face.

'One great action, lived out all the way to the sea, can change the history of the world.'

'Tell me another.'

He went into his deep silence. Then he flashed me a smile so heavenly and so radiant that all the anxieties in me dissolved.

'LOOK!' he said, pointing.

I looked, and saw them again. I saw them in the revelations of moonlight. I saw their hidden and glorious radiance. I stared in trembling wonder at the mighty procession of wise spirits from all the ages, from eras past and eras to come.

294

I watched the glorious stream of hierophants and invisible masters with their caravans of eternal delights, their floating pyramids of wisdom, their palaces of joy, their windows of infinity, their mirrors of lovely visions, their dragons of justice, their lions of the divine, their unicorns of mystery, their crowns of love-won illumination, their diamond sceptres and golden staffs, their hieratic standards and their shining thyrsi of magic ecstasy. I gazed at the royal and serene spirits from higher realms that restore balances. They were continuing their majestic procession to the great meeting-place in the mind and dreams of the world. They were moving temporarily from their adventures of infinity to our earthly realm which for centuries has cried out for more vision, more transformation, and the birth of a new cycle of world justice.

'Where are they going?' I asked.

'To the heart of the world.'

'To do what?'

'To make the world feel.'

'Feel what?'

'Feel more, think more, live more.'

'More what?'

'More love, I suppose.'

'Why?'

'Why not?'

I was silent. Then I said:

'Tell me something else that will help me.'

'Like what?'

'Anything.'

It was his turn to pause. Then, in a transfigured voice, he said:

'LISTEN!'

I listened hard, and heard nothing. But when I listened without trying to listen, I heard them. I heard the angelic music and the gentle riddles of the Blessed Souls that dad had alluded to in his exultant fever of naming. I heard

them in the eternal spaces within me and I heard them
in the moonlight. Their voices were a sublime chorus, a
concert of enigmas. I listened to the purity of a girl's voice
as she began a riddle which the others answered, one after
another, in layers, completing the circle of enchantment.
The girl began, singing:

'How does love create immortality?'

And the others replied:

'Love creates mystery.'

'And mystery creates thought.'

'Thought creates action.'

'And action creates a life.'

'The essence of your life is your gospel.'

'And your gospel is your light.'

'Your light is your immortality.'

'And so love creates immortality.'

As I listened to their songs my soul soared in the joy of
angels, and I briefly re-connected the eternal playfulness
of our mysterious inheritance. Then me and Ade began
to play spirit-games, the games of enigmas and riddles and
jokes that we enjoyed so much in the land of origins. Ade
brought the luminosity and wonderful lights of that world
with him, and its beatific grace soothed me as I sat there in
the raw world of our ghetto. And he, smiling like the moon,
told jokes that made us roll over in laughter. And I laughed in
such deep happiness because it was a long time since I had
played the sweet and innocent spirit-games of the mind. And
as I rolled about in laughter, mum emerged at the housefront
and saw me. She stared at me silently, pondering the moon
on my face.

'Who are you laughing with?' she asked with terror
in her voice.

'No one,' I replied, sweetly.

She looked around. Ade was gone. The procession of
spirits had disappeared. The voices of the Blessed Souls
were silent. The wind was cold. The air shimmered with the

dreams of the living and the dead. And the forest was sleeping badly, the trees were wondering which of them would become ghosts tomorrow.

Mum looked around, and saw nothing. She saw nothing but the ordinary poverty of our area. She came towards me, and I was tempted to run away; but I allowed her unhappiness and her warmth to encompass me. She lifted me up closer to the moon, and put me down again. Then, taking my hand, she led me into our room, where dad sat in humility and silence.

Mum laid out the mat, and slept on the floor. Dad stayed on his chair. And I drifted in and out of sleep on the bed, listening to the whispers of the Blessed Souls that dwell in the heavens hidden behind our ordinary lives.

Maybe one day we will see the mountains ahead of us. Maybe one day we will see the seven mountains of our mysterious destiny. Maybe one day we will see that beyond our chaos there could always be a new sunlight, and serenity.

March 1992
London – Trinity College, Cambridge